The Party

Saundra E. Harris

The Party

Saundra E. Harris

Published by:
Saphari Books, Inc.
P. O. Box 232
Pasadena, MD 21123-0232

This book is a work of fiction. Names, characters, organizations, and incidents are a fictitious product of the author's imagination. Any resemblance to actual persons, living or dead, events, or locales is entirely coincidental.

For information contact Saphari Books, Inc.
sapharibooks@cablespeed.com.

Cover Design by:
Keith Saunders of Marion Designs
www.mariondesigns.com

Book Layout:
Shawna A. Grundy
sag@shawnagrundy.com

First Trade Paper Back Printing:
10 9 8 7 6 5 4 3 2 1

ISBN: 0-974-5486-1-8
Printed in the United States of America

ACKNOWLEDGEMENTS

I have to give thanks and honor to God from whom all blessings flow. Mom and Dad you have supported my dream of writing from the beginning and have always encouraged me to do my best. I want to thank you for giving me three of the greatest sister's on earth; Carian, Judy and Stacey; you always believed that I was destined to write. Thanks! I love you all very much. To my big brother Billy who spoiled me and continues to spoil me so that all of the men in my life have to measure up to him, I love you and thanks.

For Tink, Karen, Lynette and Deidre you are the best sister-friends a woman could have. We have been through good times and bad times for the last twenty odd years and still remain close friends. Thanks for keeping me in check! I love you all. Tink, girl you let me talk you to death over story lines (and still talking you to death) and gave me insight on my characters and myself. You're the closest cousin that I have and I love you.

I want to thank my family for being so very loving and supportive throughout my journey. My immediate and extended family, Aunt Linda, especially, thanks so much for your love and support. I did not expect you to read "The Party", but not only did you read it, you spread the word to your friends, coworkers, and church family. Everyone has rallied around this gift that God has bestowed upon me by selling, recommending, and spreading the word about my debut novel "The Party". With their help and the help of others "The Party" continues to be successful.

Lastly, I have to thank Eleanor, for her friendship, and for believing in ME! She offered up her services as editor, and chief PARTY reader, and I cannot thank her enough.

It has been three years (time flies when you're having fun!) since the original release of THE PARTY! I wanted to be more competitive in the literary market, therefore, I have revamped, revised, and re released THE PARTY! During that time I have completed my undergraduate degree and removed myself from a couple of people. I have also extended my online family to include the Mid Atlantic Chatters, as well as increasing my presence on the web via my blog and my yahoo 360° page.

The sequel to THE PARTY will be available the summer of 2006! Hit me up on my blog for all the juicy tidbits of my dating life…LOL!
http://xcapadesofthegirlz.blogspot.com/

Take care
Saundra E Harris
aka SassyScribe

Dedication

To THE GIRLS!

Stacey, Karen, Tink, Dee, and Lynette!

The Party

Prologue

Shaeyla Andrews crossed her living room lifting the heavy platter of cocktail shrimp over her head as she swerved between guests to place the tray onto the loaded buffet table. The blinking white lights from the battery operated "Happy New Year" centerpiece bounced off of her sequined shirt. The silver and gold streamers draped around the rectangular tables accented the black table cloths and highlighted her gleaming chafing dishes. Her white pine Christmas tree sat in her bay window adorned with silver ornaments in the shape of grapes and crystal icicles. Iridescent garland dressed the limbs of the tree and shot sparkles of light around the room. As she walked along she lifted the lids to see if she needed to replenish any items. Noticing that she was okay on food, she checked the slim platinum Movado on her wrist as she made her way through the horde of guests. Her house was bursting with friends, family, and acquaintances all ready to bring in the New Year. As far as Shaeyla and her girlfriend's were concerned the New Year could not arrive fast enough. They were ready for this past year to be over, so that they could put the drama behind them. *Drama was the correct word, because they all had to pull together to triumph over the joys and sorrows of this past year.* As Shaeyla removed herself from the crowd of well-wishers and merry makers she slipped into the kitchen and headed for the staircase that led to the second level of her four bedroom home. The plush black carpet in the hallway muffled her steps as she stopped in front of the first door on her left, the guest bedroom. Placing her hand upon the doorknob, she gently opened the door and walked over to check on her now sleeping friend Benét. One look at her tear-stained face which was puffy even in her sleep made it clear for Shaeyla to see just how fretful and restless she was. Remembering, Shaeyla shook her head in disbelief at the way her friend fell into her arms when she opened her door. Benét's clothes were disheveled and her speech was incoherent, but Shaeyla was able to calm her down enough to find out what was wrong. Now as she's watching Benét's sleeping form, her story ricocheted around Shaeyla's brain, as she absentmindedly smoothed the wet hair from Benét's cheek. Lost in her thoughts, Shaeyla forgot that there was a party going on downstairs as she moved over to sit in the rocking chair beside the bed and recalled the events of the past year that changed her life, and the lives of her four friends . . .

Chapter 1 ➢ Shaeyla Andrews

Spring

The buzzing of the alarm clock broke into the erotic haze of Shaeyla's dream. Without opening her eyes, she instinctively sought out the offending device in a vain attempt to continue her dream. Silently swearing, *"Damn clock! Always going off right when I'm about to get mine, because I sure as hell didn't get it from Randall's sorry ass."* Propping her head up, she looked down at Randall's sleeping face amazed because like this he looked like the man that she fell in love with, which was a far cry from the man that he had become. Lightly skimming her hand over his toned form and solid chest, she knew that behind those closed lids, were the most beautiful mixture of hazel and brown eyes that she had ever seen. She remembered the way he used to rock her world…hmmmph, hmmmph, hmmmph, had her doing some crazy things*! Who am I kidding? I'm still doing crazy things! Hell, I do everything for him. I feed him, clothe him and pay the rent at his apartment, not to mention giving him spending money to hang with his boys. Hell, he even has full use of my new car, a sleek new fully loaded BMW 735i* .

Looking out of the skylight and into the beautiful colors of the rising sun, she reflected on the last few years. She spent two years planning the family reunion, at least ten birthday parties, countless bachelorette parties (which are always off the hook) and a spectacular wedding. Shaeyla took the advice of her family and friends and established her own business, Events to Remember. To her surprise she got more gigs than she could handle and had to quit her insurance job to keep up with her booming business.

Shaeyla has always prided herself on being a smart woman, especially in business. However, personally, she seemed to be stuck on stupid and her love life was beginning to sour. The question of the day was what to do with Randall? His work ethic was sporadic at best, but he made her laugh and as a teenager, that was enough. But as each year got worse, her dumb ass became more content. She would even make up excuses as to why he didn't work to her family and friends. She lied about everything to hide the fact that Randy was fucking up. Stealing from her accounts, and messing up her money, yet she still made excuses for him. She became so discontented with her life and what she was doing and more importantly, why she was doing it. Now his unemployment, laziness, drinking, weed smoking, crack use and her suspicions of his infidelity were getting on her nerves.

But . . . expelling a huge sigh, one question keeps popping in her head, do I keep him or do I get rid of him? She had become just the type of woman that she despised . . . one that took care of a sorry no-good, lazy, trifling man . . . but lets not forget, with a good dick. That's what she kept telling herself—"Dick is good" the mantra that she and her girls would recite because as they all agreed that it is good. But not that good that it caused her to lose her goddamn mind for YEARS!!!! FUCK IT! Truth be told, she had WASTED A LIFETIME. A lifetime of fucking drama, and then more drama, with Randall. These last few years of their relationship she had allowed herself to enter into this bottomless pit that seemed endless because of their fight-ing and raging emotions. If she were honest with herself, his body nor his mind moved her the way it used to and it had not for quite some time. Shaeyla was up half the night trying to figure out a way to pull herself away from Randall's madness without hurting him or herself in the process. She knew she was crazy for even thinking this way, but who's going to take care of him and do for him the way that she did?

Her girls would have a fit if they knew how responsible she felt for him. She knew he wasn't going to handle his business and she could just envision him sinking deeper and deeper into the world of alcohol and drugs. Throwing back the covers she padded across the room to her bathroom suite to shower for work. Stepping under the hot jets, the steady stream of water pounded away her misery it soothed her soul. As she washed the sins of what she thought was love away, she realized that her relationship with Randy had lasted ten years too long. But that was her fault and she could not lay the blame for that at anyone else's doorstep.

Thank God for her girls because they brought reality to her front door. For years they tried to tell her to get rid of Randall, even though she didn't listen, that did not stop them from being there for her whenever she had a problem or was mad and angry with Randy. They were always there, especially Benét. Shaeyla did not know how Benét put up with her being with Randy for so long. She said that they got on her nerves whenever they went out together because of the constant arguing. It was a power struggle from the beginning, between her and Randy but deep in her heart she knew that he was weak. Diandra and Worthy thought Randall was cool because they all used the same dealer to get their weed which allowed them to see right through his bullshit. Besides, Diandra and Worthy were more laid back. They liked that thug life, living ghetto fabulous and listening to rap in their own ghetto heaven. But she, Benét, and Kendra tended to lean towards more responsible friends, than Diandra and Worthy, yet all of Shaeyla's friends felt the same way, they hated the way Randall treated her and told her daily to leave him.

Shaeyla knew that what her girls said was true, but it's hard to just get rid of him after investing all of that time. She knew she deserved better and than Randall. The question she needed to ask herself was *What am I looking for?* Did she want a man that was like her father . . . strong, intelligent, charismatic, and decisive and as well as a good provider? Or was she willing to settle with Randy? Randy has none of the characteristics of her father, yet there was something that kept her bound to him. The question was, *WHAT?*

Chapter 2 ➢ Benét Grier

Benét has been feeling antsy lately. Like she needed to be doing something with herself—but she doesn't know what. Or should she say she didn't know what, until today. When she left the University this morning clutching the envelope with her admissions forms to her chest, her sense of accomplishment had her sprinting to her car and not remembering the drive home. As she pulled into her driveway she folded the forms and placed them in her purse. Benét decided that in order to soften everyone up for her news, that she should prepare everyone's favorites. They couldn't possibly be anything but happy for her with full stomachs. With this thought, she locked the car and headed for the house. The 5000 square foot mini mansion was impressive with its brick front and beautifully landscaped yard. Rose bushes and azaleas trim the paved walkway that lead to the beveled glass double doors. The large marble tiled foyer with the initials BKG in black script was the first indication of wealth. Money was not spared in the decoration of her home. This was evident by the original paintings placed strategically on her walls and the plush deep-blue carpeting that made you feel as thought you were walking on a cloud, not to mention the Italian leather living room ensemble. Her accent pieces consisted of glass sculptured vases filled with white roses which were placed upon the glass and stainless steel tables just so. Benét knew that the overall affect of her house not only showed her decorating skills but it was also very Fung Shei. The kitchen décor is that of fruit, which was evident from the tiles on the floor to the back-splash, curtains and chair pads. The game room is a man's dream with its pin ball machine, flat-screen high definition television and surround sound system. The hi-tech stereo equipment is tucked away into the recessed wall and is piped throughout the house and to the speakers surrounding the fenced in backyard. The remaining room is done in an African motif, with original pieces of Sudanese art on the walls, compliments of her husband bosses from a recent overseas trip. That accessorized with elephant tusks as curtain rods and a white Bengal tiger rug made any furniture store's set up, pale in comparison.

Placing her keys on the table in the foyer, she hangs her jacket in the hall closet and enters the kitchen. Plucking an apron off the hook in the pantry she washes her hands and sets about making the evening meal. For the next hour she effortlessly peeled, cut, sliced, diced, kneaded, and baked a tempting treat for her family. Glancing at the clock on the stove, she knows that her husband will be home soon. This thought made her nervous, because he has always been supportive of whatever she did, but it never interfered with his world before.

Wiping her hands on her apron, she pulls the thick envelope from her purse to look at the forms again. Thinking about how her life was going to change had her nervously, realizing that she now had to tell her husband Kendall and her kids Kendall Jr. and Zaria…because this is going to not only change her life, but theirs as well. She couldn't wait to tell her girls especially since they have been getting on her for the last ten years to go back to school. Originally, she laid the blame at her family's door for her feelings of insecurity and unhappiness. Hell, as much as she loved her family…she was beginning not like what she had at home. Truth be told, she was actually beginning to resent it and it wasn't their fault. Everyone had a hobby, sport, or something that they enjoyed, but she was just the chief cook, maid, and taxi driver. Won't they be surprised when that all changes Benét thought to herself as she glanced at her enrollment papers. A new start at life. "Momma, can you give me a ride to work?" Kenny asked upon walking into the kitchen. It's a good thing that dinner is almost ready, because *I swear these kids are working my last nerve!* Benét silently laments. If she had to do it over again...would she? Yes . . . but she would've finished her education and embarked on a better career first. Don't get me wrong I love my kids, but I have been depended upon for the last 19 years *(yes I started early, but I've come a long way)* never really having a chance to just be *Benét*. First, someone's girlfriend, then someone's mother and finally someone's wife she thought.

"Yes, Kenny. I will give you a ride to work after we eat dinner." The flash of black from the corner of her eye, made her realize that her husband was pulling into the driveway. "Your father's home, so go wash up and set the table for dinner." When the interior door to the garage opened, she moved toward Kendall with open arms eager to kiss his lips "Hmmm! Now that's what I call a greeting!"

"Hmmm...I do too! Mrs. Grier you are going to have to greet me that way more often."

"I know that's right. Now, go wash up for dinner. Kenny Jr. is setting the table as we speak, and tell your daughter to—" Turning to the sound of heels on her foyer, Benét eyed her daughter entering the kitchen from the living room.

"Mmmm—what's up? Mom, you have this kitchen smelling all good." Zaria sniffed appreciatively as she walked into the room. Lifting the tops on the pots she notices that her mom has made everyone's favorites. "Wow, thanks mom you know how much I love mashed potatoes."

"You're welcome sweetie, I love cooking for my family, and tonight I've made fried chicken, corn bread, roasted garlic mashed potatoes and gravy, and I finally used the bread machine that I got for Mother's Day two years ago, to make my homemade sweet honey cinnamon dinner rolls."

The ringing of the phone interrupts their jovial conversation. Benét walks over and answers "Hello" the caller with his deep Barry White sounding voice responded, "Good Evening, may I speak to Zaria? Tell her its Devin"

"I'm sorry, but we are about to sit down to dinner. I will have her call you back when we are finished." While hanging up the telephone, Benét thought, Zaria is fifteen cute as hell, an "A" student, not on drugs, isn't pregnant, and is generally a good child . . . but this Devin character sounded like a grown ass man. Looking at Zaria, she asked, "Who is Devin?"

With that teenage look of defiance for the intrusion into her personal life she responded with "See there you go all in my business"

"You are my business, so I am going to ask you again. Who is Devin? He sounded like a grown man, and you are just sixteen. Exhaling through her teeth, Zaria states "he's a friend from school." Thank God, she didn't have to worry about her daughter getting pregnant if she decided to become sexually active. Benét had put Zaria on the pill to regulate her cycle because it was becoming too unpredictable for her to keep track of. Now it comes every 28 days like clockwork. She wondered if her husband knows about Devin, she'd have to talk to him about it tonight before they went to bed.

This made her look at Kendall, Jr. He looks just like his daddy. He is seventeen, with girls coming out of the woodwork. Benét doesn't know what he tells them girls, but it seems that a different girl calls each week. Every girl in the city must have our number, that's why there will be a new line installed on Wednesday. Shaeyla told her that she called the other day and the line just rung, and rung. Had to be him—talking to one of his hood rat, ghetto tricks. They got to be the dumbest girls on earth. Yes, he is my son, but he's nothing but a playa. He already has women waiting on him, buying him clothes, lacing his pockets with money. Makes her remember what her and her girls were talking about Saturday, *women—will take a man just to say that they have one*, hell women will sell their souls to have a man. And he has learned the art of seduction and BS talking at the tender age of seventeen. Shaking her head, oh well she tried to give the young ladies as much of a heads up as she could, but he will get his . . . most men do. Unfortunately when they do, woe be tide the ladies that come after that first main heartbreak. Women will at least fall in love again, and give another man a shot, but when it happens to brothers, you can best believe that the succeeding ladies, will be tested, tested again and re-tested . . . and she may still end up by herself.

"Kenny, Jr., put ice in the glasses, and fill them with tea. Zaria, tell your father to come down for dinner please. Girl, if you suck your teeth at me one more time, you'll be picking them up off of the floor." After everyone was seated the talk at her dinner table was unusually quiet. Through the silence, Benét didn't know what to expect, she should be expecting happiness, but with this family, who knew?

"I have something to tell you all," meanwhile, Benét's heart is beating 50 miles per hour for fear of how her family will handle her news. After taking a deep breath, she says, "I'm going back to college to get my degree." She was met with complete silence and blank opened mouth stares…then everyone began speaking at once.

"Well how am I going to get to work!" Kenny Jr. yelled.

"Yeah, and what about my cheerleading practices, and, and—stuff," cried Zaria.

"Honey, that's terrific!"

The outrage from her children was expected, because kids are selfish, and she would deal with that later. But if they thought about it, maybe their selfishness was the reason why Kendall and I have yet to purchase them a car. The vexed looks upon their faces almost had her in tears. "Listen before ya'll go ranting and raving, I have to do this for me! And I think the two of you are being selfish because you only seem to be concerned about how this is going to change what you want to do. What about what I want to do, have you even thought about that? Have you thought about how running ya'll back and forth affects my life? Mmm…that's what I thought." Benét said fuming as the two of them sat in silence, sulking over how shit affects them.

"Now Benét, don't worry about Jr. and Zaria. I think it's great that you are going back to school. You know I've always said that you were wasting your talents. When do you start?"

"I start next semester," she excitedly stated, glad that someone appeared to be happy for her. "Things are going change around here. I will be in class three out of five evenings and you all will have to fend for yourselves. Kendall, you are going to have to pick the kids up from their activities during the times that I am at school."

"That shouldn't be a problem. I'm glad that you're doing this honey."

"Good, cause I want to have a party to celebrate in three weeks, if that's okay with you?"

"Whatever you want," said Kenny.

"Great, now all I have to do is call the girls, especially Shaeyla so that she can help me with the details."

Chapter 3 ➢ Kendra Thompson

The downtown offices of Kendra's accounting firm are located on the tenth floor in the Legg Mason building. The large corner office looks down to the street below which is one of the reasons why she decided to rent the space. The other factor was that it had the color scheme she could work with; a deep burgundy carpet that cushioned your steps as you walk. Her Old English style desk, was inherited from her grandfather. Although it was chipped around the edges and the pedestal feet were wobbling, she couldn't bare to part with it, and decided to restore it herself. The art work that adorned the walls of the lobby was her favorite Poncho Brown prints, which Benét hated because there was no scheme or theme to her office. Kendra liked what she liked and that was that. The sound of the telephone had her turning from admiring her view of the Baltimore Harbor to glance at her watch. Kendra's receptionist was at lunch for another thirty minutes so she happily picked up the receiver, "Good Afternoon, Kendra Thompson, how may I help you?"

"Hey Girl, what's up," asked Benét?

"Nothing much, what's up with you?"

"I have some great news to tell you. I am finally taking ya'll's advice."

With one eyebrow elevated, Kendra replied, "Oh, really, and which piece of advice would that be?"

"The one about me going back to school."

"Girl, that is great. What are you going for?" Kendra asked excitedly.

"Interior Design. What do you think?"

"I think you need to do whatever makes you happy." Kendra told her.

Just hearing the excitement and enthusiasm in Benét's voice was wonderful news to Kendra. Her and the girls have been getting on Benét for years to go back to school and get the proper credentials to fulfill her dream of being an Interior Designer. Benét hooked up each of their homes. Hell, her place was laid. Benét lived in a secluded cul-de-sac area in Baltimore County.

Damn, Kendra thought her place was nice, until Benét saw it. She was like, "You have nice stuff, but it's all jumbled together." Kendra knew that she was kind of lazy, but she hated decorating. She purchased her home three years ago, in the county about thirty minutes north of Baltimore City, yet it still bore the mark of the previous owners. The drab blue and white wallpaper in her kitchen, the purple carpet in her basement and the pealing eggshell paint on her bed room walls, all the markings of the previous owners. That is until Benét came and took one look at her place and it has never been the same.

The snapping of Benét's fingers and shrill voice into the phone helps to bring Kendra out of her daze. "Hello, Kendra, are you listening to me? See there you go again, drifting off into la-la land. What were you thinking about this time?" Benét laughs out loud and continues on before Kendra could respond, "I hope it was a man, because I know you aren't getting any."

"Actually, smart-ass. I was thinking on how you've hooked our houses up. NOW!" Kendra replied with her hands on her hips and neck moving back and forth.

"Well anyway, I'm calling everyone because I'm having a little get together and I won't take no for an answer! It's to celebrate my return to school."

"Okay, date, time and place, said Kendra because you know I have to do something with this mop of mine get a manicure, pedicure and a new outfit."

"Girl, if I had your grade and length of hair, my shit would always be tight", stated Benét. "It's on the 26th of this month, with cocktails from six to seven pm and dinner at seven thirty pm. Dress to impress."

"Alright girl, I'll be there, thanks, talk to you later."

Kendra hangs up the phone and gets back to work. Pulling her desk calendar closer to write down the date of the party, she chews on the pen tip. Damn...she has three weeks to try and lose some inches, get her mop done, buy some fingernails and maybe try to find something new to fit her big ass. Immediately thoughts of not going crept into her mind. She didn't feel like being the third wheel like the last time Shaeyla had a party. All of Randall's nice looking single friends were taken and she was all alone. Hell, she knew that she needed to lose weight, but food was her confidant, her lover, and her friend. She especially liked the fact that it doesn't talk back—and she can always count on it to be there. But Benét is always trying to find her a man. She's so tired of hearing Benét say "Dick is Good!" She knows that dick is good, hell she had some like—damn it's been a while and Henry doesn't count with his mechanical self. *You know I'm going to do something about this weight, now I know that I'll never be a size 8, but I can at least try for a 14* Kendra told herself.

With this in mind, she starts to make one of her do's and don't lists, cause she's going to be a different woman from the inside out, come the summer. "Look out ya'll!" She yelled as she danced around her office happily. She couldn't wait to share her decision with the girls.

Chapter 4 ➤ Diandra Johnson

The dream of owning a salon is now a reality. Located in downtown Baltimore, off of Charles Street, DJ's Styles is a hip, funky hair salon that caters to the ghetto-fabulous. The sounds of old school hip-hop blasted from the stereo mounted on the wall. At five foot eight, brown skin, and a size eighteen, Diandra Johnson turned out the latest hairstyles for all the thug princesses in Baltimore. Her job gave her pleasure, because she got the four one, one on just about everybody in town and that's right up her alley. Shaking her head and sucking her teeth, she listened to the women sitting under her dryers telling their man's business, knowing that if the information ever got back to them, their asses would be busted. Damn near choking on her cigarette, she blew the smoke through her nose and contemplated her next client's hair do.

Why did she schedule all of these people today of all days. She is not feeling this, her back hurts, her period is on and her vow to stop smoking is up in smoke, she thinks to herself. Damn I don't know—the ringing of the phone interrupts her thoughts.

"DJ's Styles, how can I help you?" Diandra states into the phone.

"Hey," replies Benét, "What's wrong with you sounding all down and stuff?"

"Nothing girl," replied Diandra, "I got my period, my body aches and I have too many customers today . . . but I need the money."

"Now I understand why you sound like the bitch is in residence, you sound like Shaeyla," laughingly states Benét.

"Nope," said Diandra, "one too many heads and not enough hands."

"Okay, I just wanted to call and let you know that I have finally taken ya'll's advice and I'm going back to school," stated Benét.

"Well it's about time your ass listened, what are you planning to major in?"

"Interior Design."

"Girl that is great!" Diandra squeals into the phone.

"Anyway," said Benét, "I am having a party to celebrate in a few weeks, on the 26th of this month actually, cocktails are from six to seven pm and dinner starts at seven thirty, think you can make it?"

"Sure I can make it," Diandra said.

"Good, dress to impress okay?"

Benét asked, "Hey have you talked to Worthy? I've been calling her and leaving messages but she hasn't returned any of my calls."

"Girl, you know she has two jobs," Benét's voice was heavy with sarcasm.

"Yeah right, maybe she's tired, high or both."

With hands on her hips, Diandra responds, "Stop tripping, we all used to get high!"

"Hell, I still do and I could really use one now!" Benét responded.

"Whateva, can I bring Seven to the party with me? Cause knowing you, you probably asked Kendall to invite some of his Buppie co-workers so you can set your girls up," stated Diandra.

"And what if I did?" Benét asked sheepishly.

"See that's what I thought, put me down for 2, I have no desire to meet those tack heads—oops tech head friends of Kenny's," said Diandra laughingly.

"Alright, you can bring Seven. I guess I'll put Worthy's invite in the mail. You know she's going to be pissed and cuss me out.

I can hear her nagging falsetto voice now. "How come my invitation had to come in the mail? I know Kendra, Diandra and Shaeyla got personal invites over the phone!"

With laughter in her voice Diandra replies, "And if I were you, I'd tell her to check her messages more often and she could've gotten personal attention too. Now let me go, my customer's are rolling their eyes and giving me that trifling beautician's look."

"Hahahaha! Bye!" Benét chuckled and rung off.

Chapter 5 ➤ Worthy Mitchell

Bills, bills, bills and more bills!!!! Like if I had the money they would be paid already! Shit can't get blood from a turnip as my momma used to say, Worthy said out-loud to no one in particular. The scowl on her brown skinned face makes her look older than her thirty six years. Her short hair was pulled back from her high forehead and held in place with a headband. The blue jeans she had on has seen better days, the holes that were once in style are now just holes, besides that they are two sizes too big. Pulling her pants onto her narrow behind, she remembered when she was carrying her son that the pants actually fit. She chewed on her bottom lip while her wide brown eyes continued to flip through the pile of bills and stopped as the came to what looked like a wedding invitation, she wondered *Uh oh, what's this, flipping the embossed envelope over, Benét is having something?* Tearing into the envelope, she notices a black card, scrolled with silver script writing that said:

Come and Celebrate
Date: April 26th
Time: 6 pm until
Cocktails 6pm - 7pm
Dinner 7:30 pm

Where: Kendall and Benét Grier
12489 Maple Birch Avenue
Baltimore, MD 12345
RSVP: 410-555-1859 by April 8th

Shit! What is she celebrating now! Wondered Worthy, hmmm, she decided to check her messages, because she probably tried to call her, but working two jobs, she's tired all the time. Checking messages, the first message was from her hook up, "Hey Worthy, where's my doe? Holla back, Peace!" What the fuck! Damn JJ act like she's going to runaway with his money. Just then Worthy began to panic because she did not know who she was going to borrow the money from and she was all *tapped out.*

The next message was from Benét "Hey Girl, call me when you get this message. I have some good news to tell you and I plan on celebrating it! Bye" See she knew her girl would give her a more personal invite than this mail shit. Her and her girls understand each other—somewhat! We all have our issues, but in the end, we stick together. They even tease her and call her "worthless"—because they know that she should be doing more than what she's doing. They want her to move out the downtrodden area that she's in and move to Baltimore County. But Worthy liked the city, and no, it's not the best of places, but she can afford it and it's close to the action. She loves action, she likes the constant commotion, confrontations, and conflicts that makes her neighborhood HOT. And don't let them get started on her smoking, like there, asses never did. She knew she could do better, but she liked getting high too much to take a piss test for a good 9–5 job. *Yep . . . I know I'm trifling too . . . and what? I'll change when I'm ready and not for my girls and especially not for any MAN* thought Worthy.

Reaching for the phone, she dialed Benét's number. "Yeah!" answered Benét's son Little Kenny.

"Yeah! Yeah! Is that how you answer your Mother's phone?" Worthy chastised.

"Oh sorry Aunt Worthy, but Momma ain't home. Want me have her call you?" he asked.

"Yes. And Kenny Jr., in the future answer your mother's phone with a Hello or The Grier residence. Your mother would kick your ignorant ass for answering her phone like that!" she told him.

"Okay Auntie, sorry about that," he responded.

"Bye Kenny, Jr.," Worthy had to laugh, cause that boy is just too much . . . Benét got something on her hands with him!

The invitation says Ms. Worthy Mitchell and guest. Who in the hell is she going to ask? Her son Jared, that isn't happening. Damn . . . and knowing Benét's matchmaking ass she done already asked Kenny to invite some of his boring tech head co-workers. She has no prospects that she can take. And she knew right damn well that she can't show up with JJ's ass, Shaeyla would die of embarrassment and Benét would cuss her out. He isn't exactly the type to take and mingle with the bourgeois crowd. Then again, if she got herself cleaned up and act decent (a little decent) she may make a friend of one of Kendall's friends that may just be workable for that money. See she isn't worried about having no man, at least not yet. Oh well, enough about Benét's party, she needed to feed Jared and send him out to play. Damn, stretching her neck from side to side, she wonders if JJ would be willing to let her hold something in exchange for *something.*

Chapter 6 ➤ Shaeyla

Shaeyla took a sip of her wine and looked out at the view of Benét and Kendall's home. The pool was still covered as was the whirlpool tub, but the grounds showed the first stirrings of early spring as the recent rain had the tulips sprouting, and made the deck glisten from the rays of the setting sun. The sounds of Eric Benét coming from Benét and Kendall's outdoor speakers has her tapping her feet to the beat while her and Benét sat on the deck beside the outdoor fireplace to go over the details for the party.

Events to Remember is the hottest event/party planning company in Baltimore, and Shaeyla knows it. Her clientele list consists of various charitable organizations to national and local celebrities. She also caters to the nouveau rich. For those that don't know her, they would say that she has the perfect life. But appearances were deceiving. She has all the trappings of a financially secure sister: a beautiful home nestled in an affluent section of Baltimore County, and a six-figure bank account, and a growing thriving company, which was how she was able to care for Randall. Knocking him from her mind, she can see the colors for Benét's party and the excitement she has had her bouncing on her chair.

"Girl this party is going to be the bomb! I am so glad you asked me to help, because I sure was going to ask," Shaeyla said excitedly.

"So, what do you want to serve, how many and who are you inviting, what kind of music . . . "

"Slow Down!" Benét yelled, "Damn! Do you get this excited over every event you do?"

Jumping up and down barely able to contain herself, Shaeyla told Benét a resounding, "YES! So I'll ask again, how many people and what's on the menu?"

"About 50, I've sent the invitations already, it's the menu we need to discuss." Benét responded, "And I asked Kendall to invite a few of his single co-workers. Male of course, I'm hoping that ya'll will meet an eligible."

"An eligible what"

"A man, that's what!" Benét said, "How many times do we have to tell you to get rid of Randy's sorry ass, he don't do shit for you—(stopping herself in mid sentence). Benét shakes her head and states, "Anyway, that's a dead horse, cause his ass ain't going nowhere until your ass gets tired and I mean tired with a capital T. I talked to Diandra and she is bringing Seven with her. I'll be glad when she realizes that he wants her, because homeboy has been hanging around waiting for his chance."

"Amen," I said, "And he ain't bad, but you know Diandra likes a thugged out nigga, and he is too conservative for her. But you never know, we all may surprise you and actually like Kenny's boys," I jokingly replied.

"Actually," said Benét, "Kenny's bosses are coming and one of them would be ideal for you. But since you have Randy on the brain, you'll never find out. You deserve better Shaeyla, that's all."

"I know, believe me I know . . . we all envy you. Kendall loves you. You're like the stable one out of all of us . . . and deep down inside we want what you have."

"Anyway, let's get down to business," said Benét

It took two hours to hash out the menu, Shaeyla thought on the drive home from Benét's house. Now I have to go and deal with Randall. I had my pager on vibrate and he was blowing it up . . .

which I'm glad it was on vibrate, cause Benét would've had a fit about that. I hope he had some luck finding a job, cause as good as my business is, it's just that mine—and I am tired of doing for him and not being appreciated. Hell the thought of him touching me and just his very presence is irking me . . . I need to get rid of him, but I just don't want to be alone. Damn did I sell my soul? I am exactly the type of woman that I despise. That woman that takes care of a man, doesn't want to be alone, got to feel wanted, needed and desired. The problem is that I'm too complacent and if I'm honest afraid to be alone. I am so unhappy, Randy and I have not had sex in almost 3 months, but I didn't tell my girls that. I am not stupid, I know he getting his groove on with somebody, and the funny part is that I am not even worried. Hell, half of Baltimore is sharing their man in one form or another.

But this way of living and dealing with him is not me, hell this whole relationship was never in my "master plan". Although I never really had a "master plan", just a plan and it included financial independence, love with Mr. Right, and happiness with me. I thought that was Randy, but each day I find out something else that I just don't like. I'm tired of his lies. I'm tired of being an enabler. See Randy likes to get high . . . on whatever . . . and it took me a minute to figure it out. I also think he's stepping out with someone else. Whenever I go to his house, lately he either runs to answer the phone or he just lets it ring. He has moved his caller id box from the living room into his bedroom, like he is hiding something. I don't know what to do about his cheating since I have no real proof, but like most brothers, he will trip up.

His drug habit on the other hand is another problem altogether. What do I do . . . I have hid the truth from everyone for so long and it's time to stop. I pay most of his bills—rent, gas, electric, phone, food, clothes, cars, insurance, miscellaneous . . . and it's the miscellaneous that is kicking my ass cause Randall's habit is up. I know because he is always broke and always asking me for dough. Shit, he should ask that bitch I suspect he fucking unless her ass gets high also. I wouldn't be surprised; he is a tack head so a chicken head is right up his alley. He isn't stupid—just lazy because he has a good education, and a strong head on his shoulders.

Pulling into Randy's complex, Shaeyla see's Randy's home, the sight of Tony's blue Chevrolet Blazer indicates that he is not alone. It stood to reason that if Tony is here, more than likely so are LJ, and Ice.

As Shaeyla, sits and contemplates starting her car back up and going home, she realizes that her girls are right, it's time for her to drop him and move on. She needs to learn that it is okay to be single. Besides, she deserves to find happiness for herself. But how can she find happiness if she doesn't really know what it is she is looking for in a man. I mean besides the obvious, of intelligence, education, career minded and financially independent. Oh yeah, and he has to know how to, "work the middle", in order to please me. Expelling a sigh, of dread, and knowing that she really doesn't want to go in there tonight, because all we are going to do is argue she realizes that it cannot be helped.

Banging her hand on her steering wheel, Shaeyla exclaims as she talks out loud to herself. "Damn, what the fuck do they want? Don't these niggas have a home, shit they're always at his house. Not tonight, I've had it, I'm tired and they have to go, and if Randy don't like it, his ass is going too!" She knew that technically it is his home, but as she always told Randy *"he who makes the most money and pays the bills is in charge"*, so when she walked in the door, note that his boys would be walking out the door. It amazed her that he hasn't figured out yet that his friends don't like her anymore than she liked them. Not that it mattered two fucks whether or not they liked her; Shaeyla could care less. But Randy should be tired of her constantly emasculating him in front of his boys. Hell, she would get tired of someone screaming on her in public all the time and castigating her like she was two years old, but she couldn't stop. Shaeyla has this perverted streak in her that enjoyed berating and hurting him, maybe she hoped that he would get mad or I finally *"hit that mark that breaks the camels back"* so to speak and he would leave her alone. But no, she cut him off at the balls every chance she got, and he made it so easy by constantly fucking up. Shaeyla loves being in charge that's why she run's her own business, she hated people telling her what to do. How many women do you know that can go to their man's home and regulate shit, that's right—not many. Don't judge or hate on her, but she is just beginning to open up her eyes and realize how TIRED she is. Hell, she irritates him so much, that for the past month he has slept on the couch, in his own house!! Yes, it may seem wrong, but Shaeyla does not want Randy to touch her, not even a toe touching the back of her heel. With that thought in mind, he should've been picking up on the subtle changes that she has been making. Shaeyla did not spend the night at his house like she used to. When she leaves all of her personal items and any small touches that she may have made to his home, are now at her house. Shaeyla has been saying for the longest time that she was going to leave Randy's ass if he didn't straighten up. He couldn't even see how she's pulling away from him slowly but surely. Expelling a huge breath, Shaeyla exits the car, and finds the key to unlock his front door.

* * * * *

As Shaeyla placed the key in the lock she heard Randy's pathetic attempt at whispering, "Hurry up, ya'll in the basement. She'll have a fit seeing this shit."

Shaeyla flung the door open as he was still scrambling around trying to get the smell of burning matches out of his spot. As she stood her eyes took in the sight of the sorry excuses for men in front of her before pasting her nastiest Anti-Christ snarl, upon her face. As the uncontrollable rage welled up inside of her she advanced forward screaming, "Don't take shit nowhere! Get the fuck out of my house all of ya'll!!" Turning her wrath on Randy Shaeyla, her voice curt, she lashed out, "God dammit Randy I told you I was tired of this shit and I meant . . . I want them out now . . . and I don't want them back . . . whether I'm here or not. She took a deep breath punctuated with several even gasps. "Look I can't take this! You either straighten up or your ass is out! better yet I'm done! I cannot take anymore of you or your dumb ass bull shit," said Shaeyla, and turned and walked out of the room.

The look of surprise on Randy's face at her statement had her laughing as she watched him turn to shuffle his boys out of the house. The mumbling and grumbling had her laughing even harder as she doubled over and could care less what they called her.

Shaeyla eyed Randy, as he knew she could hear his boys calling her names yet he tried to pretend like she wasn't there laughing and listening to what they were saying. But she knew that Randy never did have a back bone and if he never stood up to her she knew damn well he wasn't going to stand up to his boys. *I can't stand them*, Shaeyla thinks to herself. Tony works but is a functioning addict his damn self, and Ice and LJ take direction from Tony. Neither of them works. Come to think of it their women are taking them care of also, but those nasty looking winches did not keep themselves up enough so it wasn't a wonder they were paying for dick. Shaeyla knew she shouldn't have thought that, because she was paying for dick her damn self. Since Randy didn't want to defend her, Shaeyla decided to take matters into her own hands.

Walking behind Randy as his boys take their hats from the coat rack, Shaeyla placed her hands on her hips and let the words go, "Hey fellas you want to know why or rather how I can come over here and regulate shit? It's because I pay the bills in this motherfucker that's why. But guess what, where are ya'll going to party after next month, cause I ain't paying for rent anymore, and all the name calling and stuff ya'll did just helped me to make up my mind." Seeing the bug eyed look on Randy's face had her clutching her side because the laughter was busting her guts. *Ooh boy did this feel good to finally be strong and stand on my own* Shaeyla mused.

As the door closed Shaeyla placed her hands on her hips and started into Randy again. "You heard how they were calling me a Bitch and all, and you didn't say a word in my defense. That's the shit I'm talking about that shit got you and I'm tired of it. I deserve to be treated better than this Randy." Feeling completely disgusted and disappointed with him and herself, she continued, "Shit over ten years we been together and I cannot believe that I am still going through drama with you."

"It's obvious to me finally that I don't mean anything to you. Your boys mean more to you than I do." She spoke with quiet firmness. "Let me take that back, my money means more to you than anything."

"But you know what my eyes are open now, and you have to learn how to take care of yourself without me. As of this moment I am cutting all monies to you off," Shaeyla stated in cold sarcasm.

"And I will be going to the party solo. I think it will be the ideal time for me to 'test the water' so to speak as a single woman." As Shaeyla made this statement she could see that her words are beginning to sink in because Randy breaks down crying, begging her to give him another chance.

After finally calming him down, she explained to him that the only reason she was staying was because she was too tired to drive to her house. "So you have to understand that this is the last time that I will be sleeping under your roof, I will no longer be responsible for you at all, this is it Randy, we are over. Goodnight."

Chapter 7 ➢ Diandra

"Okay, what are ya'll getting done to your heads? I made sure to book only ya'll because when we finish, we are going shopping." Diandra stated.

"Something SEXY—something that says "SEX" Shaeyla, Benét, Worthy and Kendra stated in unison. "Okay," Diandra replied, "Kendra, you first cause you have the nappiest do, then Shaeyla, Benét, then Worthy."

Tonight is the night of Benét's party, Diandra and the girls promised each other that later that they would all go shopping together, then get dressed at Benét's. Which will be fine, but Worthy's ass is going to want to "take a ride" before hand. *Like I said I still get down and do my thing every now and then, but her ass is more now than then* Diandra thought. We have told her a hundred times about riding around getting high . . . she is not going be happy until her ass is locked the fuck up.

"Well ya'll know that I'm short on dollar's so, I'll hang with ya'll but no new outfit for me," Worthy said. "Besides I need to pay my electric and phone bill before they get cut off. I still owe the daycare provider for last week . . . shit I need to find me some money from somewhere."

"Hell," said Kendra flippantly, "I bet if you want a bag of weed, you could find some money!"

"Don't act like you ain't never get high before," Worthy told Kendra.

"I never said I didn't but damn, I grew up and out of that shit. Besides, you have a son. Why do you think his bad ass is so unruly? You too damn high to correct him," Kendra replied.

Looking at the explosive expression on Kendra and Worthy's faces, Diandra looked at Benét to step in. "Alright!" Benét yelled. "This is my night—no *our* night to party. So no more snide comments from anyone." Benét knew she had to say something so Shaeyla would not step in. Shaeyla could cut you with very few words and make you feel like shit. Now don't get it twisted, none of the girls are afraid of Shaeyla, but she has the uncanny knack for "ruining" a good day.

With hands on hips Diandra sucks her teeth and says, "True dat Benét . . . now if ya'll trying to get your napps busted before tonight . . . I suggest that somebody heads to the sink."

The sound of Diandra's phone interrupts the ladies. "Go ahead" yells Kendra, "I'll get it."

"Hello D's House of Styles," Kendra said into the phone.

"Yeah bitch—you better watch your back!" the caller said before hanging up. Kendra looks at Diandra with questioning eyes.

"What's wrong?" Diandra asked Kendra.

"There was a girl and she said, 'Yeah bitch—you better watch your back!' With a quizzical look at Diandra and asks, "Diandra, what the fuck is going on? Why is a bitch calling your shop, threatening you?" Kendra asked.

"Shit!" exclaimed Diandra.

"Alright, Diandra what's up?" asked Benét.

Damn! Of all times for her not to have answered her phone, this has to happen. Now, here comes the questions, damn, damn, damn!! Diandra knows her girls too well and she is not going to be able to blow them off. Now they all up in her business, but these are her girls—and oh hell she has to tell them at some point why not now she decided.

"Remember that dude I told ya'll I met at the club a few weeks ago?" Diandra asked her girlfriends.

"Yeah—and" they asked. "What about him?"

"His girl—or his old girl has been sweating me since she saw us at the club Sunday."

With hands on her hips Benét interrupts, "See I told you about those fucking thug friends of yours."

Looking at Shaeyla, Kendra, and Worthy, they are all nodding in assent to what Benét just said. "Fuck ya'll—them being thugs ain't got shit to do with it . . . anyway it's my business and I'll deal with it!" Diandra stated defiantly.

"Them being thugs has everything to do with it! They don't know anything else but fighting, and I hope like hell you ain't fighting over Madison's dumb ass—it is Madison isn't' it?" asked Shaeyla.

"No his name is Mason," Diandra corrected.

"You know, they are right," said Worthy.

Swirling around to point a finger in her face "I know you ain't' talking," Diandra accuses, "being that your ass got just as many if not more thugged out friends than I do!" she told her.

Clapping her hands to try to regain order, Benét yells "Alright, Alright—can we table this until later, let's get our hair done and go shopping. Besides you know what I always say . . . 'Life ain't over till it's over and you best to be glad that your still amongst the living' but on the real—Diandra, we gonna have to talk."

Rolling her eyes at her girls, she replied, "It's my business and I can handle it."

Shit, they always did pass judgment on the brothas that she dealt with Diandra remembered. "Does he own a car? To hell with the car, does he have a job, his own crib?" Are the questions they ask every time she meets someone new, especially Shaeyla, as if Randy is any better. Shaking her head, she knows that she is going to have to call Mason and tell him to he better check that bitch and get her straight before she does. As Diandra commences to wash Kendra's hair, she shakes off the gloomy feeling and tries to perk herself up for the coming night.

Chapter 8 ➢ Benét

"Ladies, its party time!" Benét shouted, and turned to show off the back of her banging ass dress that she had purchased earlier that day.

"We all look marvelous, sexy and not to mention gorgeous," Shaeyla said.

The dress that Benét decided upon was the basic black dress, but the back plunged to just above the base of her spine exposing her smooth caramel creamy back. Nestled in the middle of her back were the silver ties that were all that held the dress together. Diandra had styled her hair in the latest cut with a sexy flip in the back and Chinese bangs smoothed out to just above her brow. She was a little apprehensive about whether or not Kendall and the kids would like it, but they said it made her look younger and sexier. Oh well, as much as she disliked her hair in her face, it was beginning to grow on her. Benét also hopes that it will help to put some zest into her increasingly non-existent love life. She is going to have to talk to her husband eventually, but not tonight. Tonight is her night to celebrate the next phase of her life on the road to achieving her dream. Turning to look at her friends she smiled as she slowly expels a breath and Thank God for these four special women.

Shaeyla had on a smoking red jumpsuit with a deep vee front. The pants had sharp cuffs and with the jumpsuit, she wore red strappy sandals. Diandra was ghetto chic in her designer jersey knit ankle length dress, with a look of denim topped with a short-cropped jacket with the FUBU emblem on the breast pocket. Kendra and Worthy both opted for pantsuits, Kendra's a deep jade green with a camisole, and Worthy's was a cream color from her favorite store- a consignment shop.

"Now time to move into the living room and get ready for the arrival of the first guest. Remember please, I want you all, to be nice to Kendall's co-workers. Oh, and he said that he invited his bosses Mitchell Steele and Solomon Jackson. Please Shaeyla, no sarcastic or arrogant behavior from you, Diandra no ghetto behavior and Worthy no 'little walks'. Kendra I know I don't have to worry about you," Benét stated.

Giving a mock military salute to Benét, in unison they line up and yell, "Mam, yes Mam!" Then the ladies laughingly descended the steps into the living room.

Shaeyla used Benét's favorite colors of lavender, purple and fuschia to decorate the living room, foyer, and the banister. And she called in a favor to get the hand blown glass bud vases placing fresh spring tulips on the table in the entry foyer and in beautiful roses on the dining tables all in Benét's favorite colors. The table used a sheer beaded overlay atop the traditional linen tablecloth, with contrasting place settings. Benét wanted each person to have a nametag, so Shaeyla enlisted the help of her assistant and had nametags and holders fashioned like the initials from Benét's foyer of "BKG" to symbolize Kendall's support. The jazz band was Shaeyla's way of adding a touch of class to the party, but she also had a disc jockey, because none of her girls liked jazz. The wait staff would circulate throughout the party with Belvedere martinis, cosmopolitans, wine and champagne. They would also carry the delicious delights that Benét loved, crab balls, brushetta, crab imperial on small garlic baguettes, scallops and shrimp barbecued and wrapped in bacon. There was also a hot and cold buffet area set up with cold salads, stuffed chicken breast, salmon with tarragon sauce, steamed vegetable medley and a Caesar and house salad. The sight of the beautifully adorned room made Shaeyla smile, because she knew she had not let her friend down.

"You ladies look absolutely beautiful. I can't wait to see my co-workers response and my bosses' for that matter," stated Kendall. As he looks at all of the ladies, he instinctively knows that his bosses were going to love Shaeyla. She is the type of woman that will tempt and intrigue them. She is beautiful and independent. Damn, when Mitch and Sol spot her they are going to go in for the kill. He'll keep an eye on her tonight, just in case, because those brothers are highly competitive personally and professionally.

"Why thank you," they all said.

Striding to his wife's side he places a glass of wine in her hand, the expectant look on her face for some form of intimacy had him placing a kiss upon her temple before turning around to stride across the room and stand near Shaeyla. Damn, tonight is not the night to think about the problems that he and Benét have been experiencing in their bedroom. Shaking his head to clear it of his thoughts, Kendall turns to Shaeyla and asks, "Is Randy joining you tonight?" He senses something is not quite right as he notices the way she expelled her breath and reared her shoulders back as if she is about to deliver some shocking news.

Rolling her eyes, she informs him, "Well, I haven't said anything to Benét or any of them yet, but the other night I broke it off with Randy."

With a wide-eyed look of disbelief, Kendall silently thanks God above for this woman finally coming to her senses. Shaeyla has put up with entirely too much shit from him if the history that Benét gave him about the two of them is true. He did not understand why some women did the things that they did. Benét always says that women will do and put up with anything to say they have a man. She calls it selling their soul. Kendall called it stupidity.

The ringing of the doorbell stops the chatter as Kendall excuses himself from Shaeyla and Benét comes from the dining room to the door to admit their first guest.

Chapter 9 ➤ Trapped in the Corner

Hello! Why is it that I can never get the girls attention when I need it the most? Who is this trout mouth breath Negro hovering around me since he arrived at the party? Diandra asks herself. And where is Seven, he told me he would meet me here and be on time for dinner and it's almost 7:30 now. Benét will be pissed if her table numbers are off, not to mention Shaeyla's bourgeois ass since she 'choreographed' the event. Shit! This dude still has not taken the hint that she is not *even* listening to him, let alone *remotely* interested in his conversation. "Shoot!" Diandra silently exclaims to herself, there is no escaping him either. Diandra promised Benét no ghetto, which is hard because five more minutes and dude is about to catch a bad one.

Mentally, Diandra starts to count down from five, four, three, two, just as she is about to say "one" the voice in her hear says, "Hey girl, sorry I'm late," Seven said sheepishly. He knew how much she hated anyone being late, unless it was her. Girl this man's timing is terrific, so take that "Mr. Trout" as Diandra has come to think of him. Maybe now he will get the hint and leave her alone. Turning around to face Seven, she excuses herself to give him a grateful hug.

Diandra just hopes Seven does not blow her cover for what she is about to do, but since being nice, did not work, maybe this will show Mr. Trout better than telling him that she is not interested in him. Looking up at Seven with 'love' in her eyes, she slowly lower her arms to run her hands up and down his arms, reaching up she wraps them around his neck, she has to stifle the look of incredulity on Seven's face. Standing on tiptoes, she whispered into his ear, "Just follow my lead so I can get rid of this foul breath smelling nigga."

The look of shock on Seven's face was quickly masked by a gleam in his eyes as if he was trying to see something within her. Diandra did not know that deep down inside he had been biding his time, hoping she would see him as more than just a friend, and when she does look at him in that way, it's a ploy to rid herself of yet another man. As if coming to a decision mentally he whispered back, "No problem."

Slowly and gently, he caresses her face, as if she is the very air that he needs to breathe. Diandra can feel her heart start to race and her palms get sweaty, and a little quiver of anticipation trills down her spine. *What is going on, she wonders silently damn and the nigga ain't even kissed me yet! Well, I did ask him to help me out and this is a very convincing little scene.* Not wanting to take her eyes away from his, she attempt's to glance around the room to make sure that "her eyes" (Kendra, Benét, Worthy and Shaeyla) were all occupied, that way she would not have to answer too many questions later. These thoughts are quickly erased from her mind as he felt the first touch of Seven's lips upon hers.

Gazing at her mouth, Seven tried to calm his racing heart. He was going to make her remember this kiss for a long time to come and hopefully she will look at *him* as more than a friend. Softly, and slowly he traces his tongue around her lips before grasping her bottom lip between his own. Parting her lips with his tongue, he could have sworn later that he heard her give a deep moan of pleasure as he deepened the kiss. Breaking away from the kiss and out of his arms, Diandra swirls around to go to the bar and get herself a drink.

Talk about the kiss of death, pleasure, pain and anticipation were the words rolling around Diandra's mind as she strode across the room to the bar. Damn, Seven's kiss was da bomb. Inwardly her heart was racing thinking *who* knew he could kiss so good. *He had outlined and traced her lips with his tongue, before softly and slowly plunging his tongue into her mouth.* Damn! Damn! Damn! Just the thought had goose bumps appearing on her arms, this is Seven, she had to keep telling herself. Truthfully, she did not want the kiss to end, boy she was really feeling that kiss. No man has ever kissed her like that before, never, never, never! But Seven, damn she's seeing him for the first time now, really seeing him. He is going to make some woman very lucky, she thought dejectedly because she never mixed sex with friendship. That is her main motto, turning friends into lovers always ends up in you loosing a good friend. No way is she going to go there. Helplessly, she turns around and notices that Seven is looking at her as if he is trying to see into her soul. Wrenching her gaze from his, she turns to find her worst fear.

Across the room, she spotted Kendra and Worthy in the corner, with complete and utter expressions of surprise on their faces. They had witnessed what just transpired between her and Seven. Noticing the look of surprise in her friend's eyes, she gave them a no need to worry look, then winks and mouths that she will talk to them later. A flash of red out of the corner of her eye has her turning to see Shaeyla striding purposefully towards Benét and Kenny's den, with Randy in tow. Mmmm . . . wonder what is going on with them, because home girl does not look happy Diandra thought. Hell, they've told her time and time again to get rid of Randy's sorry behind, but she just won't do it. And we know that she is no longer in love with him, but she is content, not happy but content. She has been with him for so long that she is afraid to leave because she doesn't want to be alone. Shaeyla is her girl and she has it going on. She has finally turned her party planning into a moneymaking business, and she should be with a brother that respects her and will treat her like a queen. Someone like Kenny's boss, Diandra mused. Speaking of which, she is not the only one that notices Shaeyla and Randy walking into the den. Looks like Randy may have some competition, that is if Shaeyla will give him the chance. In one fell swoop she could go from a zero to a hero. Well the girls always accuse her of being nosy Diandra was thinking . . . might as well stay true to form. *Let me go and mingle, and the first person that she will start with is who else—Mr. Mitchell Steele and find out where his mind is.*

Chapter 10 ➤ Party Time

This party is going along really well. Kendall has some great co-workers and overall nice friends. Shaeyla knows some of them, as they have been friends for a while. A few of his co-workers went to high school with us or our parents knew their parents, and/or they're members of the church. However, she did not recognize some new faces. Scanning the room, her eyes land on the most impressive figure with his back to her near the bar with six women hanging onto his every word. He stood around six feet two or three, with a broad set of shoulders that any woman would feel safe in. His hair was a beautiful coal black, with what black folk called "good hair", a head full of black silky curls. Shaeyla could see her running her hand through that thick mane of hair while he was poised over her and about to slide into her. As she stands there imagining how good he would be in bed, she can feel her nipples harden and protrude through the fine silk fabric of her jumpsuit. *"Damn, I need to get laid,"* Shaeyla says as she shakes herself out of her reverie, *"Sexual frustration is a bitch."*

After telling Randy that she wanted to test the waters solo, Shaeyla knew that in the back of her mind he would show up eventually. If she is lucky he will not come here and ruin her night, but he is a persistent little fucker. Ever since she left his house that morning, he has been calling her begging for another chance. No chance of that happening she said. Been there done that, and she refuses to go back there ever again.

Looking down at her watch, she notices the time is almost 7:30, and they would be moving into the dining room for dinner. Thinking about dinner, she reminds herself that not only is she a guest, but she is the event planner extraordinaire. Shaeyla is looking to get some new clients from the guest, for her business. Turing to move into the kitchen to check on her staff, she is stopped mid stride with a hand to her shoulder, Shaeyla turns to find Kenny and the brother she just spotted across the room standing before her.

"Shaeyla Andrews," said Kenny, "I'd like you to meet one of bosses, Mitchell Steele, of Jackson-Steele Consulting. Mitchell just advised me that unfortunately Solomon Jackson, my other boss will not be able to make it."

Shaking his proffered hand, "A pleasure to meet you Mr. Steele." She could not believe how calmly she stated that while her insides were quivering and she had butterflies in her stomach.

"Please call me Mitch," as he took my hand in his and held it for just a minute too long.

"But the pleasure is all mine," he stated in his smooth velvety voice. This man had a voice like chocolate silk. I be damned if he didn't sound like Billy Dee in Lady Sings the Blues. *The scene where he places his hand out and ask Diana Ross "are you going to let my hand fall off."* Oooh—just thinking about it makes me hot.

Up close, she could get a better look. He stood six feet, three inches tall. He had "good hair" too. It was naturally curly, that he wore in a ponytail with a Native American clip holding his locks together. At least she was right about his height and the hair, but his eyes were a deep rich brown and his complexion was that of smooth creamy chocolate. This brother was fine, and all of the women at the party knew it, her included. He is the epitome of masculinity-sexy, virile, witty, charming and intelligent. Not to mention rich—hell she had heard the stories from Kenny on how he and his partner built his consulting firm from the ground up. This is exactly the kind of man she has always secretly desired, but instead she settled on Randy. Shaeyla knew an instant attraction to this man, and that made him dangerous.

"Kendall tells me that you are responsible for putting together this evenings festivities."

Dumbfounded by this man nothing else came to mind other than, "Yes I am."

"My partner and I were discussing earlier how we would like to do something similar to this for our quarterly meeting's, holiday parties and any other company events. We need to discuss retaining your services for our upcoming venues as well as a charitable benefit we are sponsoring."

"Fantastic, here is my card and it has my cell, pager and my office numbers on it. I would love to discuss it with you at your convenience," I told him with my sweetest smile.

The arm sliding around my waist instinctively tells me that Randy is here and has the nerve to act proprietorial! He kisses me on the cheek and apologizes for being late. Oh no the fuck he didn't come in here like we are still together. Trying to suppress the shear rage building within her, she turns to excuse herself from Mr. Steele.

"Mitchell, could you excuse us for a moment please?"

"Sure, and you'll be hearing from me soon," he said.

Cutting my eyes at Randy I turn knowing without a doubt that he will follow me. This will be the last time that she would have to deal with him! Striding across the room to Kenny's study cum office, I open the door and allow Randy to precede me in the room. Closing the door, I turn and look at him. "Clearly, I am not pleased to see you. What the fuck do you want? Why are you even here?"

As he lifts his head from his chest, he looks at me with tears in his eyes then pleads for me to give him another chance. Full of more empty promises that we both know he will never fulfill. I cannot help but shake my head at him, for he is a PI-TI-FUL sight. I hate a whining, crying, and begging man. He sounds like a little bitch, sniffling and shit.

Looking him dead in his eyes, "You know what Randy? For the longest time, I clothed you, fed you—basically took care of you, and you never once appreciated anything I did for you.

You didn't appreciate me or the time and effort I spent on making you happy. All you did for ten years was take while I gave. The sad part is that I gave you more, on the hope that maybe, just maybe, you would see the light and do something, *anything* for me." The more I talked to him the sadder I became. Releasing a sigh, I can no longer hold back the tears from years of anger, pain, and frustration. As I let the tears fall, I can feel a sudden cleansing of my soul. The burden of his love had long since left, but the burden of responsibility that I felt towards him has finally been released. I am free! Free to live my life and love myself again.

Randy mistakes my tears of joy and discovery for tears of forgiveness, which is confusing to me because I just told him that the gravy train has stopped. I do forgive him, but I will never forget the pain that I allowed myself to go through for years.

As he steps towards me with opened arms, I put up my hands to ward him off. "Don't touch me."

"But Shaeyla—," he starts.

"No Randy. It is time for you to go. Please don't call me or contact me anymore. Please just do me that favor and we will be fine."

Hanging his head, his tears wrack his shoulders, but I can no longer feel for him. As I turn away from him to go into Kenny's powder room to fix my face, I hear the door to his office open and close. Giving myself one last check in the mirror to make sure that I have wiped away all traces of what transpired in here, I open the door. Gingerly, stepping into the office, I am relieved to see that Randy took my advice and left.

Returning to the party, I am besieged by my girls and Kenny, who want to know what happened.

"Girl, what the hell is going on?" they all asked.

Looking at Kenny with a question in my eyes, he moves his head in the negative to let me know that he did not tell them of our earlier conversation.

"Look, now is not the time to discuss this. Benét you have guest to entertain and I have a party and staff to oversee. I'm sorry, but I will talk to all of you after the party and give you an explanation."

Knowing that the look on my face brooked no argument, we all moved back into the living room and made a beeline for the dance floor to really get the party started.

Chapter 11 ➢ Kendra

Niall Adams, Kendall's co-worker seemed to be nice. At six feet, 230 pounds the brother is quite nice . . . but looking down at the plate full of chips in her hand she slides it to the table before skimming her hands-down her sides. Kendra felt the dips and curves of her body and made a mental note to start her exercise program. The thought of exercising had her looking at the couple that just strode into Benét's living room to dance. They were so out of shape that it gave her the determination to change her situation. If they only knew how they looked with their bodies jiggling all over the place, they would just sit down. Their weight combined had to be close to five hundred pounds and with them being short, they resembled the weeble-wobble toys she played with as a child. At two hundred pounds herself, Kendra's spirits dipped at the malicious thoughts she had for these strangers, but her own weight has always fluctuated but now was the heaviest that she's ever been. A hand on her forearm bought her out of her silent reverie. Smiling she gives Niall her full attention.

"So are you having a nice time," Niall asks in his deep Barry White sounding voice.

"Yes," Kendra responded and to her surprise, she was. She has always been the quiet one of the bunch. She was content to follow her friends as they took charge in all of their adventures.

Returning from her musing, Kendra acknowledged that she was never one for making idle chit chat, but she was surprised to find that she and this man actually hit it off. The best thing was that Niall did not seem to be discouraged by her size. Inwardly she chastised herself as she thought, *there I go again! The girls would have my head if they know that I was thinking like this...they told her she needed to start thinking positive about herself and that a man is either going to accept her or not, but she had to accept herself first.*

The laughter from the dance floor became louder and she could see that the other party goers had started a soul train line. Arms were in the air going from side to side, while everyone paired up to take their turn down the aisle. The sight of gyrating bodies bumping and grinding to the old school funk started Kendra to doing the bank head dance.

Her dancing made Niall hold his hand out to her and pull her towards the dance floor. She attempted to tug her hand free but he just stopped and looked at her and as she noticed his mouth about to question her, the imp inside of her said go for it! Niall's smooth moves matched her booty shaking as she lost herself in the music. Maybe it was those apple martini's that Shaeyla's wait staff had floating through the crowd. Or maybe it was the fact that Niall seemed like such a nice guy. Whatever the reason, Kendra let herself go for the first time in a long time.

As the evening wore on, Kendra found out that Niall was the head accountant at Jackson-Steele Consultants, and has been employed by that company from its inception.

While making small talk, Kendra finds that although he is single and very handsome, the truth was that he only dates occasionally. Kendra remembered what the girls told her about being able to find out the most important information about a person within the first 20 minutes of conversation. That is if the right questions are asked.

Clearing her throat, Kendra asked, "So, do you have any children?"

"No, I don't." He was irritated by her question. "I distinctly remember saying that I date occasionally and that I am single. What would possess you to ask if I have children?"

She swallowed with difficulty and found her voice, "Well, at the age that we are, it's kind of hard to find a man that does not have any children. Regardless of how casual or non-casual his dating schedule is."

Looking her dead in the eye, he responded, "Well I could ask you the same question, but I figured that I would get to know you before delving too deep into your personal life."

She knows now that she has once again put her foot in her mouth, by saying the wrong thing. Damn, she knew she was lacking in the "chatting" department. Apologizing to him, Kendra turns to walk away.

As she turns to leave, Niall grabs her by the hand. The chemistry between the two of them had Kendra snatching her hand back in disbelief. Her breath caught in her throat and had her heart pounding.

"Just because I did not appreciate your question, does not mean that I want the conversation between us to end." Her answering smile was mirrored in his own face as she could see a smoldering spark in his eyes. At that moment the disc jockey put on Heat Waves hit song *Always and Forever* which cleared the dance floor leaving plenty of room for couples to get close. Kendra could not remember how or when she realized that Niall had maneuvered them onto the dance floor, but she felt the flex of his forearms tighten around her as she slowly relaxed into his body. Mmmmm, Kendra purrs to herself as she closed her eyes and inhaled the crisp scent of his cologne. Her attraction to him combined with the music, had excitement zinging along her spine and she was sure that he could feel it as well because it was evident as his growing manhood pressed up against her. Pulling away from him slightly to stare into his eyes, she was amazed and shocked to discover that a big girl like her could arouse such a viral and handsome man like Niall. Exited yet embarrassed she runs a hand over her now red face, looking for a place to compose herself. Turning away from Niall, she sees the eagle eyes of her girls staring at her with looks of shock and joy. The burning in her cheeks deepens and she silently curses her mother for having inherited her fair complexion. In desperate need for air, she suggests to Niall that they step outside onto the patio. Standing directly behind her, Niall placed a comforting hand on her shoulder before sliding it down her arm to clasp her hand in his. The warmth of his hand warmed her cold palm and Kendra silently thanked him for not saying a word as she worked through the dizzying effects of his presence.

Damn, Kendra silently exclaims, this man is so out of her league, but she would love to get to know him. Hell, who is she kidding, this is just the kind of man that would rock her world, and she has chills running up her spine at the thought of the two of them being intimate. The girls would not believe that she was thinking like this. Well they would because the look of shock on their faces when they saw her dancing left no doubt in her mind that she would be bombarded with questions. Out of all of the girls, she is the last one to go in for one -night stands, regardless of how 'hot' she got. Pulling herself together, she looked down at her small hand cupped in his large one. As she slowly looked up into Niall's eyes, she saw understanding and wanting. Then as he had her mesmerized he slowly moved their clasped hands upwards, while opening her hand to place a hot, wet kiss upon her palm. The feel of his lips on her moist palm made her close her eyes for a moment and when she opened her eyes his answering smile made her heart skip a beat. As the doors behind them opened the sounds of the party broke the spell between.Grinning stupidly they turned to rejoin the revelers, while each of them were thanking their lucky stars that they were forced to attend this evenings event.

* * * * *

As the last of her guest left and the clean up crew arrived, Benét joined the girls and her husband in the living room. She had informed Kendall that the girls and she were going to play a little catch-up, as they did not have the chance to gab during the party. However, from the faraway looks on their faces, she was pleased to see that everyone appeared to have enjoyed themselves.

Worthy was the first to start as she asked Diandra, "So what was that kiss about?"

"Girl it was nothing. I was trying to get rid of that foul breath smelling coworker of Kendall's," replied Diandra with a look of innocence. "But, damn girl, let me tell you, Seven has a tongue that would make a sista's panties soaking wet."

Rolling her eyes Benét stated, "Girl when are you going to open up your eyes and recognize a good man when he is in your face? That brother has been sniffing around you for a while now under the auspices of being your friend. We can all see the way he looks at you, as if you are *the one*. But no! You want to roll with the ballers, thugs, gangster-ghetto fabulous brothers and we just don't understand that. Seven is an entrepreneur, good looking and child free, what more can you ask for? With Seven, you seem to have blinders on. But guess what, you can bet that he is not going to wait forever, so you need to jump on that before some other less deserving female has your man."

Ignoring what Benét just said to her, Diandra turned to Shaeyla and said, "Enough about me, I noticed that a certain sexy gentleman had his eye on someone. Who I might add was too busy dealing with a zero to even notice the hero that was feeling her."

Averting her eyes from the girls, Shaeyla said, "I told you all that I would explain what went down between Randy and me, so here it is. My relationship with Randy is over." She then went on to explain about the incident that took place at his crib after she left Benét's house.

"What everyone witnessed tonight was Randy not believing a word that I told him," Shaeyla told her girls, "And to answer your question, yes I did feel the hero tonight."

"Girl, you know that man was feeling you. His eyes followed you around the room, so what's up?" Kendra asked.

"And how would you know," Worthy said to Kendra, "You were occupied with 'Mr. Barry White' all evening."

"He was a fantastic man and the conversation was great," sighed Kendra. "His name is Niall Adams, and he works with Kendall." Cocking her head to the side she said, "How would you know

Worthy? You were too busy trying to sneak out and get high. I saw you slip back in through the French doors, a couple of times I might add." Kendra said to her rendering her speechless for a minute.

As the girls laughed out loud they thought that Worthy had no response then Worthy put an 'I don't give a fuck' look on her face and said to Kendra, "You are a nosy bitch." Then she flipped her the bird.

"I thought I told you that I didn't want you taking a walk during my party!" Benét exclaimed. "Damn girl . . . you need help!" she said to Worthy with a look of exasperation.

"Overall I think the party was beautiful," said Shaeyla. "Of course, under my expert advice I had no doubt that it would be a success."

As everyone agreed to that statement, the girls gathered up their items and headed for their cars. Hugs and kisses went all around. Benét embraced Shaeyla and told her that she would call her over the weekend.

Locking up the house after the clean left, Benét could not help but think of the reason she had this party to begin. She was going back to school!! She still found the reality of her decision hard to believe. The wistful look on her face had Kendall asking her what she was thinking. She told him how she could not believe that she was fulfilling her dream of returning to college.

"Baby, I am behind you one hundred percent. I will make sure that me and the kids do our parts. You have a natural talent for decorating. Look at our home; you have turned it into a show-place of understated elegance, yet it still has that lived in homely feeling. You have worked wonders with Kendra and Shaeyla's homes and not to mention what you did for Diandra's shop. We have all been telling you that you needed to be paid for what you do and stop giving away your talent for free. See how Shaeyla turned her love for organizing and throwing parties into a thriving business? I have faith that you can do the same."

"It's not so much of you and the kids not believing in me," Benét intoned. "Your love and support were the two things that I counted on when I signed up for classes. Do you know that I am probably going to be the oldest person in my class?"

"Probably, but you will be the finest sister on campus. Those young girls have nothing on you," Kendall lovingly stated.

Hearing these words come from Kendall has tears in her eyes. Here lately the tension between them has been thick, especially in the bedroom. Ever since Kendall was promoted to the Director of Engineering, their sex life has been non-existent. Either it is too late when he gets home or he is too tired, which leaves her frustrated as hell. The last few times she tried to entice Kendall into making love, he had trouble getting an erection. She told him it was okay, that the stress of a new job could have that kind of effect on men. Nevertheless, Kendall was not trying to hear that. Therefore, she waited three days, hoping that he would want to try again, but he didn't. On the fourth day, Benét put on her sexiest nightie and initiated the sex between them but to no avail because he still could not get an erection. It seemed that the harder she tried the softer it became if that is even possible. Her man has never had that problem, but lately she has been self-manipulating to the point that her eyes were beginning to stray. That combined with a campus full of men would not be a good thing because she loves her husband and she has too much to do to be distracted by looking at her professors The thought of the possible distractions had her wondering when they will be able to make love. As she voiced her fears to Kendall about them maybe spending even less time together once she started school, he wrapped her in his arms and said "we will survive and find a way through this". As she turned in his arms to kiss him, Benét hoped that tonight would be 'the night'.

As she started to move down Kendall's body, kissing, caressing, sucking and licking all of the spots that she knew would get him in the mood, she lead a path straight to his manhood. That is when reality set in, tonight was not going to happening. Kendall was as limp as a wet noodle.

Pushing her away, he stormed into the bathroom and slammed the door. Benét attempted to talk to him to tell him that it was okay, but he would not listen nor talk to her.

Knocking on the door, she depicted an ease she didn't necessarily feel, and stated, "Kendall, baby? It is okay. We can work through this. There are other ways to make love." Damn why did she say that? He couldn't even get it up and here she was talking about him going down on her to give her some release.

"Benét, leave me the fuck alone! I need to handle this on my own, and in my own way!" He yelled through the closed door.

"Baby, don't get mad at me when I say this, but have you thought about seeking professional help? I mean a doctor or a psychiatrist could probably help us."

"Us, this is my problem Benét, not yours."

"On the contrary Mr. Grier!" Benét yelled through the door, because right about now she's getting pissed. "This affects the both of us. We have not made love in over a month, going on two months now, Kendall. That is how long this problem has been going on. I am so sick and tired of apologizing to you about this situation and all you do is turn and take your frustrations out on me. I am willing to go to the doctors with you, but you have to be willing to first accept that there is a problem. I miss being intimate with you so much Kendall, I just want us to get back to the way we used to be."

Turning from the door, she climbed into bed and waited for him to come out of the bathroom. As she pulled the covers up over her head, she heard Kendall moving around and then the sound of the shower being turned on.

Benét must have fallen asleep, because the sun was shining through her bedroom window and she found herself in bed—*alone*. The only sign that Kendall did eventually come out of the bathroom was the imprint of his head on his pillow.

Chapter 12 ➤ Kendall

Shuffling the papers on his desk, Kendall looks up upon hearing the knock on his office door. "Come in," he said.

His boss Mitchell Steele walked in. After the obligatory greeting, Mitchell Steele states, "I wanted to stop past and thank you for inviting me to your party. I thoroughly enjoyed myself."

Kendall wondered what he was getting at. He knew that his boss did nothing and said nothing without a reason. Mitchell Steele, is the ultimate cause and effect person. Kendall would be his last dollar that Shaeyla was involved. Kendall saw how his boss monopolized her at the party. Not that Shaeyla looked like she was bothered, not in the least. If his memory served him correctly, the party is the first time that he has seen her truly happy and without Randall, the albatross around her neck.

Mitchell goes on to state, "Your wife has some beautiful friends, especially Ms. Andrews. Why haven't you mentioned her before?"

Ding, Ding, Ding, Ding, Ding, the bell just went off in Kendall's mind. Bingo! He knew a woman was involved. "Because she just recently broke up from a relationship," he told him.

"Not that brother that showed up late and looked like he was on something?" asked Mitchell.

"One and the same," Kendall replied as he wiped his hand across his chin. "So what do you really want?" *As I said, there is a reason for everything with his employer.*

"I would like to see her, if she is willing. Do you think you or your wife could help me out?" Mitchell asked.

"Well I would have to talk to Benét, although I've known her for a while, she is Benét's friend. Besides man, she was with that man for about ten years. I know, he is a loser, but for some reason, she stayed with him. Benét and I could not figure it out, nor could her family or any other friends, but she finally got out. We are all just glad it was not too late."

"Benét and I feel that were it not for him, Shaeyla would be a lot further along in life. I tell you, she lavished so much love and attention on him, it was not funny. I tease Benét all the time and tell her she needed to be more like Shaeyla."

"She is absolutely beautiful and that is not just on the surface. From our time spent together at your party, I have to tell you that Ms. Andrews is a fascinating woman."

As Kendall digests what his boss just said, he knew how long the two of them talked. Before Randy showed up and after Shaeyla escorted Randy to the door, she made a beeline straight for Steele.

"Look, Shaeyla has to agree to meeting with you first. Besides, I thought you asked her to do the company's annual affair?" inquired Kendall.

Shaking his head Mitchell said, "Man, I forgot about that, I'll have my assistant call her and set up a meeting today."

Shaking hands, Mitchell exits his office. Kendall reaches for the phone to share this news with Benét. His boss interested in Shaeyla, now brother is a playa so he needed to make sure he does not hurt home girl or his shit at home is going to be in the doghouse. Yeah he best let Benét know so she can have a one-on-one with Shaeyla.

He dropped the phone back on its cradle. The conversation that he had had with Benét after the party hit the forefront of his mind. Thing's have not been good between them since. Benét just did not know how right she was about seeing a doctor. He is so glad that she could not see his face, because he did go to the doctors and was diagnosed with temporary impotence due to stress. He asked him about his lifestyle, activities and his job. Kendall told him about his promotion to Director of Engineering, Doctor Charles nodded his shiny bald head and asked Kendall if he had an active and healthy sex life up until he received his promotion. Answering in the positive, Kendall remembers telling the doctor since the promotion that he has had problems with achieving an erection. Doctor Charles told him to talk to Benét and inform her of his diagnosis, but he just could not bring himself to tell her that he was suffering from Erectile Dysfunction which is the reason why he could not make love to her.

Hell, he loves his wife, but they have never, ever, had a problem in the bedroom. He considered himself a lucky man, because after the year's they have been together and married, Benét has remained a loving, generous, erotic, sexy, sensuous woman. She could also be a freak when he asked her to be. She loves sex and her appetite was just as voracious as his, or at least his was voracious. Now he couldn't even satisfy his baby physically. Pushing away from his desk, he decided to take a walk to clear his thoughts.

"Regina, hold my calls, I am going out of the office for a while. If Jackson or Steele needs, me page me," Kendall told his secretary.

Chapter 13 ➢ Worthy

Worthy placed the key into the door of her shabby apartment, and kicked off her sandals all the while grabbing a beer from her fridge. Glad to be home from one of her part-time jobs she strides across the room to check her messages. Pushing the pile of dirty clothes from her worn couch she sits down and punched in a series of codes and passwords to retrieve her messages. First message said:

"Ms. Mitchell, this is Patricia Smith, calling from Central Collections, it is imperative that you contact our office as soon as possible regarding your utility bill. Please contact me at 410-555-1398 extension 227."

Slamming down the phone before listening to the rest of her messages, Worthy realizes that she is yet again short on cash. She knew she should've checked her voice mail sooner because the message from gas and electric was from three days ago. Every time she picked up the phone, it beeped to let her know she had messages, but she just never took the time to listen. Leaning up to click on the light switch, she slammed her beer down when nothing happened, so she got up and walked over to the kitchen and hit the switch there. When nothing happened again, she realized that those bastards had cut her electric off sometime in the wee hours of the morning. Sneaky Fuckers! No wonder her son Jared had crawled in bed with her, there was no heat. Now what!!! Fuck!!! She yelled in frustration, then she took a deep breath to try to calm down. Raking her fingers through her hair, she wondered who she could hit up for some dough to turn her shit back on. She knew that she could borrow the doe from Shaeyla or Kendra, but Diandra and Benét are out because she already owes them money. Needing to clear her mind, she rolls up a fat one and sparks it up. Inhaling the sweet aroma of her blunt, she knows that she is going to get a lecture on responsibility regardless of whom she called. Shit they would get mad at her for getting high now, instead of having a clear mind and trying to figure her shit out right. "You need to stop getting high" she could hear Shaeyla saying. "You need to spend more time with Jared" Benét would say. Worthy didn't feel like hearing that shit, not just yet. Jared can't stay here with no lights or anything. She could always send him to her momma's house- but naw, shit!! Decisions, Decisions! Don't get me wrong the money that I do have is owed to JJ, that's my hook up. But I ain't about to give that up, especially now, because I am going to need me a hit after I finish with this bullshit.

Reaching for the phone, she dialed Shaeyla first.

"Events to Remember, Shaeyla Andrews speaking."

"Hey girl."

"Damn," said Shaeyla, "What's got you up this early?"

Cutting to the chase, Worthy quickly explains the situation to her.

Shaeyla asked, "Worthy when is your ass gonna wake up and grow the fuck up? This is just irresponsible—you have to start worrying about Jared and not JJ!"

"Look are you going to lend me the doe or not." Shit, she knew she shouldn't have called Shaeyla's high-falutin ass.

"No, I am not giving you the money, because your ass needs to learn a lesson. I'll come and get Jared until your gas and electric are back on."

"You ain't taking Jared anywhere you snooty bitch. You act like you never got high, but we all know different don't we? And as they say 'birds of a feather, etc.'."

"What do you mean by that statement?" asked Shaeyla.

"I mean Randy's crack smoking, weed smoking ass. Or have you forgotten that JJ supplies both of us? And as Randy's ass wasn't working in a pie factory, we all know who supported his habit, don't we?"

I see that statement shut Shaeyla's ass up. But I'm sorry, someone had to tell her that her "secret" was never a "secret" to begin with. Shit her complaints about money stemmed from her supporting him and his habits.

"You know what Worthy."

"What?"

"You're right, and I'm sorry, but I still ain't lending you the money. And just to remind you, Randy and I are no longer an item. Look girl I love you and you can do better and if you can't we can help, but you have to want the help first," Shaeyla said. "And not just when emergencies happen, like today."

"So you're not lending me the money, yet you say you love me. I don't understand why you think I even have a problem, shit its just weed!" Worthy said.

"Regardless of what *it* is, you're not paying your bills, but you'll buy a sack of weed. All I'm saying is get your act together."

"Alright, whatever, see ya," Worthy said and hung up the telephone.

Reaching for the phone she started to call the next name on her list—Kendra.

Chapter 14 ➢ Kendra

Kendra kept good on her promise to herself and began exercising three times a week. When she couldn't make it to the gym she always got up an hour earlier to ride her exercise bike prior to going to work. Being overweight and sexually frustrated was nerve wracking. She was tired of her girls telling her that they wanted to purchase the dick for her. Even though she had Henry all was well. She knew that they hated "Henry" (her mechanical friend) but "Henry" was okay to use in a pinch. All that changed after meeting Niall, now she had a need to feel his arms wrapped around her while he was knocking her back out. Kendra knew that she was not ugly, as she gazed into the mirror of her guest bedroom. Her short cropped hair stopped just above her ears and her slim neck leveled off to a healthy chest and small waist, but her hips were her main problem. That is where the majority of her weight was which is why she lacked confidence when it came to meeting men. As she picked up the pace on her stationary bike, the sweat poured down her face to pool between her breasts.

The ringing of the phone penetrated her brain and interrupted her exercise. Glancing at the clock, she wondered who was calling her at this time of the morning.

"Hello!" she said gasping for breath into the receiver.

"Hey girl, what's up?" asked Worthy.

Between breaths, Kendra answered, “Getting my exercise on. What's up, why you up so early?” Kendra asked her suspiciously, cause if Worthy was up at this time of the morning she needed something.

“I have a favor to ask you,” she said.

Bingo, she knew she needed something. “How much?” Kendra asked.

“Why do you assume its money?”

“Cause I know you girl, your ass ain't up until after 11am, unless you need something, so how much and for what?”

“I need five hundred dollars. They cut off my electricity and I need that much to turn it back on,” she said.

“Five Hundred!” Kendra exclaimed. “What the fuck are you doing with your money Worthy?”

Kendra doesn't even know why she asked Worthy that question, because she isn't going to tell her the truth anyway.

“Look I know I fucked up, but I promise to pay you back,” Worthy said pleadingly.

“Okay, but we are going to have to talk. You can't keep doing what you’re doing and expecting us to bail you out. I'm doing this for Jared, not you do you understand?” The sound of her huffing and sucking her teeth over the phone didn’t matter because Kendra knew that she didn't want to hear a lecture, but somebody's got to tell her about her trifling destructive ways.

“Okay, I'll make the check out for you, better yet, give me your account number and I'll do it over the phone,” she told her. She wasn’t getting her money to give to JJ's sorry ass Kendra thought.

“Damn, thanks for the trust,” Worthy said to her sarcastically. Then read the account number and the phone number for Patricia Smith at Central Collections at gas and electric company.

“I'll handle it for you and we'll talk later, so bet on it,” Kendra told Worthy.

“Okay, thanks girl, I owe you big time,” Worthy said before she hung up.

Shaking her head in disgust Kendra clicked the phone, and immediately ring's the utility company to have Worthy's shit reconnected. But she is going to talk to the girls. Worthy just ain't doing what she should. Jared deserves better. The poor boy has a druggie for a mother and his father is strung out on that shit too. We heard that he was sucking dick to get hits. What a shame because Nico was fine as shit. It's a shame what drugs can do, shaking her head in disbelief.

Walking back into her exercise room, she switched off her VCR. The bullshit with Worthy used up her workout time and now she has to get ready for work. Walking into her bedroom the soothing baby blue walls always brought her peace. Taking off her sweats, and throwing them into the laundry bin, Kendra plucks a fresh towel and washcloth from her linen closet. Thanks to Benét, her bathroom is done in a contrasting blue, with a southwestern appeal. Kendra knew that her taste was slightly different than her girlfriends. They were more into style, fads, trends, a casual yet elegant atmosphere for their homes and offices. She on the other hand is more into harmony and peace, more of a retreat like atmosphere for her home, which is cool, because it suits her. Stepping into the round cubicle shower, with the three jets protruding from the wall to give her body a full force shower, she smiled to herself. Her thoughts had turned to Niall Adams, *again.* She has wanted to pick up the phone and call him ever since they met at Benét's party. But, that is not her style, if he was interested in her, then dammit he should call her.

Her girlfriends on the other hand, would have a serious problem with that, because they are the types to call if they were that interested. The only problem is that they are about fifty pounds lighter in weight than she is and more secure. Niall didn't seem to have a problem with her weight, especially when Kendall's co-worker, Nina came sauntering over to talk to him. Nina, what a piece of work. She was nice and polite, but she came over shaking her skinny body like everyone was supposed to just stop and drop at her knees. Please, it gave Kendra great pleasure when Niall placed his arm around her waist, and steered them deeper into the corner of Benét's living room. He had no idea how good that made her feel!!! Kendra turned off the shower taps, dried herself off and strolled into her bedroom to get dressed for work.

Grabbing her briefcase and keys from the foyer table, she made a decision to call Niall Adams and ask him to lunch for tomorrow. Feeling good about herself, she slid into her pearl colored Land Cruiser, and headed to the city of Baltimore to begin her workday.

Chapter 15 ➢ The Meeting

Preparing for the meeting with Mitchell Steele of Jackson-Steele Consulting had butterflies in Shaeyla's stomach. Catering Benét's party threw a lot of business her way. The contract with Jackson-Steele could hike her company's revenue up by over fifty percent, if she can secure a retaining fee for future conferences and meetings for his company. Her presentation is laid out and ready, she even printed out handouts in case she was meeting with the board. The idea that she had for the first quarter meeting are both innovative and eclectic. After doing research on the company, Shaeyla found that their first quarter earnings were three points more that the two that had been projected. That is why she created the concept "Five on Time". Her plans involved getting huge decorations of a nickel to hang from the ceiling, with nickel napkins, plates, and party favors. The favors are over size coffee mugs with the company logo on one side and the party theme on the other. Inside of the mug would be a company pen with the company logo and theme emblazoned in black. She just hoped he went for it, because even though in a sense it was corny, it would remind the employees and shareholder that the magic number was five. After preparing for her presentation she quickly took one last look in the mirror, what she saw told her that she was successful in achieving the perfect look. The chocolate brown suit made of soft jersey knit and the cream colored silk blouse was feminine yet professional. The skirt fell mid-calf just skimming the tops of her designer cream-colored boots. The French cuffs of the blouse with a deep v-cut brings out the smooth dark brown complexion of her skin and made her pearl necklace stand out. Diandra did her hair over the weekend in an up do, to make her look more professional, yet sexy. Gathering up her briefcase, and keys, she lock's up the house and headed to her car.

Yes, her car…this baby is mine, she took it from Randy the week before Benét's party, when she told him she was through with him.

The Beemer eats up the miles to the city in record time. Turning into the parking lot of the building that Jackson-Steele is housed in, was impressive. The beautiful pearl green Jaguar that she parked beside had to be either Mitchell Steele's or his partner's. The thought of his partner had her hoping to meet him, because she wanted to present her presentation once, but if she had to she would do it again. As she parked the Jaguar, she took notice of its powerful and elegant sleek lines that screamed wealth and class. Must be nice she thought as she headed towards the entrance.

The rich smell of leather and furniture polish surrounds her as she enters the foyer. She was greeted by a perky young woman sitting behind the desk.

"Good Morning, How can I help you?" the receptionist asked.

"Yes, I'm Shaeyla Andrews and I have an appointment with Mr. Steele."

"He is expecting you. Take the elevators behind you to the top floor. When you exit the elevator, you will see his assistant, Ms. Croghan, she will direct you through to Mr. Steele's office."

Crossing the foyer to the bank of elevators, Shaeyla advised the attendant to press the button for the 12th floor. As the elevator takes her to the top of the building in record time, she steps off, turns to the left as instructed by the receptionist, and announces herself to Mr. Steele's assistant.

"Mr. Steele, Ms. Shaeyla Andrews has arrived," his assistant said into the phone.

Returning the phone to the cradle, his assistant turns and replies, "Please have a seat, Mr. Steele, will be with you momentarily."

As Shaeyla turns to have a seat, she admires the elegant décor of the reception area as she tries to calm the butterflies floating thorough out her stomach.

Girl, get a grip on yourself. You're a successful entrepreneur. This company will benefit greatly from your expertise she thought. Just at that moment, Mitchell Steele appeared. His dark blue suit screams of superior quality. Shaeyla has always been able to tell a man in a cheap off the rack suit and a man in a designer suit because next to planning events she loved fashion. The subtle hint of a yellow pinstripe, with a soft blue shirt and yellowish-gold tie was cut in the classic Ralph Lauren style that accented his shoulders and size. Oh boy, was this going to be a hard meeting. Shaeyla needed to keep her mind focused on the business at hand and not the man.

"Ms. Andrews, a pleasure to see you again." Mr. Steele states with an outstretched hand and warm smile. Damn, his teeth are sparkling white. She drank in his smooth light brown complexion with jet-black wavy hair. *Calm down Shaeyla.*

"It's a pleasure to see you again and I want to thank you for meeting with me."

"No problem, as I informed you when we met, our intention was to have someone else coordinate the annual meeting and the meetings thereafter. Unfortunately, that didn't work out. Also, I must apologize as my partner is tied up in delicate negotiations and will be unable to sit in on this meeting."

As he escorts her into his office, she can see the beautiful view of the Inner Harbor. The plush navy carpet and soft gray and navy pinstripe wallpaper, is masculine yet warm. The expansive cherry wood desk is impressive in its style, with claw feet and gold accents. Lowering herself onto the soft gray silk chair in front of his desk, she attempted to wipe her sweating palms by smoothing out her skirt. As she opens her briefcase to retrieve the report, she asked him if they would be meeting with anyone else. He informed that he and his partner made all of the decisions therefore, it would just be the two of them. Handing him the folder with the business proposal and presentation,

Shaeyla began. Halfway through the presentation, Mitchell asked, "Shaeyla, would you like to break for lunch, then we can resume afterwards?"

Nonplussed, she did not know what to say. Mainly because she found Mitchell Steele a distracting presence on a professional and a personal level. Although, the night of Benét's party Shaeyla remembered that she was a little tight, and her mouth was a little looser than normal. Yet, at this moment he was making her feel horny and desperate, which were feelings that she was not comfortable with. Mitchell noticed her hesitation and said, "If you would rather work straight through that's okay with me."

"Well I don't mind, I just don't want to take up your entire day or take you away from other appointments."

"I have cleared my schedule for the entire afternoon. Especially for you," he tacked on.

Giving him her million-dollar smile, Shaeyla replied, "Well in that case, I would be delighted to have lunch with you."

Thankfully, the elevator ride down was not done alone, as other members of his staff were headed out to lunch. As they stepped out of the elevator, they ran into Kendall about to get on.

"Hey Shaeyla, Steele, how are you?" Kendall says as he gives her a warm embrace. Then he turns to shake Mitchell's hand.

"I am meeting with your boss, to discuss my company doing some event and conference planning in the near future," said Shaeyla.

"Good luck." Kendall then turns to his boss and says "No one can organize an event more effectively or efficiently than Shaeyla."

After parting with Kendall, they make their way to the parking lot and stops at the Jaguar. Mitchell walks to the passenger's side and opens the door. "Thank you," says Shaeyla.

"You are more than welcome," says Mitchell. Then he proceed-ed to the driver's side. After he is seated he starts with idle chit chat.

"So do you have a food preference?" he asked.

"I am an avid seafood lover." Shaeyla wondered where they were going because they traveled south from 695 to I97. Mitch pulls into the valet area of a quaint restaurant situated on the

Chesapeake Bay. The smooth sound of jazz was playing as they entered.

"Good afternoon Mr. Steele. Will you require your usual table today sir?" The maitre'd inquired warmly.

"Yes, thank you."

Shaeyla felt him place a proprietary hand in the small of her back to guide her to their table. From the looks that she received from the male patrons she wondered if it was also an act of ownership. With this thought in mind she pulled slightly away and knew from the fine hair rising on her neck that he was avidly watching the seductive sway of her luscious backside.

Arriving at their table, he held the chair out for her to sit down and crossed around to take his seat beside her. As the waiter handed them the heavy leather bound menus, Shaeyla caught Mitch staring at her from the corner of her eye. She knew exactly what she wanted him to see, a beautiful confident woman whose smooth brown complexion set off her deep brown almond eyes. Her coal black shoulder length hair shone like spun black silk, and was just as smooth to the touch. As she felt him moving his way over every feature of her face he came to her lips and licked his lips in admiration. Her lips were not the traditional full lush lips of many black women, but they were perfectly shaped, with a broad beautiful smile that encompassed her entire face.

"So, what do you recommend?" Shaeyla asked.

"I would suggest the broiled crab cakes, but the ravioli stuffed with mushrooms in a creamy red garlic sauce is equally appetizing."

"I was looking at that. I love mushrooms, but I don't think garlic would be conducive for me to tell you about the plans that I have for your first quarter meeting," Shaeyla laughed.

Picking up her menu, she wondered what his thoughts of her were, because he seemed duly impressed with her quick wit and sense of humor. This was a plus in her factor because she knew that people assumed the worst when they first met her. Her deep brown almond shaped eyes appeared black at times, which is why many told her that at first glance she had the look of a 'takes no shit sister' AKA bitch. Truth be told, Shaeyla knew that she had that look, but deep down she was a sentimental fool.

She loved romance and flowers, and was often told by her girls that she was more in love with the idea of love rather than love it self. The presence of the waiter beside Mitch made her concentrate on the menu.

After placing their orders, they exchanged information on each other's backgrounds, education and hobbies over the meal. Mitchell told her about his partner Solomon Jackson and how they started their engineering consulting firm. He stated that it came about in their last year at Morehouse College where Solomon worked for a merchant generating company in their employee development department. Solomon noticed that there were few blacks in that industry and informed his mangers of this fact. He was then placed in charge of recruiting. Solomon also noted that the company contracted a lot of their work, especially dealing with environmental and mechanical issues. Upon graduating they offered Solomon who was summa cum laude with a double major in chemical engineering and economics, a full time position. He got Mitch a job working in their environmental department as an engineer, and after five years, they both quit to establish their own consulting firm specializing in training and development for merchant generating companies nationwide. They each took turns talking to junior and senior college students majoring in electrical and nuclear industries, informing them of the numerous opportunities available to them.

Shaeyla found the conversation stimulating and commented on the fact that she new nothing at all about the industry but could see where it was probably a white male dominated field. Mitchell also informed her that Solomon was not only his closest friend but more like a brother.

Shaeyla told him about her girls and how close they were and also about her company. The one subject they stayed away from was that of each other's love lives. Shaeyla knew he saw the exchange between her and Randy at Benét's party and was probably wondering about her situation. However, she was not going to broach the subject unless he did. He must've had the same thought to keep the conversation neutral, because he asked her who her favorite musician was.

"My favorite musician of all time is Prince," Shaeyla told him.

Shaeyla saw how this information brought Mitch up short as he stated, “Prince! What do you see in his effeminate ass?” Just as she was about to respond to his question the bleeping of his cell phone stopped her from taking his head off. Shaeyla sipped her water and couldn't help but listen to the one sided conversation as she realized his call was business.

Shaeyla watched as he snapped his phone shut and signaled for the check. “I'm sorry but some important business has come up that I have to tend to. I would like to continue our discussion, so would you care to do so over dinner, say Saturday evening?”

Taken aback by his request, she took a nervous sip of her water, “Huh. Well, huh, sure Saturday would be fine.” After handing him her card with her address scribbled on the back Mitch pulled her chair out and guided them through the restaurant and out the doors to his waiting car.

The drive back to his office building was done in companionable silence, as they each thought about their lunch and forthcoming date.

Chapter 16 ➤ Back to Work

On Shaeyla's drive back to her office, she couldn't believe that she had agreed to meet with Mitch again on Saturday. Thinking about how sexy the man is, isn't going to do her any good. Not only is the man fine, but he is intelligent and financially secure. There is so much more she wanted to find out about him. Shaeyla thought, damn, I need to keep my mind on business, besides momma always said 'you don't get your meat where you make your bread', and that is the truth. Look at how many people that I know that hooked up at work and when the romance was over, someone had to end up leaving, or asking for a transfer. It is never a good idea to mix business with pleasure, but damn—this time is going to be hard. Thinking ahead to Saturday, the sound of her own cell phone halted her thoughts.

"Shaeyla Andrews speaking. How can I help you?"

"Shaeyla Andrews speaking. How can I help you?", Benét mimicked in her best 'white-girl' voice.

"Hey, girl. No, you did not go there. You know I always use my business voice. Besides, that's what I get for not looking at my caller-id. What's going on with you?" asked Shaeyla.

"No, no, no! The question is what's going on with you?"

Playing dumb, Shaeyla asked, "But whatever do you mean?"

"Well a little birdie told me that you had lunch with Mitchell Steele. So how did it go?"

"A little birdie huh? I bet his name was Kendall. Damn, your man can't hold water. He worse than an old woman."

"Hey now, watch it. Seriously, how did your meeting go?"

"I think it went okay. Or rather, it ended before it began. He asked me to lunch to go over the details. We went to this seafood restaurant in Annapolis on the water. A really nice spot. We had a somewhat secluded table- you know to allow for some privacy. But, before we could even order our meal, his cell phone rang and we had to leave. He asked me to if I would be willing to meet him Saturday evening to discuss it further over dinner."

"Well, I know you can do whatever job he asks of you. Now as for this meeting on Saturday, where is he taking you?"

"I don't know yet, he said he would call me, but wherever it is, it is going to be around six-ish." Thinking how handsome Mitchell Steele is, she admonished her friend for not telling her about him sooner. I could hardly eat for looking at him. My pussy did about 20 flips per minute. All that did was remind me that my ass ain't had any in a minute. I don't know how I am going to get through Saturday night." *Actually, Shaylae had some a couple of weeks ago when she went out on a blind date. She didn't dare tell Benét or Kendra that she was having one night stands and she knew that Diandra and Worthy could care less. But she still decided to keep this to herself, because she would never hear the end of it. Besides, since she left Randy, she was getting her freak on. No reason for her not to explore now that she was single, plus, she had to feel what it was like to be with different men, to learn different styles and methods of sex. Hell, there were a few that she went back to a couple of times.* As she smiled to herself, she had to stifle herself from bursting out laughing and returned her attention to Benét.

"Yes he is fine. As for Saturday night, you make sure you don't drink any wine or spirits of any sort. You know how you get when you imbibe too much."

"What do you mean by that?"

"Your ass knows exactly what I mean. Since you left Randy's sorry behind, we know you haven't had any relations—at least not with a man. We're not talking about the times that you do yourself. So, don't go getting drunk and falling on a dick. Ya dig?"

Shaeyla could not help but laugh. Benét was her girl, and that's what she loved about her. She always keeps shit real. Benét isn't the only one, all of my girlfriends keep it real. That is one of the reasons why we get along and love each other so much. There is no hesitation in what we say to one another or how we say it. We agree that if we have this attitude or if we can't say what's on our minds then no one can. We don't care how mad or upset you get, you will get over it.

"Enough about me how are you and Kendall doing?" Shaeyla asked Benét.

"Girl, I don't know how much more I can take. It has been almost three months since we last had sex—and I am tired of bringing my shit out of the closet to do myself," Benét said bitterly.

"What seems to be the problem? Have you all seen a doctor?"

"I asked him to see a doctor but that nigga had the nerve to say that it was his problem not *our* problem. I tried to get him to understand that it is our problem but he doesn't see it that way. Shaeyla, I ain't gonna lie, my ass is getting weak, and my eyes are wandering, so he better work it out and soon."

"Benét, I know that you and Kendall have had your ups and downs, but work with him. Don't fuck up what the two of you have."

"Do you honestly think that I want to fuck up what we have? I don't even like feeling the way that I do, but I have needs too. Hell Shaeyla, we don't even have to have intercourse, we used to have intimacy and now we don't even have that."

"Benét, I'm going to tell you some good shit—so listen up. Diandra, Kendra, Worthy and I, would love to have a man that loves us as much as Kendall loves you. I thought I had that with Randy at one point in time until drugs took him over, but here the four of us are, and we are over thirty and still single. I thought I would at least be happily married by now. Instead, I or shall I say we all have to face the facts that we may never get married. And although that may not be a bad thing, an empty bed can get pretty lonely. Sometimes I wish I had a solid pair of shoulders that I knew without a doubt and without question had my back. I would love to have a man, that special someone to help me share my burdens and problems with. That is what you have so don't go thinking that getting some strange dick is going to change anything. All that is going to do is make it worse."

"Shaeyla, you just don't know—," Benét started.

Cutting her off, Shaeyla said, "Believe me, I understand your pain girlfriend. Hell I stayed with Randy in a loveless relationship for the last few years, and I had plenty of opportunities to cheat and didn't. But you have a good man, give it some time, talk to him and don't go taking in no stray dicks."

"I get your message, damn! Look, I have to go Kenny, Jr. is beeping in. Take care and be careful okay sis."

"Okay girl, later, love ya."

"Love ya back."

Chapter 17 ➢ Shopping

Saturday morning arrived sunny and bright. Opening the blinds to let the light in had Shaeyla feeling anxious over tonight's meeting with Mitch. He had phoned earlier on Friday, to ask if it would be a problem meeting him at his house, because he wanted to do something special and prepare a meal just for me. How could a girl say anything but yes to an offer that sweet?

Walking on cloud nine with anticipation of this evening, Shaeyla moved into the kitchen to prepare a protein shake and noticed the light flashing on her answering machine. Retrieving the message, Kendra's excited voice was bubbling over with excitement about having a date tonight. She went on about desperately needed help deciding what to wear. This is a welcome distraction. Knowing that Kendra is an early bird also Shaeyla picked up the phone and returned her call.

"Good morning!" Kendra said all sunny and bright into the phone.

"Well aren't we chipper this morning," said Shaeyla with a big smile on her face. "So who is the lucky man?"

"Shaeyla, girl thank God you got my message. Niall Adams, a co-worker of Kendall's. I met him the other night at the party."

"Damn, Benét's party seems to have been match making heaven that night," said Shaeyla.

"Who are you telling? I have been talking to Niall since the party. Due to various commitments we are finally able to get our schedules to mesh so that we can go on a date! That's why I figured I'd call you to see if you wanted to go shopping," said Kendra.

"Well it just so happens that I have another business meeting with Kendall's boss, Mitchell Steele, so I could use something more relaxed for tonight's meeting. I can be ready in an hour, you want me to pick you up or what?"

"Well I was thinking we could go to Georgetown, I want something to really knock his socks off," Kendra said.

"Yeah, they have some great upscale boutiques there. Hey! Let's call Diandra, Benét and Worthy to see if they want to hang out."

"Diandra is working—you know Saturday is her busiest day. Benét has to take Zaria shopping for a dress for a school dance and nine times out of ten, Worthy's ass is broke."

"So it is just going to be us," said Shaeyla, "On second thought, Benét could probably find Zaria a beautiful party dress. Hold on, let me call her."

Clicking over to conference mode, Shaeyla dialed Benét's number. "Hey Kendall Jr., where's your mom?"

"Hi Auntie Shaeyla, here she is."

"Hello," Benét said.

"Good morning," Shaeyla said smilingly into the receiver. "Good Morning!" yelled Kendra.

"Good morning to both of you. What's got ya'll all happy first thing in the morning?" Benét asked. "Especially you Shaeyla, cranky as you are in the morning. That's why I don't call you before noon on the weekend."

"Kendra and I are going shopping in Georgetown and were wondering if you and Zaria wanted to go. Kendra told me that you have to take her shopping for a party dress and you know that they have some bad ass shops over there—so what do you think."

"Alright, what time should we be ready and are we meeting somewhere?" asked Benét.

"Well since you and I live close to each other, why don't you and Zaria come to my house then we can drive over to Kendra's and can go from there," Shaeyla replied.

"Cool, we can be there in an hour is that good?" Benét asked.

"Yes," said Shaeyla.

"Cool," said Kendra.

"Okay, we better go and get ready. We'll see you all in an hour," Shaeyla replied.

"Okay, later," said Kendra.

Hanging up the phone, Shaeyla retrieved the mail from the mailbox and moved into the bathroom to run her bath. Adding 'Tranquil Sleep' her favorite scent from Bath and Body Works, she traveled to her bedroom to inspect her closet. All of her clothes were neatly lined up, blouses, dresses, suits, pants, blazers, and casual clothes. Placing a black jersey knit halter jumpsuit and a pair of black and white slides across her bed, she returned to the bathroom to finish her ministrations.

Slipping into the hot soothing water, relaxes her body and mind. Damn, I could sure use a good massage right about now, she mused. The last few months have been somewhat stressful. A good stressful, because it was dealing with work and not Randy, but stress is stress. Business is booming and if she lands Jackon-Steele Consulting as a client, other engineering firms will be eager to jump on board.

Thinking back to the first time she decided to quit her job in the insurance industry and plan events professionally had everyone calling her crazy. Especially her mother and sisters, they thought she was really nuts, to leave the security of a job to the insecurity of being an entrepreneur. The first few years were very lean. All money that was made went directly to daily living expenses and the back into her company. Today she has her very own office, with an assistant. It may not be a fortune 500, but its all hers, lock, stock and barrel!

As the water began to grow tepid, Shaeyla grabbed a towel from the heated towel rack, releases the drain, let the water out and exit the tub.

Fastening the halter straps around her neck, the sound of the doorbell had her stepping into her shoes, and going to get the door.

Peeking through the side window of the door, Benét yells, "Shaeyla, it's us!"

As she let them enter, she could not help but notice how tall and beautiful Zaria was. She is really going to break some hearts—sooner than we want, Shaeyla thought. Throwing open her arms for a big warm hug Zaria said, "Hello Auntie Shaeyla. Thanks for asking us to go shopping with you and Auntie Kendra. We never even thought about Georgetown."

"No problem sweetie. Besides, you know we won't settle for you not being the best dressed not to mention most beautiful girl at the party," Shaeyla said as she held her away from her to look at her. "When is it anyway?"

"In two weeks," Benét responded.

"Two weeks!" exclaimed Shaeyla, while giving Benét the 'eye'.

"Don't even go there Shaeyla, I know we should've been more on point, but with registering for school and all, I just lost track of time. That is why I told Zaria that I would devote this and next week to finding her the best dress in town," Benét said.

Grabbing keys and purses from the foyer table they headed to the car to pick up Kendra.

As they drove along Shaeyla said to Benét, "Girl . . . Kendra has a date tonight."

"With who?" Benét and Zaria asked simultaneously.

"No way, I'm not telling you anything else. Kendra is going to have to drop that bombshell on ya'll," replied Shaeyla.

Pulling up to Kendra's house and tooting the horn, Zaria moved to the passenger seat behind her mother.

"Hello everyone," Kendra said looking like she was on cloud nine.

"Hello Aunty Kendra," Zaria said and gave her a hug and a kiss.

"Benét, what are you and Kendall going to do with her? This girl is gorgeous. Whatever you get today is going to knock your dates socks off," Kendra said to Benét and Zaria.

"Speaking of dates," Benét questioned, "I hear that you have a date tonight. So, who is the lucky man, because Shaeyla wouldn't give up any information on the way over? So, come on with it . . . give us the dirt."

Blushing like she was Zaria's age, Kendra said, "His name is Niall Adams and he works with Kendall. We met the night of your party and have been talking just about everyday since."

Benét tried to think back to that night and the number of people that were at the party, but, she couldn't place him in her mind. "Niall Adams, Niall Adams," Benét said out loud. "I don't remember him, but that isn't important. The important thing is that I am so happy to see that look in your eyes."

"Thanks," she responds with the widest grin on her face. "Girl he is so nice, good-looking, smart, I like him a lot, did I say good-looking?" They all burst out laughing.

"Well that's all that's important," Shaeyla told Kendra.

"Shaeyla's right," Benét seconded. "Women are always trying to make everyone happy but themselves. Don't worry about what we think, your mother thinks or anyone else for that matter. The only one you need to make happy is yourself."

"I know that," Kendra went on to say, "But I have been out of the loop for so long, that I am actually nervous about this date." Looking over at Zaria, she said, "I feel like a teenager again on her first date—isn't that is ridiculous?"

"What the fuck? That's why I hate driving in DC!" yells Shaeyla. Turning around, she apologizes to Zaria for using such foul language.

"Where is Aunt Diandra and Aunt Worthy?" ask Zaria shrugging off her aunts apology.

"Well you know today is the biggest hair day of the week, so Diandra is working and I have no idea where Worthy is," her mother replied.

Stepping out of the underground parking garage in Georgetown, the ladies began to get excited as they were all are on a mission to splurge. The object is to look their best and knock their man's socks off.

Turning to look at Benét and Shaeyla, Kendra stated, "Now I am trusting ya'll to make me look good. Don't let me choose my normal dowdy outfits with those drab colors. Deal?"

Benét, Shaeyla, and Zaria, rolled their eyes and simultaneously yelled, "Deal!"

"Girl, it's about time you got out of that old-maid, spinster clothes anyway. I am going to burn those fucking earth tone outfits of yours when we get back," said Shaeyla.

After several hours of shopping, everyone had an outfit except Shaeyla.

"You should've bought that outfit that you tried on in *Sadea's Hype,"* Benét said.

"I was just thinking that everyone has what they wanted except for me. I did like that outfit, but you know I'm trying to stay away from black."

"You can try all you want, but you and black are synonymous. Hell girl, we rarely see you in anything other than black." To emphasize her point Benét pointed to her clothing, "Look at what you're wearing now."

"We were shocked when you wore that red jumpsuit to Benét's party," Kendra added.

Looking down at her watch, and sighing Shaeyla said, "We have to start back home, I am not trying to be late tonight. Let me run back to *Sadea's Hype* and get that outfit."

Chapter 18 ➤ Crack Time

The weekend always brought out the itch in Worthy to catch a hit and since last night was pay day her last twenty dollars was burning a whole in her pocket. Chewing on her fingernails she paced up and down her living room as she anxiously awaited the ringing of the phone from her contact JJ. "Damn! Where the fuck is he? Any other time, you page his ass and he calls back with a quickness. Here it is going on thirty minutes and I haven't heard from him yet."

Kicking her sons toy truck against the wall in anger, the sound that it made and the scowl on her face made her son Jared ask "Mommy what's wrong?"

"Nothing, Jared! Damn, take your ass to your room and don't come out until I say so," Worthy yelled at him. "Shit fucking kids, getting on my damn nerves, they always fucking underfoot, begging and wanting shit.

I want shit too! I need shit too! Don't nobody try to help me or try to give me shit. I'm the mother-fucking single mother struggling with his ass, no one else. His fucking father split as soon as she told him about the baby—the black bald headed bastard. But as Shaeyla told her *"that is no less what you deserved for fucking a stranger*", that bitch always acts like she knows everything, her and Benét. Worthy could hear their *voices "Worthy you need to do this, stop getting high so fucking much and maybe your ass could keep a job. Hell, you are 36 years old and you haven't worked for one company for more than one year. That shit is pathetic!"* Putting her hands over her ears to stop the sounds of her mind chatter, she picks up the phone to page JJ again. Damn, she needed a blast, now!

Worthy remembered the first time she tried crack. It was at the lowest point in her life, right after she had Jared and his father came to see him the day she brought him home and then told her he was leaving and would never be a part of their lives. She loved that man so much and thought he felt the same about her, but obviously, that was not the case. Worthy had gone *to visit a girlfriend and her sister was there. She knew that her friends sister smoked some different shit, meaning crack, but she was just looking to smoke a vanilla Dutch master with some green leaves. When Worthy arrived at the house, she did her normal of knocking then trying the knob on the door because it was usually unlocked. This time when she walked in, she caught her girlfriend Brenda hitting her sisters' crack pipe. This surprised here, because as far as she knew, her girl only drank and smoked weed, not that shit. But the look on her face and the way her mouth twisted up, she knew at that moment that that shit had to do something to make you feel awfully good. Well you know the saying curiosity killed the cat—well Worthy's ass should be dead, because after Brenda told her that she should try it before she should condemn it, she let curiosity win and tried it. Been hooked ever since. Nothing compares to the very first time you get that blast. The hard part was trying to make sure that her girls didn't find out about what she was doing, but now, she didn't give a fuck! Hell, they have already started to question her, she doesn't hang out with them like she used to and when she does, she doesn't have shit to say to them. They are always lecturing her, like she's a fucking child.*

The ringing of her phone snapped her back to the present and she snatched the receiver on the first ring. "Hello," she said frantically into the phone.

"Damn, shorty," JJ said with laughter in his voice, at the same time, thinking this bitch is feigning like a son-of-bitch. Damn, that saying never get a woman turned out on this shit is true.

Cause Worthy is down for whatever when she ain't got no doe and want that hit up in her. "I got your page. What's up?" he asked.

"Man, you know what's up!" Worthy yelled, and then stopped herself before she cussed him out and would be ass out with no hit. Changing tactics, she seductively asks, "JJ, how come you took so long to call me back? I have paged you a few times today. Can you come and see me?"

"I dont know, maybe I could slide through there later, but I'm getting my grind on right now," JJ told her.

Worthy did not have time for JJ's games. He was either going to bring her the shit or not. "Look, JJ, you know damn well what I want. So can I meet you down the block or you wanna come to my house?" JJ asked her how much was she working with? She knew how he hated to come out for less than fifty so instead of lying she decided to tell him the truth. As she waited for his response she could hear voices in the background that he was shushing. JJ told her if she could help him out with a little something, something then maybe he could see fit to selling her a twenty-piece of rock. She knew this nigga was up to something, but the question was what? Honestly at this time she didn't care what he was up to as long has he came through. Shit who was she fooling? No one but her damn self, because it ain't no secret that she would do just about anything for a blast.

Replacing the phone to her end, Worthy felt like she has just been played.

Kicking her sofa again, her eyes strayed to the clock on her cable box, noticing how much time had passed really pissed her off. Almost 1:00 AM and JJ still hadn't shown up or returned her pages. "Fuck it! Let me take my black ass to bed." That bullshit she copped from that dude downstairs wasn't shit, didn't do nothing but make her madder. That's what the fuck I get for dealing with JJ's lying ass. Wrenching off her shirt she grit her teeth, because just thinking about JJ's shit and that first blast . . . had her feigning all over again. Damn it, she said. Getting into bed, she fell asleep around 4:00 AM to the sounds of the television.

The banging on the door at 5:00 AM, made her think she was dreaming. Who da fuck was knocking on her door at this time of morning? Stumbling her way to the door, she peeped through the peephole and saw JJ.

Opening the door she let him in, and noticed is that he was not alone. He had two other dudes with him.

"No you didn't come to my door at this time of the morning," Worthy said.

"Bitch calm down! You are lucky that I came at all," JJ said, pushing past her to enter the apartment.

"JJ, you said around 11:00 last night, and here it is damn near dawn."

"Look, do you want the shit or not?"

Mad at herself for wasting her money earlier on bullshit she calmed down to say, "I don't have the money now. When you didn't show up, I got some shit from this dude downstairs. And that shit wasn't as good as yours. He must've cut it a thousand damn times. You think you can spot me until pay day?"

Worthy watched him turn around to look at his boys, and then he turned back to her with a sly grin on his face and said, "I tell you what. Let me think about dat, but in the meantime, how about you hit me and my boys off with a little something, something?." Turing to the left he introduced Ray and to his right, Kai.

"So is this the favor that you asked me about earlier?"

"You could say that. So you down or what?"

Scratching the back of her neck, she reached down for a cigarette. This nigga knows he has her, she wanted a hit so bad!!! Damn it JJ. Coming to a decision, Worthy turned back around and said, "Aiight, let me take a shower, then ya'll can take turns."

Shaking his head, "You must've misunderstood, I said hit *us* off, meaning at the same time. See let me run it down to you. I done fucked you already, but my boy's here well now they want a piece too. Besides, they the ones wit da shit, I sold out around three this morning."

"I heard that you can suck the skin off a nigga's dick said, Ray "I just love having my dick sucked."

"And I like pussy," Kai chimed in.

These nigga's are a little over six feet tall; she couldn't believe that she was actually contemplating doing all three of them at the same time. Hell, it's not like she hasn't done dudes for a blast or rent before. Squaring up her shoulders, she heard herself agreeing to it. "But, I still want to take a shower," she stated.

Exiting the shower, she opened the door to find Ray and Kai in her room sitting on the bed. Simultaneously, they both reach for her and began to move their hands over her body. Ray unfastens his pants and stood up and wrapped his hands around her head and thrust his dick into her mouth. And oh, what a beautiful dick it was, long and thick, just the way she liked them. Wanting some of what Ray is getting, Kai unfastened his pants, and twisted her head guiding her mouth to his thick shaft. *Damn, two long and thick dicks she thought,, at least the shit that I will get from them will be good, cause I'm about to let the ho out.* Stuffing both dicks in her mouth at the same time, she generously shined both of them up. *Oh fuck, this feels so good! Her mouth was watering so fast that their juices were running down her chin to her neck.* Taking Ray's dick, she rubbed it over her face, as she continued to deep throat Kai.

She turned over on her back, so they both can take turns dunking their dicks down her throat. Ray leaned over and fingered her pussy, which was wetter than it has ever been. The sound of the door opening was JJ coming into the room. The site of seeing the cum from her pussy running down her legs, has him so excited that he took off his clothes and climbs on top of her. Towering above her like the God Mandingo, he made her beg him to fuck her. "Fuck me JJ- please. Give me that juicy big dick of yours!" she heard herself telling him. She didn't know she had so much ho up in her. He slapped her a couple of times, cause he knew she likes the feel of the sting on her ass cheeks, then he slowly slide inch by tortuous inch of his dick into her pussy. *Damn, this shit feels good, she thought. JJ was always a good fuck.*

Flipping over onto his back so that she can ride his dick, Worthy felt Ray pouring some oil onto her ass. As she turned around, she saw him oiling up his dick, which made it look like a shiny spear about to pierce her body. And that is exactly what he did. *I'm riding JJ, sucking Kai and got Ray in my ass, damn all holes stuffed and still I want more* Worthy thought to herself as she reveled in the moment. "Damn, girl, we heard about you from the niggas around town." Ray said in her ear, "But they didn't tell us that you were all of this."

Kai could barely stand, so she opened up her throat even more and took his dick all the way in her mouth. All the time that she was doing that, all she can think about, is the amount of shit that she is going to get for being so good at what she does. As they all climaxed together, she reveled in the moment and then went to the bathroom to clean up. When she came out the bathroom, they were all still lying on her bed.

"Aiight, now I want my shit," Worthy said with hands on her hips. As she took the rock from JJ, he whispered in her ear, "I got you boo, don't worry."

He had her all right. JJ and his boys fed her crumb after crumb, and for the rest of the day, they fucked her, and had some other friends come over and fuck her too. For the rest of the weekend, she was used, abused and violated. But guess what, she got high, *for free* and that's all that counted.

On Monday, her home became JJ's headquarters, and she became his ho. He took care of her bills, and all she had to do was take care of him and whomever else he bought to the house. In her drug induced haze she thought, *It feels good to have a man love me enough to take care of me, and he the dope man too, so I don't have to go far for my shit. And Shaeyla and them said I didn't have my priorities straight. That's how much they know., Jared is at my mothers, so I'm straight for now . . . time for me to start living my life.*

Chapter 19 ➤ Diandra's Beauty Shop

Looking around at what seems to be a never-ending line of customers, Diandra became pissed, because now she was going to miss the first half of Mason's party. Mason's birthday is tomorrow, and his family is throwing him a party to celebrate tonight, Mason just told her about it on Wednesday, making it too late for her to call a sub for today. She thinks his ex is going to be at his party tonight. She didn't even know why she's tripping over this, but she feels he has been lying to her all along, because home girl called her shop with some drama. She also has been calling her house leaving her threatening messages, but Diandra ain't the one. She refuses to have to look over her shoulder for the rest of her life. Diandra is just as, if not more ghetto than she was and her motto was to bring shit straight to you. Nobody fucking threatens Diandra Johnson and then don't follow up on it. Shit, she could have her boys plant that simple minded bitches ass right now if she wanted to, but she wasn't going to jail over no trifling stank ass ho. It was just her bad luck that she was on her way to the shampoo area when Kendra answered the phone. Kendra is still worrying her about it to this day.

The bullshit gossip that goes on in the shop is where Diandra got the majority of her information anyway. Although, she knew that she should set an example for the girls that booth rent from her, but the two ladies sitting under the dryer were having a conversation that the whole shop cannot help but hear. These girls were new faces, and had appointments with Nakia or Lisa, the new stylist's Diandra recently hired.

"Yeah girl," said the hoochie in the baby blue two-piece booty short set. "You know she told me she called her on her job and told her to stop fucking with her man. I told you that bitch was crazy. She does stupid shit like that."

This tad bit of information had Diandra's ears burning, Talk about déja vu because the same thing had just happened to her.

"Why won't she just leave his ass alone? He always been a ho, she knew that going in. First, he is the top hustler around, secondly he is fione, and third I heard that he can split your back. You know what I mean," the girl she was talking to responded.

"I know right. Anyway—," said the girl in blue, "his family is throwin' him a party tonight cause his birthday is tomorrow, and they are going to be there together."

"What? How did she know about it?"

"Girl, Mason's mother loves Andrea. Besides that, she is the only one that he has ever taken to his house."

No, they are not talking about me! Ain't this a bitch, they are in my motherfucking shop, clowning my ass over Mason. The fucked up thing about it is that I can't say anything to these ladies, as Shaeyla would say 'don't shoot the messenger'. Well if he is attending with Andrea, he's going to have both of us there? That way I can kill two birds with one stone. Especially since his mother loves his 'ex' so much. As the ladies continued their conversation, Diandra reached into her smock pocket and dialed his cell phone—no answer. Diandra didn't want to talk to voice mail but left a message anyway.

"Andrea said that bitch he's fooling with owns some kind of business. All I can say is that she better never find out what kind, cause she's the type to have your shit torched or held up. I'm telling you the bitch is crazy," Booty shorts said.

"I know, you don't have to tell me. That's why Mason ain't going nowhere. Hell, girl he is a nigga with money, these chicken heads don't care how they are treated or mistreated so long as they can say '*I got a man*'. He would have no chance of keeping a real woman this long, regardless of how much money he has." The other girl said, "Why doesn't she realize that Mason ain't shit and is never going to be shit? He always got some trick ass bitch on the hook somewhere, and she been putting up with it for this long . . . why is she tripping' now?"

Shrugging her shoulders all booty shorts could say was, "I own' know."

There conversation was halted, as Lisa one of the girls that booth rents, beckoned booty shorts from under the dryer, telling her to sit in her chair.

Picking up the salon phone, Judy the receptionist that Diandra hired tells her that she has a call. Excusing herself from her customers for a moment, she motioned for her shampoo tech to finish up the wet set.

Making her way to her office, and closing the door, she picked up the extension "Diandra speaking."

"Hey boo! I got your message. What's up?" Mason asked.

Arching an eyebrow and shaking her head, she said "Nothing much. I just wanted to know what time are you picking me up? I should be done by six, because my last appointment is at four." Never giving him a chance to speak, "So how about around eight-ish?" Let's see what the motherfucker has to say, cause I know its going to be good she thought.

Sighing, Mason said, "Look I need to talk to you about tonight."

"I'm listening—."

"Something went down, and I lost something. And one of my boys got knocked in New York City, so I'm on my way up there now to bail him out."

"What! Which one?" I asked him sounding surprised.

"Uh, Uh, Uh—Lil' Man," he stammered. *I swear niggas ain't shit.*

"So you're going to miss your own party tonight. What is your family going to do? Did you tell them you had business to care of?"

"Yeah, Mom's is upset, but it's cool. She said she would make me a big dinner tomorrow."

Diandra knew he was lying. His mom's ain't never cool about shit. She couldn't go into it with him any further because of her clients, but she would talk to him later—in person.

With the promise to hit her up later, she rang off with Mason and lay her head down on her desk. This whole conversation had her thinking. Why is he playing her like this? Diandra asked out loud to the empty room, *"It wasn't supposed to be like this. I was going to fuck him and forget em . . . just like I always do."* Standing up and kicking the trashcan, *"Fuck! That got-damn Shaeyla and Benét told my ass he was no good, and I understood that in the beginning. Yeah well if I understood so much, then why is it upsetting me now? Why do I always fall for the wrong type of brother?"* Shaking off these pitiful feelings she returned to her shop and her customers.

* * * * *

The ringing phone had Diandra rushing to enter her downtown apartment, running to the end table in her living room the phone stopped ringing as soon as she picked it up. Her initial thought was that it was Mason's psycho ex girlfriend. But looking at the caller ID, she saw Seven's number. Damn! She hasn't said two words to him since Benét's party. After that slam-dunk of a kiss he laid on her, she had not worked up the nerve to call him back. *Seven has called a hundred times since that night.* Her girls say that he wants her, and after that kiss, she wondered if they are right. Just thinking about his kiss, and those juicy suckable lips of his has goose bumps on her arms. Her nipples start to tighten up as well. Deciding that the visual was too much, Diandra decided to call Seven back. Picking up the phone to call him back, the beeping tone indicated that she had unanswered messages. Instead she dialed her mailbox code and password to retrieve her messages. The system told her that she had three new messages. Two messages were from Kendra and Benét, calling to see what was up. Then she heard, *"Hello Diandra. This is Seven. Since I have not talked to or seen you in a minute, I just called to see if you wanted to hook up and grab a bite to eat, maybe catch a movie. Anyway it's almost seven o'clock now, so give me a call when you get in. I'll be waiting."*

Damn . . . does he have to sound so good? Let me stop this. *Seven is a friend, and good friends are hard to come by, so why mess up a good friendship with him just because he made me sweat one time* she thought. Straightening her back, she decided to call him back and take him up on his offer. She just decided not to let that kiss ruin their good thing. Besides, she liked kicking' it with Seven, he's mad cool, and it feels good to have a male friend. Especially one that isn't expecting sex at the end of the night. With Seven she felt comfortable.

After the third ring, Diandra was just about to hang up when she heard, "Hey girl! What's been going on?"

She was about to ask him how he knew it was her, but she realized that just about everyone has caller id now. The sound of his voice had her insides tingling, but she tried to play it cool, so she just responded with, "Nothing much. What's going on with you?"

"Same ole, same ole. Another Saturday night and I ain't got nobody," he said, singing the old Sam Cooke song.

"Yeah, neither do I. I was supposed to go to Mason's house for his birthday party, but he cancelled because one of his boys got knocked."

Somebody got knocked my ass Seven said to himself. Out loud, he said, "For real." He knows she just got smoke blown up her ass, because his boy Noble is on his way to the party as we speak. But I'm going to let her have her fantasy, and I'll just be there for her when the shit hits the fan. If you haven't figured it out by now . . . I love this girl and have been in love with her almost from the first time we met. That was around six years ago, and she still only sees me as a friend.

"Yes he's on his way to New York to bail him out now," Diandra explained.

"So does that mean that you are free to kick it with me?"

"Sure, I don't mind going out. What do you want to see?" she said, accepting his offer.

"I figured we could check out that new action flick with Denzel Washington, then grab a bite to eat or vice versa. It's up to you."

"Aiight, bet. What time do you want to meet?"

"I'll pick you up in an hour. Is that enough time for you to get ready? Or are you ready now?"

"That's enough time. I just have to shower and get dressed," said Diandra.

After confirming that her he would pick her up in an hour, he ended the call smiling. Thinking to himself, he wondered why did she tell him about the shower? If she only knew, how many times he'd seen her in his mind butt naked, and dripping wet . . . damn! His dick was getting hard just thinking about her. He is going to have to do something soon, or else cut his losses, because he wasn't sure how much more he can take of loving someone that doesn't love him back. Hours later, as Seven drives back to Diandra's home, she realizes that this has been one of the best times they have had since they've known each other. Something is going on with Seven, she thought. Throughout the night, when she would look up or turn around, he would be looking at her with the oddest expression on his face. Not wanting to spoil the evening, she let it pass, but it still had her curious what that was all about.

In the driver's seat, Seven, lost in thought remembered how many times Diandra licked her lips, or walked ahead of him giving him a view of her sweet round ass. She caught him eyeballing her a couple times, but either she didn't see how he was looking at her or she didn't want to see, because she never asked him about the look on his face. As he was about to turn into the underground parking garage of her building she turned to him and said, "Hey, you can pull right up front. Remember the building is controlled access as well as twenty four hour security."

"Now where did that statement come from? How many times have I walked you to your door? Over a thousand, and now you want me to drop you off?" Seven asked her irritably.

Damn he sounds pissed, "Why are you giving me attitude Seven. You know what, I've been sensing this all night, but something about you is different. I just can't quite put my hands on it. Anyway, I ain't got time for you to park, cause Mason called while we were in the movies and I want to call him back before it gets too late," she said.

"You really like this one don't you?" Seven asked her somberly.

"What do you mean *this one*, like I didn't like the rest?" Diandra replied not liking the tone of his voice.

"You didn't like the rest of them the way you like him. I thought your motto was 'fuckem and forget em', so what's so special about Mason?" he asked.

Damn, she thought he busted my ass right out, because he is right, for as much as I tried not to like Mason, this niggas gotten under my skin. "I tried that with him, but he's different, he knows how to work the middle," Diandra said with a wistful smile on her face.

"Is that what you females like about his punk ass?" Seven asked.

"He is far from a punk and why are we having this conversation?"

Seven paused before he responded to her as the thought of her with another man made him see red. "You're my friend and niggas like that, all they do is take and never give. I ain't saying not to get your groove on or have your toes curled or whatever you women call it, but don't get serious about him. He is only going to hurt you in the end. Besides, the word on the street is that he already has a woman that he has been with for years."

"I know all about his girlfriend. Although the nigga did lie and tell me she was his ex. I have been hearing a few tales in the salon about that not being true, and it doesn't make a damn bit of difference to me one way or the other. Anyway, a man like Mason cannot be held by one woman, unlike my girlfriends, I don't mind sharing my man, so as long as he's kicking out the doe . . ."

Looking at her like she was crazy, Seven said, "You don't mean that. I know that you think more of yourself than to be some hoods woman on the side, or is what my mother say is the truth? Women will put up with anything just to say 'I got a man'. Don't you understand that, that is just like selling your soul? Isn't that what you and your girls say you shouldn't do? Isn't that what you said Shaeyla did with Randy?"

Diandra replied, "Look its' my life and I am the only one that has to live it. And for your smart ass information I am not selling my soul!" she rolled her eyes, opened the door and strode into her building. In her heart of hearts, she was hurt because she knew that what Seven had said with the truth, she had already sold her soul.

Chapter 20 ➢ Kendra's Date

When Kendra arrived home from their shopping spree, she started to call Diandra, but knew that she was probably still at the shop. Saturday's are the busiest days when it comes to doing hair, so Kendra let the thought go as she strode into her bedroom and laid her new outfit down on the bed. Turning to move into the bathroom, she added cucumber melon bubble bath to the tub and turned on the water. Tying her hair up, she pulled the lone cigarette from her pocket and stepped onto her balcony. *I am actually going on a date, with a fine ass man in about two hours, releasing the smoke through her nose and mouth, Kendra could not believe that she bummed a smoke from her neighbor's boyfriend. They looked at her in surprise because she hasn't smoked a cigarette in almost three years, yet here she was on her balcony smoking!*

Stubbing the cigarette out, she returned inside to shower and change. Niall is going to take her to a jazz club in D.C., which is supposed to be very good. She's not really into jazz, but tonight she is going to fucking love it.

The white Capri pant set is a vast difference from her usual wardrobe of drab neutral and earth tone colors. Benét, Shaeyla and Zaria and the sales clerk at Bloomingdale's all told her the same thing—she looked fantastic. Turning from side to side to view herself once again in the full-length mirrored closet door, she has to admit that they were right. For the first time she actually believes them. Smiling to herself and doing the bank head dance, she couldn't help but be happy over the fact that this outfit was a whole size smaller. She gave herself a high five and patted herself on the back, because she now realized that her diet and exercise program was working.

The pink sandals and matching kidskin purse pickup the pale pink beads around the hem of the pants and top, a silver choker with an iridescent pink mother of pearl charm and earrings completes the ensemble.

The doorbell rang as she was applying her lipstick. Completing the task, she turned and walked as calmly as she could down the steps to her front door. Checking herself in the mirror one last time, she placed her hand on the knob, took a deep breath, added her dazzling smile and opened the door.

The first thing she saw was a beautiful bouquet of tropical flowers. Appearing from behind them is Niall. Taking in how handsome he looked, she notice's that he was wearing a pair of Kenneth Cole brushed suede mules in a soft cream color to match the Ralph Lauren khaki pants and top. Damn, she still could not believe that he is actually here to see her.

"Welcome."

"Good evening beautiful," Niall said, handing her the flowers, "These are for you."

Taking the flowers with the dumbest grin on her face, she said, "Thank you, they are beautiful. Please come in while I put these in water."

As he stepped into her home, he complimented her by saying, "You have a very nice place. It has a warm and comfortable feel."

"Thanks. But I can't take the credit for it. Benét, Kendall's wife, did all of this. She is one of the best interior decorators around. I should just be a minute and then we can be on our way."

"Take your time," he said.

Escaping to the kitchen to find her favorite vase, she placed the flowers in the 24 kt gold trimmed Makasa vase and added a little water a dab of sugar and her secret ingredient—a little Sprite. This will help to preserve the flowers. She then decided to place them in the center of her dining room table so that they would be the first thing she sees when she walk's in the door.

Crossing to pick up her purse and wrap from the couch, she opened her purse to pull out her keys. Opening the door for her, Niall stood back and allowed her to precede him. "Aren't you going to lock up—at least set your alarm?"

Holding up the device, a keychain remote, she said, "I am sort of a computer geek, so I had the whole house wired. With the press of a button, it locks the house and sets the alarm."

"Now that's impressive," Niall replied.

Parked at the end of the drive was a champagne colored Range Rover. After he assisted Kendra into the passenger seat, he made his way to the drivers' side and got in. He turned to her before pulling off and said, "If I haven't already told you, you look absolutely gorgeous tonight."

Not knowing what to say, other than, "Thank you," she just settled in for the ride smiling to herself.

The drive down 295 to DC was done with animated conversation as they took that time to get to know each other. They discovered that they had a lot in common. They enjoyed the same types of movies, books, music and generally, they shared the same type of family values and beliefs. They even had the same thoughts about settling down and eventually having children.

"The fact that we both love science fiction movies and books is great, because it's like pulling teeth to get my girls to go see a sci-fi flick with me," Kendra told him.

"Well that can be fixed, because now you can just call me and I'll go see anything you want," Niall's responded.

"Don't say that, because although I like sci-fi, I like romance, drama and comedy too."

"Ahhh, the romance we can take in doses, but I have no problem with suspense or comedy. How about horror movies, do you like those?" he asked.

"Yes, I love a good horror movie. Now my girlfriend Shaeyla, she doesn't do horror and even dramatic suspense are a little too much for her sometimes. I usually end up seeing those with Diandra and Worthy."

"Now, that's the first time you've mentioned her," he said.

I didn't get the chance to respond to that statement because he pulled into the valet parking area of the jazz club that we were going to.

Stepping out of the car, he hands the valet his key, takes the ticket, makes his way to Kendra's side, and opens the door. He put his hand into the small of her back as they make their way into the building to the maitre d'. "Good evening, reservation for two, for Adams," Niall told him.

"Yes, if you will please follow me," the maitre'd said, and turned to walk into the main room of the restaurant.

Niall looked around and noticed that a couple of brothers eyes was all trained on Kendra She looked great tonight, and he was proud to be seen with her. Stepping closer to her, he placed his hand on her forearm, to show that they were together. He thought back to after the party, when his friends asked him what was up, because he normally did not fool with women over size sixteen, but there was just something special about Kendra, that he could not explain.

Arriving at a table overlooking the Potomac, he was approached by the wine steward and handed a wine list. He asked the wait staff to give them a few minutes.

I wonder what the prices are in here Kendra thought, as she picked up the black leather bound menu, that offered an array of dishes from steaks, chicken, pork, seafood and even soul food. Looking in the seafood section she knew that she couldn't have anything that was stuffed because of the calories. Her diet has been going well so far, but she was not going to tempt fate. Deciding on the garden salad with the grilled chicken breast to start, for her entrée she decided on the broiled orange roughy in a lemon butter sauce with fresh steam vegetables and garlic-mashed potatoes.

"That sounds good," said Niall. "I think I am going to have the stuffed chicken breast, with a Mediterranean salsa topping, baked potato and broccoli."

"Mmmm . . . that sounds good also," she agreed.

When the waiter arrived, Niall didn't give her the chance to order as he ordered for both of them. He tasted a cabernet and

Chablis and decided on the Chablis, as it would compliment both meals.

The meal was excellent, and the conversation stimulating. Which was a testament as to why when the sinful dessert was served, they noticed that there were only a few diners left in the restaurant.

Looking at his watch, Niall said, "Okay, I think its time for us to get on the road."

Helping her out of her chair, they crossed to the door, retrieved his vehicle and made their way back up 295 to her house.

Chapter 21 ➢ Dinner with Steele

The black and white dress that Shaeyla purchased earlier was hanging on her valet. Going through the other outfits in her closet, she pulled the red jumpsuit from the party. "Uh, naw, he has already seen me in this one." She decides as she talks out loud to herself. The black and white dress is cut out in the back, and again dips to just above her ass. She wonders if it is it too sexy for a business meeting.

Applying African Musk oil, her favorite scented lotion and perfume, she stepped into the Manolo Blahnik pumps that cost her an arm and three legs. Why did she listen to Benét's ass, she knew good and damn well that the money she spent on this one outfit today, should've gone back into her business. But no, her dumb ass listened to Benét and wham—here is this sexy ass outfit that makes her look like a million bucks, which damn near cost her as much. Rounding the bed to the valet, Shaeyla stepped into the dress and tied the straps around her neck. She didn't know what it was with her and halter style outfits lately, but there was something sexy about them. Come on Shaeyla, she silently muses who are you kidding? You are going to dinner with a handsome eligible bachelor, and that's why your ass is going over there all-cute and stuff. Well a girl's gotta eat, and what's a little harmless flirting going to do? Besides, if she got the vibe right at the first meeting, homeboy wouldn't mind having a piece of her either.

Giving herself one last twirl in the mirror, she grabbed her matching purse from the bed, her keys from the foyer table and headed towards her car. Shaeyla had placed her briefcase and laptop in the car as soon as she got back from her shopping trip. Looking at her watch, she wondered how Kendra was making out on her date. She sure hoped home girl didn't mess up; because her date looked genuinely interested in her at the party. Pushing those thoughts out of her mind, she follows the directions that Mitchell given her to his home. Interstate 83 North towards the Pennsylvania border. She continued until she arrived at a gated community of grand estate homes. Stopping at the gatekeeper's station, Shaeyla give her name and Mitchell's address. Once the gatekeeper reviewed his list, security cleared her entrance and she noticed that as she was leaving the gate, the guard was jotting down her license plate number.

Keeping straight, she made the second turn on the left, to a beautiful sprawling mansion. Letting out a whistle, "Well I'll be damn! This brother is paid." Wait until I tell the girls about this house, Shaeyla thought immediately impressed. Obviously Kendall has never been here because, she was sure Benét would've mentioned it to her. Entering the circular drive, she passed a four-car attached garage on the left, and stopped in front of the stone pillar entrance. The vast double doors had an 'S' etched into the glass pane, with beautiful brushed silver handles. While parking the car and retrieving her materials and purse, the door opened. She looked up only to find the man himself, looking oh so handsome.

The gray silk shirt and white pants was an incredible look on him. On any other brother it might look gay, but nope not this guy. The butterflies started to flutter in her stomach as he places her hand in his and pulled her in for a brief hug.

"I didn't believe that it could be possible, but you are even more beautiful than the last we met," Mitchell said.

Not one to disregard a compliment, she said, "Thank you, you're looking mighty handsome yourself."

They both turned at the sound of running feet to see a whirlwind come flying down the steps. Dressed in a Barbie nightgown, the little girl flew into the waiting arms of her father, "Daddy, you said you would tucking me in," his daughter said indignantly.

Brushing a kiss on her forehead, he replied, "I am sweet pea, but first let me introduce you to Ms. Andrews. Remember I told you about her and our business dinner?"

His daughter's eyes traveled over Shaeyla from head to toe. Shaeyla tried to put on her friendliest smile, but there was no secret, that she would do almost anything, but one thing Shaeyla Andrews did not do was kids.

"Malina, this is Ms. Andrews."

Holding out her hand, his daughter hesitantly placed her hand in Shaeyla's. Suddenly, her eyes grew as wide as saucers as she looked at the color blocked, black and white nails. "Daddy, look at her fingers. Is she a witch?" she asked wonderingly.

Laughing, "No sweetie, she is not a witch. Now let's get you into bed."

Shaeyla never noticed the maids quiet entrance until Mitchell said, "Anya, take Ms. Andrews into the study and get her a glass of merlot. I will join you as soon as I put Malina to bed."

Turning to follow his maid through to the study allowed Shaeyla a chance to scope out his home in his absence. He has a thing for windows, because his study was located on the back of the house with floor to ceiling glass panes overlooking the pool. To the right of the pool there was the pool house and a mock Cinderella castle, which she assumed was his daughters. In fact, as she looked further his entire back yard had an "Alice in Wonderland" theme to it. If he spoils his daughter like that, Shaeyla wondered how he must spoil his women. As Mitchell's maid escorts her to his den, she heard the ringing of the doorbell. Anya excused herself and Shaeyla turned her sights back to the wonderful backyard view. The sound of angry voices had Shaeyla turning to see Mitchell angrily talking to a tall dark skinned brother. Not wanting to look like she was eavesdropping even though she was, Shaeyla turned back to look out of the windows while straining to hear what was going on outside.

Minutes later Mitchell entered the room with the newcomer and introduced him "Shaeyla Andrews, this is my partner Solomon Jackson." As the newcomer stepped forward with his hand outstretched to shake her hand, she stepped forward with a friendly smile saying, "Hello, It's a pleasure to meet you."

Staring into her eyes a moment too long, the Mr. Jackson then turns toward Mitchell and says, "No wonder you wanted to keep this beautiful lady all to yourself."

Blushing Shaeyla replied, "Really, each time that we've met, you've always been away in meetings."

"Well that's about to change, because I will be sitting in on tonight's meeting," said Solomon.

Looking past him Shaeyla noticed Mitchell's mouth tighten ever so slightly, but then he shrugged off his ire and informed them that they would be having there meal on the veranda. He excused himself to inform the maid that there would be three for dinner instead of two.

As the three moved to sit down, Shaeyla immediately took a seat on the settee, and Solomon sat down beside her.

This turn of events did not sit well with Mitchell as he moved to the bar to pour himself a drink. Shaeyla jumped as he slammed his tumbler down and dropped three cubes of ice before pouring himself what looked to her like scotch.

Seeing her jump, "I'm sorry. I didn't mean to startle you," he apologized.

"No problem," she said.

It is at this point that Solomon asks Mitchell to pour him a drink as well. Mitchell mumbles to himself, but grudgingly turned back to fulfill Solomon's drink request. Shaeyla could feel the tension in the room as if the two men are in a battle of wills. Not wanting to have the night end on a sour note, she attempted to break the ice.

Fidgeting she filled the silence, "Your daughter is very pretty and your home is beautiful."

"Thank you. I completely renovated the grounds after my divorce. As you can see, I gave Malina her dream as she has a very active imagination," he said pointing outside to her play area.

Before she could acknowledge that statement, his maid announced, "Dinner is served, Mr. Steele."

As the two of them rushed to help her out of her seat, they crossed through the French doors of his study, to see a lavishly set table awaiting them on the Veranda. Flicking a button near the door, the outside lights surrounding the property perimeter came to life and a waterfall appeared. With the flick of another switch the smooth sounds of Santana reached their ears.

Shaeyla gasped in delight at the sight of the waterfall, "That's beautiful," she replied.

As they took their seats, the maid served them a meal of beef Wellington, parsley potatoes, and steamed broccoli. The dessert was baked Alaska, and the entire meal was served with a bottle of Kristal. The light conversation had slight undertones of a tug of war between Solomon and Mitchell as they vied for her interest. Shaeyla had never been the object of two such handsome men before and she has to admit that the feeling it gave her was wonderful. She felt like the most beautiful girl in the world as they each jockeyed for her attention.

After dinner, they moved back into the study to go over her proposal. Before Shaeyla could open her portfolio, Solomon informed her that they had decided to do an in house function for their first quarter meeting. He also informed her that the company would be sponsoring the annual Black Charities gala later in the year. Solomon proceeded to tell her that she would be working with Mitchell on the first quarterly meeting but that she would be working with him regarding the Black Charities gala as he was a member of the board. Nonplussed at the chance to do the gala, she was completely overwhelmed and elated to have this opportunity to coordinate such a function. The Black Charities gala drew hundreds of prominent citizens of Maryland, which would give her company much needed exposure. Taking all of this information in her stride she informed them of her "Five On Time" theme for the quarterly meeting and explained how she had come up with the idea. Each of the men listened to her intently, and with a few minor changes instructed from Solomon, they informed her that they would love to retain her company's services.

Crossing over to a hidden wall cabinet, Mitchell produced another bottle of Kristal to cement the agreement. As he poured glasses for the three of them, Shaeyla noticed a look in his eyes that she couldn't quite discern.

Downing the crisp liquid, she knew that it was time for her to take her leave. "Gentlemen it has been quite an evening, but I must get home so that I can start working on your campaign." Mitchell informed her that Solomon was about to leave as well. This statement made Solomon swiftly turn to his friend bringing on a mental test of wills between them. Shaeyla saw Solomon come to a decision as he stood and informed her to stay and he strode towards her and took her hand in his and thanked her for a pleasant evening. As he turned towards the doors to make his exit, Mitchell placed his hand on the small of her back and steered her outside.

As they stood there listening to the sounds of the waterfall, he ran his hands up and down her arms and whispered in her ear, "Shaeyla can't you feel the chemistry between us? I know you can, because I feel it too. I want nothing more right now than to kiss you." His voice had dropped to a deep huskiness, that sounded as if he couldn't catch is breath.

The sound of her name on his lips had her thinking of how it would sound were they to make love.

Her eyes got as big as saucers. "I'm sorry Mr. Steele, but I do not mix business with pleasure," she said, while thinking how badly she wanted him to kiss her.

"I can respect that," he replied and released her from his hold.

Moving to stand across the room from him, she gathered her belongings, which made it clear that her intention was to escape as soon as possible. "I believe it's time for me to go. Thank you once again Mr. Steele, I promise that I will not let you down. I'll make the changes to the contract and have a courier deliver them to you first thing Monday morning."

The scowl upon his brow at her air formality told Shaeyla that he was disturbed by this turn of events. Walking her to the door and seeing her into her car, he advised her that he would be awaiting the package and that he would contact her midweek.

Closing the door to her car, Shaeyla took a deep breath and tried to slow down her heart rate. It was beating triple time, because she knew that had she not escaped soon, she would've made passionate love to Mr. Steele, and would have enjoyed every minute of it. But that was not the impression that she wanted to leave regarding her business.

Chapter 22 ➢ Love is in the Air

Shaeyla was awakened to the sun streaming through the penthouse window of Mitchell's downtown condo. The sounds of running water told her that Mitchell was in the shower. His entire place was designed for the hedonist.

I cannot tell a lie, the man wore down my resolve with a relentless campaign to get me. After that meeting at his home, he sent flowers and candy daily. When they didn't work, he called the office several times, until she finally broke down and accepted an invitation to dinner.

Talk about charm personified! When this man wants something, he will stop at nothing to get it.

In the last month and a half, he has shown her a whole new world; a culture and a way of life in which Shaeyla always wanted to live. Never having to ask for anything, but receiving everything that her little heart could imagine.

As Mitchell strode into the room soaking wet from the shower, he smiled that Billy Dee killer smile of his, and said, "Good morning beautiful. Do you want breakfast?" he asked, as he lightly rubbed his beard along the side of her neck and ear. Moving Shaeyla's arms around his neck, she pulled him down on top of her. "I am ready for breakfast," she said with a naughty look on her face. Are you the appetizer or the main entrée?"

"I will be whichever you want me to be or both," he replied. Reaching down to remove his towel, Shaeyla grab his dick, and started rubbing it up and down. Pushing him onto his back she said, "I was wondering if I could get my protein drink?" She proceeded to place her lips upon his dick. Licking his dick all over to get it nice and slippery, Shaeyla stick its full length into her mouth. Trying to take it all in was difficult, because it was first thing in the morning and her throat hasn't opened yet. But that didn't matter, because she loved the feel of him in her mouth. Randy had never gotten it like this; in fact it was a chore to for her to do him at all. But with Mitchell, she couldn't wait to surrender to her knees before him. Just the thought of his throbbing member had my mouth watering.

The sound of Mitchell's moans get her hotter and wetter. Moving her hand down to finger herself, she insert two fingers into her pussy and pulled them out, placing them in his mouth to lick off her juices. That little transaction had him jerking and thrashing on the bed which sent me on a natural horny high. Shaeyla could see that he was clutching the headboard in all attempts to stem his release. Reaching up, she pulled his hands from the headboard and place them on her head, "Feed it to me," she begged.

Kneeling between his legs, she straddled his right leg and rubbed her clit over it while she tasted his savory love. She wanted him to feel how wet she was getting just by pleasuring him. As he guided her head back down, he slowly began to penetrate her mouth and throat. She assisted him by bobbing her head up and down. "*Got damn I love this shit," she yelled out loud.* Seeing his balls tighten up told her that he was about to cum. "Cum for me baby! I want to taste you!" she said. She knew that that statement alone would him cum faster, because he loved when I talked him through. He thought only white women swallowed, and who knows they probably do, I only started swallowing with him and I told him that the first time I did it. After that, I was hooked. I never knew that the taste of a man's juices was so good. The first time that I tasted his cum, it was like manna from heaven, it was smoother than I thought and in actuality it had no taste to it all.

As his hands tightened around her head for the final thrust into her mouth she eagerly awaited her prize. Releasing him from her mouth for a moment, she said "Yes baby that's it, I want you're cum down my throat, NOW!" Shaeyla felt the first burst hit the back of her throat and exclaimed, Yesss, YES! She couldn't seem to swallow it fast enough as it was seeping out of her mouth, and running down her chin. Shaeyla proceeded to wipe off the rest of his cum with his rigid staff and then softly licked it. She was very gentle because she knew how sensitive he was at that moment.

Just the feel of him throbbing and pulsating in her mouth ignited a burning deep inside.

"Damn Shaeyla, you amaze me," He said as he felt my juices running down his leg. Pulling me up to sit on his face, he licked me dry of the first of many orgasms for that day.

Later as we are lying in each other's arms, he asked me about my plans for the day.

"Well today is the day that I meet the girls for our monthly lunch. We have a lot to catch up on and I cannot wait to tell them about our relationship."

Framing her face with his hands, he asked, "Can I persuade you to change your mind?" Then he traced her lips with his tongue.

All that man had to do was touch, her or even look at her and she'd go up in flames. '*Damn, Shaeyla, what's wrong with you?* She muses silently to herself. You vowed to yourself that you would have a fling with this man and get going. Now you want to settle down and he said he wanted to get to know you with no strings attached, because he isn't getting married anytime soon. Fuck! I knew this, but that didn't stop my feelings from getting involved. I have fucked up and fallen in love with this man'. Snapping herself out of her musings she said, "Persuade me how?"

"I'm picking Malina up and we are going to the Inner Harbor and I thought you could spend the day with us?" he said.

Damn, he has never once had his daughter *and* me in the same place. He must feel something for me, why else is he doing this? It didn't matter. I would do just about anything to be with Mitchell even if it meant forsaking my girls.

And just like that, Shaeyla forgot all about her girl's lunch and thought of spending the day with Mitchell and his daughter. "Of course I will spend the day with you," she happily replied.

Chapter 23 ➤ Girls Lunch

The beautiful summer sky was the perfect setting for the girl's monthly luncheon. The breeze blowing off the Chesapeake Bay provided a refreshing coolness to the heat and humidity of the day.

"Hey, girls what's up?" Benét asked Diandra and Kendra, as they seat themselves at the table. The monthly "girls" meeting for lunch was at their favorite restaurant at the Inner Harbor, The Cheesecake Factory.

"Where's Shaeyla?" they both ask.

"Girl, you know Shaeyla, since she dropped Randy's tired behind she has been seeing someone," replied Benét.

"Well how dare she miss our lunch? If it was me, she would have a fit," Worthy stated.

"Well actually since you mentioned it, I am surprised to see you here," Kendra said to Worthy. After all, their friend had been missing from a lot of their get together's of late.

To diffuse the situation and to stop Worthy from responding to Kendra's jibe, Diandra added, "Well you know what I always said about Shaeyla, and I love her to death, but you know that girl got GDGD syndrome."

"GDGD—?" the ladies replied in unison.

"Yeah, you know Get Dick Get Dumb. Shaeyla's ass is famous for that. Look how she was with Randy. Trying to pretend like she didn't know what his ass was doing, then he had the nerve to have a bitch on the side. He played her . . . but let her tell it, it's the other way around," said Diandra. "You know whoever he is that she always ties herself up into him instead of the other way around."

"Well all I know is that this is the third time in the last three months that she has missed our luncheon. Now I want to know who this mystery man is?" Kendra intoned.

Fishing in her purse for her cell phone, Benét decided to call her. As she punched in the code for Shaeyla's cell phone, her friends looked on expectantly hoping that Shaeyla would answer. Seeing the look on Benét's face, they realized that the answering machine picked up. "Shaeyla, girl where are you, this is the third time you've missed lunch with us. You have some explaining to do. Who is he and we want an introduction-soon!" Benét said into the phone.

"Yeah, one of us needs to have something at our place and invite them over," said Diandra

"Well my place is out," Worthy exclaimed.

"Girl, your place wasn't even in the picture," said Diandra. "Hell you won't clean the place up, plus it's not in the best of areas, now is it?"

"But it's mine," Worthy said.

Diandra leaned over towards Worthy to whisper, "Oh Really? That's not what I've been hearing, but I'll holla at you later about that."

Kendra intervened, "All right now ladies, not today, please this is our day. Let's try to remember that and get along, like we really love each other!"

Seeing the waiter approach, they all decide to look at the menus. "Are you ladies ready to order?" he asked.

"Can you give us like 5 minutes? Benét asked.

"Sure he replied, can I get your drinks while you decide." They give the waiter their drink orders and Kendra almost knocked the table over in her rush to get up.

"What the—"

"Look, there goes Shaeyla," Kendra pointed out the window toward a couple walking hand in hand, looking disgustingly happy. Benét and Worthy both looked out of the window and saw Shaeyla with a fine specimen of a man and a little girl. She was completely oblivious to her surroundings, strolling hand in hand, as they smiled into each other's eyes; the picture of the perfect family. You can tell just by looking at them how much they are into each other. In his left hand were several shopping bags from the high-end boutiques and she was holding the hand of the little girl, dressed in a summer dress and sandals.

"Huh" gaspsed Benét.

"'What's wrong with you?" they ask Benét.

"That's Kenny's boss—Mitchell Steele".

"I thought he looked familiar, but I couldn't place him to save my life. When did they hook up and how?" asked Kendra

"Look at her, just as happy as a lark. He is fine, but she could have at least called one of us to tell us that she would not be able to make it instead of just not showing. Now we know what she's been doing with her time—damn, that man is fine as shit!" exclaimed Diandra thinking there should be a law against a man that good looking.

"Yes, he is," replied Benét. "I wonder if Kenny knows that they've been seeing each other? Anyway, I don't care who Shaeyla is seeing so long as our girl is happy. Hell ya'll, Randy wasn't worth a damn, so let her have this happiness."

Looking around the table at her friends, Diandra said, "I am happy for Shaeyla. He must be good because we all know that Shaeyla does not do children." Shaking her head earnestly, Worthy was in complete agreement with Diandra.

"Oh, don't misunderstand me," Benét said, "I will have a talk with her myself about not calling or showing. It seems like it is the only time that we can get together and catch up on each others lives is at lunch."

"Well, I say, lets enjoy the rest of our day. We can get on Shaeyla later about dissing us, then get the scoop on what's been going down between her and Mitchell Steele," Kendra said to them.

Summoning the waiter over to the table, the ladies placed their orders and continued with their luncheon.

"I'm going to the ladies room, be right back," Worthy chimed. Turning back to her girls she said, "Get me another iced tea and strawberry daiquiri."

Putting on a bright smile, but missing her girl Shaeyla, Benét informed the girls that her first day of school begins in two weeks.

"Damn, that was quick! Are you sure you want to start in the spring/summer session? Diandra asked. "I mean, if I was you, I would want to enjoy my last summer instead of sitting around doing homework."

"I understand what you mean, but having put it off this long, I don't want to waste anymore of my time. I am so excited about it, ya'll just don't know," Benét told them.

"Uhh, excuse me, but I did go to college okay," Kendra told Benét. "Besides your missing the best part of it all and that is living on campus. They were some good times."

Looking at Kendra, the girls notice that she had lost weight since Benét's party, and that she was beginning to display a little more confidence about herself. Looking around, the three ladies realize that Kendra had a certain sparkle in her eye too. Her relationship with Niall Adams must be going good, because she appeared to be truly happy.

Seeing the look on Kendra's face, prompted Diandra to inquire, "Why are you smiling like that?"

"Look at us looking at Shaeyla. Why are we surprised?" Kendra asked her. "Hell, I'm happy for her. She hasn't looked that happy since before she first started seeing Randy. And now that she is happy, we are sitting here upset because she *is* happy? What's wrong with us?" Kendra asked them shaking her head.

"Nothing is wrong with us, but this is the third time that she has not shown. All we are saying is that she could've called. We haven't seen each other or spent time together as a group since Benét's party," said Worthy with a look of exasperation on her face.

Over lunch, they all questioned Diandra about the statement she made about Randy having a sidepiece. She explained that Shaeyla didn't tell us the real reason for leaving Randy was because of his infidelity, and not his drug abusing, no-good laziness. Benét said that is unfortunate that she couldn't confide in us, but who cares about how or why she dropped Randy, I am just thankful that she did.

Sitting back in her seat Benét was trying to think back to the last time Shaeyla and her had a good girl talk. It's been a minute.

Chapter 24 ➤ Kendall's Speech

Rush hour traffic as always was horrendous. Benét thought that she should've stayed at the restaurant and had a couple of more drinks instead of rushing to Kendall's lecture. Baltimore's traffic lights must be the only fucking lights that are not synchronized. She knew she should've taken the back way home. Everyone was blowing their horns and still getting nowhere. She glanced down at her watch and figured she would be late. Kendall was talking to junior and senior college students at Harris State College, to line up interns for his firm. He had reminded her a week ago that he would be there and asked her to attend. Although their sex life was still non existent, she took this as his way of breaking the ice between them and decided to go. She knew that her husband loved talking to the students and was actually hoping that their son would follow in his footsteps. As the light turned green, she traveled to the north east side of Baltimore to the campus. The cars parked along the road in front of the Ernest F. Coates, engineering building was a good sign that Kendall would have a good turn out for his lecture.

Benét was silently praying to the parking God in the hopes of getting a space close to the door, when she spotted a car pulling out from in front of Kendall's Cadillac Escalade. As she put her blinker on, she bobbed her head up and down happy to find a close parking lot and right in front of her husband to boot.

Parking her Lexus, she turned the car off, pulled down the sun visor to freshen up her lipstick, grabs her purse and exits the car. Her beige skirt, highlight her slim waist, and the red paisley blouse with its key-hole front, accentuated her full chest. Three inch red sandals emphasized her well-toned legs. The matching polish on her toes gave her feet the look of a sexy confident woman. Glancing at her watch, she realized that his lecture started thirty minutes ago. The sound of her heels tapping on the concrete brought about many admirers, which secretly brought a smile to her face. Benét knew that she looked good. She stepped through the double doors and headed up the staircase to another set of doors which lead to the crowded auditorium. Removing her Anne Klein shades from her eyes, she looked around for a seat. Looking down the rows she caught a pair of eyes appraising her. The eyes belonged to a man with the complexion of a smooth cup of coffee. He was sitting down but he his legs were long and stretched out in front of him. Moving her left hand up to lightly touch her brow, Benét saw his eyes land on the princess cut Diamond wedding ring. Yes he was fine, but she was silently telling him that she was unavailable. As she didn't care to register his reaction at that point, she moved her eyes away from his gaze, and noticed a person leaving their seat and moved quickly to sit down.

For over an hour, Kendall dazzled the faculty, students, and other interested parties with his spiel on his company and the electronic and nuclear industries focusing on their need for educated brothers and sisters. As he concluded his lecture, he asked for questions and for another thirty minutes he advised and guided those interested on his contact information. Benét watched as his eyes shined his excitement and she loved the way he mesmerized the audience with his voice. She felt the familiar stirrings of longing well up inside of her. Benét and Kendall had made plans to go to dinner after the lecture. She was taking this as an opportunity to rekindle the spark that seemed to have fizzled from their marriage.

Hearing Kendall announce that his question and answer session was complete, she turned her cell phone back on and watched people start moving towards the exit doors while some made their way to the stage to talk more with her husband. She noticed that one of the gentlemen walking to the stage was the same young man that had given her the eye. Just as she was about to walk towards the stage, she heard the bleeping of her cell phone.

Looking at the caller ID, she notices that Shaeyla is finally calling her back. Good because she can't wait to tell her what just happened, and to ask her what was going on with her and Mitchell Steele? Walking through the exit doors into the crowded hallway, she rushed down the steps and outside to the sidewalk so that she could talk.

"Hey, stranger. We missed you at lunch today," Benét told her.

"Hey girl, I know and I'm sorry. Was everyone there but me?" Shaeyla asked.

"Yes, all of us were there including Worthy, but she had to leave early. Speaking of which, have you seen how much weight home girl has lost?"

"No, I haven't seen her in a while. Every time I call her, I get her answering machine. One time I called and this dude answered the phone, so I figured she was getting her groove on and hung up."

"Well Diandra said she looks like she is on that shit. The weight loss, even her skin tone looks bad. She was a nice size before she had Jared, but now she is a pale version of what she used to be. Her hair isn't as healthy looking, as it used to be. She keeps it pulled back with that damned head band but you can see that it doesn't shine and it's limp. Diandra goes crazy when she sees it because she had her hair growing. But I hope she is wrong. I'll tell you what, lets get together and talk to her so we can see for ourselves what is going on. I mean, we know something is up, because my mother was talking to Worthy's mother the other day and said that Jared as been at his grandmother's for the last month or so. I think we need to do something, because she is our girl and we cant just let her go out like that," said Benét.

"You know I hope you're wrong, because when a woman gets turned out on crack, her ass will do anything and I do mean *anything* for a hit. You know anytime it can make a straight man wanting to suck a dick for a hit, what do you think it will make a woman do?"

Benét huffed, "I know that's right. We can get her and take her to Kendall's study before the guests arrive at my summer fest party. But I can't talk about that now, because it upsets me so much that I'm crazy enough to run up over there without ya'll and then all hell would break loose if I actually find out that its true."

Needing to change the subject Benét asked, "So, tell me about you and Mitchell Steele. Last, I heard, you hadn't seen or heard from him since that meeting at his house a while back, when his partner showed up unexpectedly. So come on—tell me what's up?"

Flabbergasted, Shaeyla asked, "What do my mean what's up?"

"Come on now Shaeyla, you're talking to me. All of us saw your happy ass at the Harbor today with him. You were holding hands, and looked like ya'll had been shopping. Me, Kendra, Worthy and Diandra all saw you." No my girl is not trying to play us for dumb, Benét thought.

"Okay, I guess this means I'm busted."

"Uh—*Yeah*. So what's going on?"

"Girl, Kendall's boss is the *man*, the *one!* I mean he is charming, witty, funny and exciting. He is everything that I have always wanted in a man. It's just amazing the way he makes me feel," Shaeyla said breathlessly.

Benét could hear the happiness in her voice. "Damn girl! Your ass is all scrambled up over this man. I was just thinking in the car that he had your ass wide the fuck open."

"You are right about that, my whole body is open. Girl I do shit for this man that I said I would never do again after Randy. I'm in love," Shaeyla happily said.

Ahhh shit. "Shaeyla, he is not the type of man that looks like he is about to settle down," stated Benét. "Kendall told me about his reputation with the ladies. He's the love'em and leave em' type who only wants one thing from a woman. Now his partner Solomon Jackson is more your speed, because Kendall says he isn't dating now, but when he was he only dated one woman at a time."

"Well yes, Solomon is sexy as hell, but I don't care about that love'em and leave'em shit, I love him and that's all there is to it."

"Okay, let me ask you this? Are you the only woman that he is seeing?" This statement is met with silence. "See your ass can't even answer that question. Your M.O. is too conventional. You're too straight to date or see anyone else, so again I'll say Solomon Jackson is perfect for you. Plus, I've met him several times over the years and I can see that what Kendall has told me was true." Actually, Benét thought to herself, she never really cared for Mitchell Steele, because he would tell Kendall some bullshit about what a woman's role or place in relationships and society should be and then Kendall's dumb ass would come home and try to pull it on her. Kendall said he had archaic beliefs when it came to relationships, because he said that Mitchell believed that men could see as many women as they wanted to and that women had to deal with it. In Benét's opinion, no man could do better than Shaeyla. Benét knew that her girl was a softy, even though she tried to act tough, Shaeyla was the type to crack under pressure. The fact that he has a child is interesting, because Shaeyla's thoughts on children are well known. She didn't want any, and doesn't fuck with niggas that have em. So, she must really like this Steele fella based on those facts alone, Benét surmised.

"Well you're entitled to your opinion. You know me Benét; you know that I love being a part of a couple. I feel better about myself when I have a man, plus I have never felt like this with Randy. I don't like being alone. To be honest, when I first met his daughter it was daunting, but she's a great kid."

Quickly changing the subject Shaeyla continues, "Did I tell you about the dick spree that I went on trying to get with a man"?

"First of all when will women stop worrying about being alone and needing men to love them? We have to love ourselves first," Benét told her. She wasn't letting Shaeyla get off the subject that easily. She has always wrapped herself up in the lives of the men she was dating. But it's her life. Hell, we couldn't tell her ass about

Randy, so I know we can't tell her ass about Steele. "Yes you told me all about your dick spree," Benét said.

"I only told you some of them. I was fucking anything that moved. If he looked at me, twice I was fucking him. Did I tell you about the dudes I met over the Internet?"

"No you didn't meet niggas from online and fuck them," exclaimed Benét.

"Didn't I? I did four of them," Shaeyla said.

Laughing out loud Benét said, "You nasty bitch. I knew your ass was nasty."

"Girl every last one of them ate pussy like you wouldn't believe. I mean this one dude told me 'I'm going to make that kitten purr' and he damn sure did. He was tonguing my pussy and moving his lips to make these vibrating noises girl! That shit get's me wet just thinking about it. Then the second one had this tongue ring, lets just say, when that ring on his tongue touches the clit . . . damn I must've came twice just from him eating me!"

"Hmmm, Hmmm, Hmmm, sounds good to me," Benét replied. "Whatever floats your boat, but your ass should've been more careful." The thoughts of sex had Benét telling Shaeyla, "You know Kendall and I *are* still having issues. So this is like having sex vicariously through you."

Shaeyla was still full of stories, and therefore didn't hear Benét's last statement. "This one dude was a basketball player. Now this dude, had my mouth watering to suck his dick, and he wouldn't let me. All he wanted to do was eat my pussy, lick my ass and fuck me. He fucked me well too . . . and would you believe I lost his number?"

"What do you need his number for?" Benét asked, then quickly switched topics. "Speaking of sex I think I might be getting some tonight. As a matter of fact I am standing at the HSC campus waiting for Kendall to come from a lecture he just finished."

"What!? Girl that's good right?"

"I hope so. We are going out to dinner tonight and I hope it helps to bring the spark back into our relationship. When he asked me a couple of weeks ago, I looked at it as his way of meeting me halfway. So I am hoping that I can talk him into going to a counselor. Up until now he still won't consider it," Benét told her friend.

Shaeyla could hear the pain in Benét's voice, she knew she loved her husband, but she was right. If Kendall doesn't meet her halfway at least, she's afraid that Benét is going to get the love and attention she needs from someone else.

"I feel you on that Benét. Isn't it funny how the two of you are trying to get it together? As if the good Lord is trying to tell you something?"

Benét spotted Kendall coming through the double doors of the building and walking towards her with the young man she saw making his way to the stage after his talk, "Hey, Kendall just walked out of the building, so I'll talk to you later. Wish me luck."

"Good luck. Take care . . . luv ya."

"Thanks girl . . . luv ya back."

Chapter 25 ➢ Reunited?

Placing her phone back into its case, Benét turned to her husband, "Hey sweetie!" His answering smile was encouraging enough so that Benét gave him a hug and kissed him on his lips. Kendall turned to the young man and introduced him as Christian Kane. Shaking his proffered hand, Benét smiled in acknowledgement, then she focused her attention back to her husband.

He thanked the young man again before turning back to her. He smiled down into her eyes, then grabbed her hand and tugged them towards their parked cars.

"We are going to leave your car here, and take the truck," Kendall said to her.

"What about dinner?'

"That's where we are going."

As they make their way to the truck he depressed the alarm and popped the trunk to place his briefcase in the back. Benét spotted their carryon and garment bags and gave her husband a perplexing and confused look as to the luggage.

"I have a surprise for you," he said before kissing her again and escorting her to the passenger door. He helped her into her seat, palmed her behind and smiled as she jumped slightly at this newfound playfulness. After belting her in he closed the door and made his way to the drivers side, strapped himself in, starts the engine and proceeded to pull out into traffic.

Benét noticed that they are driving into downtown Baltimore when Kendall pulled into the valet area of the Renaissance Hotel. Helping her from the car the bellman retrieved their luggage from the rear and escorted them to the elevators. Benét turned questioning eyes to her husband but all she got was him smiling like a Cheshire cat and she decided to save her questions for later. The elevator swiftly moved them to the top floor to what looked to be a suite of rooms decorated with rich colors of deep green, gold, and burgundy. Benét placed her purse on the huge California king sized bed and immediately turned to Kendall who was tipping the bell man and then closed and doubled latched the door.

"What is this?" Benét asked smiling. Trying to figure out what was going on in her husbands mind because the excitement filling the room was electric.

Walking to her he pulled her down on top of him and slowly penetrated her mouth in a deep long wet kiss. As his hands moved up and down her body bringing it to life, her hands ran over his head and face as she tried to get closer to him. Benét's awareness of her husband was strong as she began to pull his shirt from his pants and anxiously started unbuttoning his shirt. She was all thumbs as her long nails make her fumble with the small buttons on the shirt and frantically rips the shirt to expose his sleek chest. She placed her tongue upon his hairless chest and she heard Kendall groan. She was startled as he pushed her from him and strode across the room leaning on the temperature control unit near the window.

Jumping from the bed, Benét moved behind him and wrapped her arms around his torso, and ran her hands over his still exposed chest. Inhaling his scent she took several deep breaths until her rate returned to normal. Guiding her to the bathroom door, he said, "Go and shower because I have dinner reservations for us in the hotel dining room in one hour."

Reluctantly letting his hand go, Benét picked up her toiletry bag that Kendall had thoughtfully packed and walked into the bathroom with the shower built for two. Stepping into the stall she turned on the water and let the eight showerheads bathe her body and cool her heated flesh. Minutes later she turned off the water, opened the glass doors and stepped onto the thick bath mat. Pulling the large bath sheet from the towel rack, she wrapped it around her body and wiped the steam from the mirror. Looking at her face she smiled to herself because she just knew that tonight they would make love. Pulling her toothbrush from her bag, she cleaned her teeth, before entering the room to see Kendall sitting in the chair watching television. Her first instinct was to drop the towel in an attempt to change his mind but she didn't do that because she wanted to prolong the yearning until after dinner. She didn't know how she was going to make it through dinner because she wanted him now.

Picking up his own travel bag, he moved into the bathroom to shower without saying a word to her. While he showered, she lotioned her body and applied her favorite fragrance to her wrists and neck. The garment bag that was lying on the bed when she went into was now hanging in the closet. Moving over to the closet, she found a beautiful strapless baby blue sheer georgette dress with a fitted waist. Attached to that was a small bag which held a matching purse and high heeled mules along with a beautiful French cut lace bustier and thong in the same shade. Pulling the items from the hangar she hurried into them and after she was complete she turned around to see herself in the mirror. The outfit hugged her curvaceous figure and the shoes showed off her toned calf muscles. Except for holidays, birthdays, and anniversaries, her husband had never went out and bought her clothing before. Shocked at the fact that he would do something so out of the ordinary showed her how much he cared for her and to her it symbolized how much he wanted their relationship to work. She was so lost in her own thoughts that she didn't hear the shower stop or the bathroom door open until she heard Kendall gasp at the sight of her.

Grinning from ear to ear he knew that he would be the envy of everyone who saw them tonight. Women would wish they had a body like hers and men would wish that they could take his place. "You have never looked more beautiful," he stated proudly.

Moving around the room he hurried to dry himself and dress in his new navy blue suit with a matching baby blue silk shirt and tie, matching hers.

Benét watched her Kendall's fluid movements across the room. As he put his shirt on, his muscles flexed in his arms showing off his toned and fit torso. Finally complete, he turned to her with his eyes asking for approval. "Damn, you look good," she told him before meeting him halfway in the room to take his hands. They stood staring into each others eyes when his watched beeped startling them. Hands still clasped, in silence they moved towards the door, and took the short trip down the hall to the elevator. Hitting the button for the top floor to the restaurant the gleaming gold interior of the elevator reflected their stunningly handsome appearance. As the compartment stopped the doors slid open to reveal a bank of windows overlooking the Baltimore Harbor. Kendall gave the maitre d his name and after checking the list he escorted them to a table that provided a view of the star studded sky and the twinkling lights of the cars below. The black leather bound menus offered Mediterranean delights and sinful desserts. After ten minutes they had decided on their meal of braised lamb with a cranberry jelly sauce and asparagus tips with a hollandaise sauce. The bottle of Merlot was the perfect accompaniment as the bold flavor opened the palette with each bite of the meal.

The conversation between them came easily bringing nostalgic thoughts to each of their minds. Two hours later their meal was complete and Kendall signaled for the check. Benét excused herself to use the ladies room.

Benét gave the restroom attendant a tip after using the facilities and replacing her lipstick. She opened the door to see Kendall standing there waiting for her. Taking her small hand in his he turned directing them down the hall. The sounds of Kenny G could be heard as they moved closer to the doors. Upon entering through the doors they could see the couples dancing to his smooth melody. Kendall never stopped to get a table he took them straight to the dance floor and for the next few hours they danced and held each other, which heightened the desire between them. Finally they made their way back to the room, and immediately fell into each others arms.

As she pulled his tie from around his neck he released the zipper on her right side allowing the dress to flutter to the floor. Quickly they undressed and followed the clothing to the floor. They didn't care about the comfort of the bed. It had been too long since they held each other in this way. As Kendall moved down her body he placed kisses from her neck to the top of her thigh. Hooking his fingers through the band of fabric at her waist, he pulled them down her legs throwing them across the room. He then he placed his tongue where the small scrap of lace used to sit and lathed her core in slow strokes.

Grabbing him by the head Benét's flesh burned from the desire she felt for him and pulled his head up for a kiss and tasted her own sweetness which turned her on even more. Wanting to please him as he was pleasing her, she attempted to push him to his back but he stilled her saying "Tonight is for you Benét," before moving back to take his place between her thighs. His hot tongue speared her moist lips and then he lifted her higher giving him a perfect view of her backside. To her surprise and delight he placed his tongue there rimming her hole that had her body pulsating. She had always wanted him to lick her there but in the past he felt that it was dirty. Moving his tongue he paced himself as he switched from her fragrant apex to her rear. As she moved her hips in tune to his tongue, her climax built to the breaking point. Taking his hand he placed it upon her abdomen slowing her hips and moved his body beside hers as he slid one, two, then three fingers within her. Benét wanted to feel his thickness in her hand, she moved her hand towards his middle only to find him not erect. Her eyes widened and offered a questioning look.

Benét moved too fast for Kendall to stop her from knowing that he was not erect and the intentness of her stare shouted *whats wrong*? The need to take the question out of her eyes raced through him as he increased the pace of his hand and wiggled his fingers around. Closing her eyes he saw her loose herself as her moans became louder and her hips moved faster. Leaning down he kissed the bulging nub of her clit. That was her undoing. He felt her legs tremble and she held his head and hands in place as she climaxed. He removed his fingers and caught the essence brought forth from her spasms into his mouth.

Picking her up, he placed her between the sheets and slid down beside her.

Benét had wanted to question him but when she did he placed a finger over her lips and turned her around to spoon their bodies together. He knew that he would not get off so lightly in the morning and slowly rubbed his hand along her thigh. Kendall could feel his wife's body become heavy as the sounds of her even breathing told him she was asleep.

So as not to wake her, he eased himself from bed, sat in the chair and got lost in his thoughts, remembering the look in her eyes when she realized that he was not erect. Tried as he might to will himself to an erection, it would not come. He remembered the once incredible appetite they had for each other was now non-existent because of his problem. He believed it to be mind over matter, and after having several talks with himself, he decided to make tonight the night he would renew the flame. Leaning his head back in frustration at the unfairness of the situation, he closed his eyes as a thousand thoughts, ideas, and solutions bounced around his head. However, the one solution that remained constant was the solution his pride would not allow him to accept. As he watched her sleep he knew that he should, no needed to, seek counseling yet his pride rejected this thought each time.

Chapter 26 ➢ Kendra

Summer

Kendra stood in front of her mirrored closet in the sheer black chemise that Niall presented her with as a gift for her recent weight loss. The outfit had matching thongs which tickled her because she could finally wear them. Before, they were so uncomfortable and the cellulite made her too self-conscious to wear them for herself let alone a man. The look that Niall gave her had her smoothing her hands over her once dimply curves that are now beginning to take shape. So far, she has lost twenty-five pounds and Niall has supported her by eating low fat low calorie meals with her when they are together. Last night on their date, Kendra could tell he wanted to order the steak but out of difference to her, he ordered the same meal as she did—grilled chicken Caesar salad and baked fish. As she danced toward him, she counted her blessings of having met a man who wanted her for herself whatever the size. As Niall reached up to grab her to him, she hit the small radio on her night stand and the sounds of Sade emanated through the air. Kendra moved her hips from side to side and started to strip for him. Pulling the hem of her chemise up to give him a glimpse of her center in the thong, and while he continued to gaze she raised it just to the top of her thong straps and pulled them up separating her throbbing cherry lips. Licking his lips Kendra saw the sheet extend around his middle creating a tent like formation. Seeing how aroused she made him, she turned around to give him a quick view of her plump behind. He told her after several dates that he loved her ass and could not wait to see her in a pair of thongs. As he threw the sheet to the floor he jerked her towards him and released the shoulder ties to her chemise letting it fall between them. Releasing her enough to step out of the gown pooled at their feet, he rips the thong and dropped to his knees to place a kiss at the apex of her thighs.

Kendra's legs began to quiver because Niall could make a meal of her every time he touched, stroked, or kissed her hot center. Grabbing onto his shoulders he pushed her back onto the bed never once breaking his hold on her and brought her quickly to a climax. As her insides vibrated, he slipped inside of her in one long deep thrust. "You're my woman, right?" Niall moaned in her ear. It almost felt as if he was trying to meld himself inside of her, because she felt him all over, and wanted to join her soul with his. Her recent weight loss enabled her to get closer to his body because her stomach, hips and thighs were smaller.

"Yes, Niall, I'm yours and only yours!" As he stroked in and out of her, Kendra contracted her walls around him making his body jerk in ecstasy. With one final deep thrust, he pulsated deep inside of her spasmodic walls making her scream out in ecstasy as they climaxed together.

Resting his head upon her shoulder, Kendra wiped the sweat from his brow, thinking how happy he has made her. As they both got their wind back, she intertwined her legs around his and he pulled her closer to him to cuddle. Yes cuddle, a lot of brothas don't like to do that, but Niall does and she's wasn't complaining. Turning to face him, he pulled her closer, and dropped a kiss on her forehead before falling to sleep. *Hey, she said he liked to cuddle didn't mean the nigga don't fall asleep like the majority of men.* Drifting off into a light sleep, the sound of the phone awakened her. Reaching for cordless off the nightstand, Niall hands her the phone. "Hello," she answered groggily.

"Kendra!" says Benét. "I know your ass ain't still sleep at this time of the day," chastised Benét, "You know I'm having my Annual End of Summer Fest today and none of you mother-fuckers are here."

Damn! "What about Shaeyla, Diandra and Worthy?" Kendra asked.

"I just told you none of ya'll were here. It's just a surprise that's all, because we normally get together and hang out before the other guests arrive. So get your ass up and get over here," Benét said.

As if it was a second thought Benét asked, "Hey, what are you doing in bed anyway?"

The deafening silence that this statement was met with had Benét continuing, "Fuck! Were you doing it? Girl, you know the rule. Never answer the phone when you're getting some." Benét laughed.

"No problem at all, we were sleeping, so you didn't really interrupt anything. Besides, you know that we never answer the phone, that's the rule. But give me about an hour and we will be there. Do you need me to bring anything?" Kendra. Asked.

"No take your time. Okay."

"Cool. We'll see you in an hour or so," Kendra replied as she replaced the phone back onto the cradle.

"So where are we supposed to be in an hour?" Niall asked.

"Remember I told you about Benét's Annual End of Summer Fest. Well she's been having them for a while now, and I normally go alone, but this time I'm taking you with me," she stated.

Nuzzling her neck, he moved his hand up her leg to her damp center and started to finger her again. One touch and her walls constricted, she needed to stop him before it got out of hand she thought. "Stop boy. You keep this up and we will never make it to the party."

"Hmmm that's the whole idea. I want to stay just where I am," he said, taking her hands and pinning them above her head. He proceeded to place his knee firmly between her thighs, and slid down her body to partake of her sweet nectar.

Well maybe just a little longer won't make a difference, Kendra thought to herself as she succumbed to her desire for him.

Chapter 27 ➢ Benét's Annual End of Summer Fest

The Isley Brothers could be heard throughout Benét and Kendall's upper-class neighborhood as Shaeyla pulled into the driveway. She smiled because she knew that some of their neighbors had to be having fits over the noise; at least the ones that were not invited. The cerulean blue sky and the eighty-degree temperature was perfect for the days festivities. Outside events were known disasters as far as Shaeyla was concerned. Having catered several outside affairs that were ruined by either a brisk wind making it seem like forty below or the torrential rains that drowned out many a parties. If she had her choice, she would only do inside events, but this being her girl and all, how could she turn her down? As the light summer air blew her glossy black mane into her eyes, she pushed it back and ran into what she thought was a wall of steel only to find that it was a solid chest, with strong arms that kept her from falling. Once she got over the shock of almost falling and embarrassing herself, she tried to look away, but the shine from a set of the prettiest white teeth that she had ever seen caught her attention. She glanced up and found a handsome face. Dark complexion, close cut beard and mustache and a pair of dreamy brown eyes that danced with flecks of gold.

"Excuse me are you all right?" Although he said something, all Shaeyla heard was the deep well-modulated voice, because she could not stop staring at him. As her eyes widened behind her dark sunglasses, she recognized Mitchell's partner Solomon Jackson. He looked better today than he did the night she met him at Mitchell's. Seeing his brow furl in consternation she knew that she had to say something before he thought her to be a complete imbecile. Shaking her head from side to side, "I'm sorry. Yes, I'm fine," Shaeyla stated while at the same time releasing herself from his strong grasp. Damn, her heart was racing like a pubescent teenager. Confused by her immediately and sexual reaction to him, she did not want to make a fool of herself, so she quickly excused herself and re-joined the party in the back yard.

When she stepped around the corner, she saw Kendall with his chef's hat on and his famous black apron with "The Grill Mastah KMG" emblazoned in red flamed letters on the front. Lifting her hand up to acknowledge him, she walked towards him, while avoiding getting too close for fear of smelling like smoke and appreciatively wiggled her nose. "Hmmm boy you got those ribs and steaks smelling good!" Moving on she made her way over toward Benét who was setting out salads on the overflowing buffet table. As her stomach growled she realized that she had skipped breakfast, so she picked up a carrot from the vegetable platter, and popped it into her mouth. She couldn't help but admire the setup of the yard. The tiki torches sat on the boundary of the yard to ward off mosquitos. The decorative citronella candles placed on the individual tables were an added measure to ward off the other outdoor pest. Shaeyla had offered Benét her assistance but her friend insisted on doing the fest alone. Always with an eye on design and style Shaeyla noticed that Benét purchased three new tables that were placed around the kidney shaped pool. Looking at the bodies of people frolicking in blue water reminded Shaeyla that she left her bag with her swimming suite in the car. Deciding to get it later, Shaeyla walked toward Benét.

* * * * *

As the music changed to the sounds of Earth, Wind and Fire, Benét sat the salad bowl on the buffet and turned to survey her surroundings. Looking around at the various family, and friends, she saw Shaeyla coming towards her at the same time that Diandra rounded the corner with some thug,. Benét and Shaeyla both turned watching Diandra and shaking their heads, neither of them could believe that Diandra would brought his punk ass after the way he just dissed her. Benét thought to herself if that were her man, she would cut him with the quickness.

"Hey! Let's get this party started!" Diandra yelled as she spotted Benét and Shaeyla and ran over to give them hugs and kisses. Diandra's friend just stood back looking over his sunglasses at the bikini clad ladies lying around the pool. Turning to Mason, Diandra said, "Benét, Shaeyla ya'll remember Mason."

Benét and Shaeyla held out their hands to shake Mason's but his ignorant ass, just nodded his head saying, "What's up." Not liking the way he spoke to them both Benét and Shaeyla looked at each other and without words thought the same thing. *Damn, what does Diandra see in this ignorant Negro.*

Shaeyla walked away from them making her way to the house while Benét chose to ignore his rudeness and be the gracious hostess by saying, "I hope you two bought your swim suits with you?"

Holding out a straw bag, Diandra said, "Girl, why do you think I had my hair braided last night? I knew I was coming to your party and wanted to be able to get my hair wet."

"Its party time!" Shaeyla screamed from the top of the deck waving a bottle of Dom in the air. Running down the steps of the deck to the patio below, she swayed to the beat of the music.

"Damn, Shaeyla, what got into you?" her girls asked.

"Nothing. Can't a sister be happy? Besides I love a good party," Shaeyla replied.

"So no date today?" Benét and Diandra questioned.

"No, not today, Mitchell had to work," Shaeyla said although she really didn't believe that but refused to let it ruin her day or give her girls a reason to say *I told you so*. Even thought she was sure that Mitchell's absenteeism was certain to be commented on soon.

"You know the last few times we've gotten together you have been the odd girl out. What's up with you and Steele, are you still seeing him?" Benét asked.

"Yes, we are still seeing each other, but you know the man is busy. And you know that I am not about to beg anyone for their time . . . not anymore," replied Shaeyla.

Before Benét or Diandra could respond to that, Benét felt a tap on her shoulder and turned to find Kendra and Niall beaming at her.

"Well, it's about time you made it," she said good-naturedly.

* * * * *

Kendall spotted his wife and her friends, "Ladies, Ladies, whats going on? We have a party to enjoy . . . so go mingle, grab a drink, eat and enjoy!" Grabbing his wife by the shoulders Kendall planted a hot wet kiss on her lips, prompting Benét to look at him with hope in her eyes.

"Well Big Daddy, what was that all about?" asked Benét.

"That was about how much I love you," Kendall said smiling into her eyes.

"Well . . . " putting her hands beneath his shirt to caress his back and chest, she whispered, "Then I cannot wait for later on this evening."

Moving to circulate amongst her guest, Benét couldn't help but think that tonight she was going to get FUCKED! Hot damn, she silently exclaimed. It has been too long since she felt Kenny's loving arms, hands, and lips upon her body. The gasp from her elderly neighbor made her realize she had actually voiced her thoughts. Quickly apologizing, she turned and headed to the bar to grab a drink.

* * * * *

"Hey!!! I saw you and your man over there all hugged up . . . does that mean ya'll are back on track?" Shaeyla asked.

"Girl, I sure hope so, but tonight will tell," Benét replied gleefully.

"Ah shit, that's what I'm talking about," Shaeyla laughed out. "Turn around and check out who just joined your party."

Turning to view the new arrivals, Benét recognized Seven with a cute dark skinned woman. This immediately had Benét and Shaeyla turning to see where Diandra was and to gauge her reaction of Seven arriving with a date. Shaeyla called Diandra come over.

As soon as she arrived, Diandra spotted Seven and was immediately engulfed in outrage and jealousy and a feeling of betrayal. She just could not believe that he would *come to her girl's affair with some trick bitch knowing that she would be here.* She had to calm down because she did not have the right to be angry or jealous. Seven was her hanging buddy and that was it. Nothing more, nothing less.

Stiffening her spine, she approached the group amid introductions, hugs, and handshakes, Seven turned to introduce her to his co-worker Leslie Fordham. "Nice to meet you," Diandra heard herself reply. Kendall joined the group, at which time the ladies excused themselves, because now was the perfect time for them to go have their talk. Also they noticed that Diandra seemed a little pissed about the situation. Before she could blow a gasket, they swiftly moved her into the house and headed to Kendall's office.

Once inside the room Shaeyla started, "Alright Diandra." With her hands on her hips, she said, "Why you looking all pissed? Could it possibly be because Seven brought a date with him today?"

"Fuck you Shaeyla," Diandra spat.

"Hahahaha, that's just what your stupid ass gets. What did you expect him to do, trail around after you for the rest of his life? He is a handsome eligible man, and apparently someone else agrees. Besides, you have always acted like you didn't want him. It looks to me like he found someone that does," Benét said wickedly.

Not to mention that you only seem to call him when you need something from him added Kendra. So I don't see what your problem is. I say good going Seven, it's about time he showed let you know that you aren't the only fish in the sea".

"Fuck all of ya'll," Diandra said as she turned and headed to the other side of the room.

Still standing where Diandra left them, Shaeyla said, "I'm glad he brought someone with him. Let her ass know that he ain't waiting around for her to make up her damn mind about whether or not she wants him. The sad part is that you can see the love he has for her every time he looks at her, but she is too stupid to recognize how lucky she is. I wish I had some man looking at me like that she said with sadness in her voice."

"Well Diandra's problem is that Seven is a good man. Meaning he isn't into the thug life, and he isn't trying to be in the thug life. She should snatch him up before someone else does," said Benét.

Diandra walked to the other side of the room, but she could still hear her girls talking about her. She listened to them talk about her as if she wasn't even there. Enough was enough, so she placed her hand in the air and said, "Okay ya'll Damn! Enough about me, shit! I have something more important to talk about I have to talk to you all about Worthy."

Hearing the seriousness of her voice her friends incessant chatter stopped as the smiles on their faces were replaced with looks of concern. Diandra began with, "There really is no easy way to say this, but lately, I've been hearing about Worthy and how JJ has her strung out on that shit. My customers mumble about how she let him move in with her and the fact that she is down for whatever as long as she can get a hit. From the conversations that I have been able to piece together, he pimpin' her for hits! She's sent Jared to live with her mother, and is letting that trifalin JJ sell his shit out of her place. Which means that five-o is probably watching her and her stuff."

"What!" the ladies exclaimed in unison.

Kendra's look of fear and Shaeyla and Benét's looks of disbelief and concern, mirrored Diandra's worried expression.

"What are we going to do?" Kendra said, "Ya'll know we have to do something, we can't let her go out like this."

"To answer your question we cannot do anything unless Worthy want's the help or hits rock bottom. We all know people that we went to school with that grew up and got hooked on that shit. Randy and his friends are the perfect example of how crack can control your mind, body, and soul," Shaeyla voiced.

"You're both right, so I think we need to just roll up on her and see for ourselves. I mean I'm not trying to discount what Diandra heard from her customers, but as her friends, NO sisters, we need to see the situation for ourselves," Benét stated.

Diandra threw her hands up in the air, "The whole situation is just fucked up if what we've heard is true."

"I say, we next Saturday we go pick her up unexpectedly on the pretense of taking her out," suggested Kendra.

The women digested this thought for a minute before agreeing to hook up next week to see what the deal was about their girl. After agreeing Kendra and Diandra returned to the party stating that they had to get back to their dates.

* * * * *

"Is everything okay?" Niall asked Kendra as she returned to sit beside him on the lounge.

Not wanting to tell him of Worthy until she saw her, she turned and pointed in Diandra's direction, "You know my girl Diandra, right? Well you see that couple at the buffet table? Kendra asked Niall as she pointed out Seven and his friend, "That's Seven, a friend of Diandra's and his friend."

"Oh, okay," Niall said sounding confused. He didn't understand the significance of the situation. "So what's the point to you pointing them out to me?"

"Well we all know that he is in love with Diandra. I mean you can see it, but she doesn't see him in that way, she only see's him as a friend."

"Well it looks like he has gotten over her, or at least trying to if he brought a date here," Niall observed.

"Yes, but the point is Diandra is disturbed *because* he brought a date. I mean she has Mason with her, but she is so used to seeing Seven alone, that this has thrown home girl for a loop.

We think it's great because he's a good guy and Mason is a thug. We were just telling her that she better recognize it before he gets scooped up by another woman."

Pulling Kendra closer, Niall kissed her on her cheek, "Well that may be true, but why don't you concentrate on *us* and let the rest of them worry about them," Niall said.

Giggling like a teenager, Kendra happily puts her friend and their problems out of her mind for the moment to concentrate on Niall.

* * * * *

The door hadn't closed good before Benét turned to Shaeyla, "Now, what's going on with you? I know something is wrong, because of that last statement you made."

"Well it's Mitchell and I. Girl, I think he trying to play me and I do mean *play me*," Shaeyla said.

"What do you mean play you? Play you how?" Benét asked.

"Basically, he wants to see me and other people too, when I haven't been seeing anyone else but him. He says he doesn't want and isn't ready for a relationship, but he is willing to be my friend and fuck buddy until such time as I meet that man wanting a commitment," Shaeyla explained giving a summary of the last conversation, she had with Mitchell.

"No he didn't!" Benét exclaimed righteously. "Who the fuck does he think he is?" Deep down Benét knew something like this would happen and if Shaeyla was honest with herself, she knew it too.

"Mitchell Steele is who he is," Shaeyla said sarcastically.

"Well I'm glad you're getting rid of his ass," Benét said to her happily.

"Wait now, who said I was getting rid of him? I don't mine being his fuck buddy," Shaeyla said knowing deep down that she was lying to Benét and herself.

"Shaeyla who are you trying to kid? You can't be that man's fuck buddy and you know it."

"Why not?"

"Because you have been wrapped up in his entire life since you started seeing him and you wouldn't be able to be objective about it. Come on Shaeyla honestly, is that what you want from him? Is that what you want for yourself?" Benét asked.

Expelling a huge breath, "No it's not what I want from him or for myself."

Benét listened with rising dismay. "So why are you sitting here contemplating his outrageous suggestion?"

"I am not contemplating—," seeing the look on Benét's face Shaeyla stopped talking in mid sentence.

"Yes you are! Don't ever give a nigga that much credit! Understand. Dick is a dime a dozen, Shaeyla and you deserve better!" Throwing her hands up in the air, "The sad part is that your dumb ass is going to try it his way. And as soon as you realize that he is actually *actively* fucking someone else is when your ass is going to be sitting a corner in the dark crying somewhere," Benét said distastefully.

"See I knew I shouldn't have said anything to you," Shaeyla said disgustedly.

Benét relented, because despite how negatively she viewed his disrespectful comments Shaeyla was her girl. Plus she needed to remember that Shaeyla has always been hard headed in the man department. "Okay, point taken. I just wish that you would learn not to wrap yourself up in men and remember to put yourself first, second and third. Sadly Benét knew that Shaeyla was going to end up hurt before she saw the light. With that said, Benét stood and walked over to the door. She put her hand on the knob blurted "But I think you should leave him alone and find somebody else like, like—Solomon Jackson. Now you know he is not my taste but I figured he'd be perfect for you."

* * * * *

As Benét walked out of the room Shaeyla realized that they had been in the study for over an hour. Deciding that she needed a drink Shaeyla stepped from the room directly in the path of none other than Solomon Jackson. "Whoa, where's the fire?" he asked and for the second time that day she felt the warmth of his hands upon her. She also felt the strong pull of attraction, but she continued to chastise herself for her feelings, because she remembered that he was not only Mitchell's partner but also his best friend.

Snapping herself out of it she said, "I'm sorry. I need to watch where I'm going." Then she turned to walk over to the bar. After ordering a glass of Merlot, she could feel him standing behind her. Shaeyla tried to compose herself and taking another sip of wine she turned to see the handsome face that she could feel behind her. Shaeyla watched as Solomon's eyes traveled over her body in admiration. Simultaneously, behind her dark lenses she admired his physique, all the while comparing him to Mitchell and was surprised to find that it was Solomon's body she found wanting and not Mitchell's. The pale yellow silk T-shirt he wore with black linen shorts displayed his solid form. Knocking these thoughts from her mind, she let the business woman in her take over.

"So Solomon, Mitchell tells me that you sit on the board for the Black Charities Association." At the mention of Mitchell's name, Solomon's eyes locked with hers and she could see the question mirrored in his eyes as to what was going on between them.

Inclining his head, he walked towards the pathway leading around to Benét's small garden. The wrought iron benched seat faced a small rock fountain which was the focal point of the area. The wind carried the pleasing scent of densely planted colorful flowers to their noses. "That's right. It helped me gain a scholarship to Morehouse and as a member of the board it allows me to give back to my community."

Falling into step beside him he motioned for her to sit beside him. There was something about him that put her at ease allowing her to be completely comfortable in his presence. For the next hour they talked about his role with the charity and how he always had a hand in helping to plan the annual gala. The more he talked to her the more comfortable she became and before she knew it they had rejoined the party. Relaxed and at ease, they laughed, danced, and enjoyed each other.

Chapter 28 ➢ Partying at Summer Fest

Standing on the veranda, Kendall looked down his lawn to view his guests. Taking a sip of his drink, something out of the corner of his eye turns his head to the right. The site of his wife standing talking to some of his co-workers had him pissed. It's not the fact of her talking to his co-workers, but the fact that she looked to be openly flirting with them that outraged him. The shrill sound of her laughter carried up to him on the deck and at that point that she looked up and saw him standing there. With a wink of her eye, she blew him a kiss, while at the same time keeping her audiences attention. The firm hand on his shoulder had him turning to find Christian Kane, the associate professor of the chemical engineering department as well as chairman of the math department at Harris State College. Since Christian's request for him to lecture students on the availability of jobs in the industry, the two of them had become good friends.

Offering his friend a warm greeting, Kendall said, "Christian Kane. I'm glad you decided to come. Can I get you anything to eat or drink?"

Christian didn't answer and Kendall laughed, Christian was staring out over the veranda looking like a lovesick teenager. "Man who are you staring at?" asked Kendall.

"That woman with the long hair and jeans talking to Melvin Tetford," Christian replied

Kenny felt the rage return. "That's my wife, Benét," He said tightly.

He watched Christian's eyes widen and his face fill with embarrassment.

"I'm sorry man, I . . . I . . . just thought I recognized her. She's beautiful" he fumbled. I mean, you should be proud . . . or."

Kendall turned to look down at his wife as Christian's voice trailed off. "Yes, she is gorgeous isn't she?" *Somehow I almost forgot how beautiful and vivacious she is.* That's what prompted him to kiss her earlier. Now as he looked at his wife he for the first time noticed that, she was surrounded by men, and his blood started to boil with jealously and possessiveness. Those brothas aren't slick. He saw the lust in their eyes, especially, that Melvin character from advertising. He is the office lothario and has put his hand on her arm one time too many for Kenny's liking. "Would you excuse me?" he asked Christian. Turning, he strode briskly down the steps intent on removing his wife from the clutches of those men.

Maybe it was his look or maybe it was his belligerent stance, but the group parted like the Red Sea to permit him access to Benét.

Grabbing her by the hand, he turned to the men and said, "Gentlemen, excuse us for a moment." The look in Benét's eyes was one of anger and embarrassment. At that point, he didn't give a fuck about her feelings. What he did care about was why the fuck was she openly flirting with his co-workers?

When they were far enough out of site, Benét wrenched her hand from his, "What the fuck is wrong with you?" she asked through clenched teeth.

"What the fuck is wrong with me? What the fuck is wrong with you?" Kendall reposted.

Obviously perplexed by his response, Benét asked, "What do you mean?"

"I mean, how can you sit here and openly flirt with my co-workers?"

"I was not openly flirting with your co-workers. I was talking to them; just having friendly conversation," she replied.

"Friendly conversation my ass," Kendall scoffed. "Your ass was flirting with them? Do you want to fuck one of them?"

At this point, Benét was really confused because she was starting to get tired of his mood swings. Earlier he kissed her with promises to come and now he was jealous of her conversating with his co-workers. "Come inside, where we can talk in private."

When he didn't move, she said, "*Please!*"

Kendall followed her into their study. Benét turned on him before the door closed.

With hands on her hips and lips compressed, she said, "I don't know what your fucking problem is. But I cannot believe that you have the audacity to come out your face and ask me if I wanted to fuck one of your co-workers." Banging her fist on his mahogany desk, she continued, "What if I told your ass yes? What if I told you that if you don't get your problem fixed, that I am going to find a man that can do what you can't?" Just then she started pacing around the room, because she didn't want to go there but he had pushed her too far. 'Since the day that Kendall surprised her with the hotel, dinner, and clothes, they were slowly trying rebuild to their intimacy. When she woke up on the morning after, she kept her questions and thoughts to herself, because he broke the ice with his thoughtfulness and unselfish behavior of that wonderful night.

That last statement cut through Kendall like a hot knife slicing butter. Turning away from her spiteful words, he braced his back replying, "You know what Benét. At this point, I don't give a fuck who you fuck." Seeing her eyes start to tear up, he realized that he had cut her deeply with that statement. Well good he thought, twisting the knife even more, "Have you ever thought that maybe you're the reason why I can't fuck? Have you? Your ass is never satisfied. I work all the hours that God allows to keep your ass in the style that you are accustomed to living and it still doesn't seem to be good enough."

Shaking her finger in his face she said, "Hell naw nigga, you ain't going to turn this shit around on me. You can't fuck because of whatever is going on with you, but it is not because of me, or the demands that you may *think* I place on you. Everything that we have is because we *both* wanted a better life for our kids. So no way mister, you need to come better than that. You have major psychological problems."

When Kendall did not respond, Benét moved to stand in front of him. Putting her hand on his arm, she felt his muscles contract, as he jerked away from her.

"Regardless of what you think, our sex life was fantastic. We enjoyed exploring different things and bringing excitement into our bedroom. You know it. Right now I don't know what your problem is, but unless or until you get counseling…our situation is going to get worse, before it gets better," Benét sadly stated.

Knowing that his wife was right did not make him feel any better. How could he tell her that he saw a doctor and that he advised him to seek counseling? But his pride would not allow it. Hell, he was a young man and only old men have problems getting hard. His ego won't let him see a counselor, and his dick won't let him make love to his wife. Somehow, he had to overcome this problem if he wanted his marriage to survive.

Benét must have read his thoughts, because as she opened the door to the study to return to their guest she said, "The question you need to ask yourself is whether or not you *want* our marriage to survive."

Quietly closing the door behind her, Benét leaned against the gleaming mahogany finish of the door. Shortly after, Kendall crossed to the door and placed his hand on the knob to call Benét back into the room. As he opened the door, he watched her retreating figure walk through the French doors and back to their guests.

Chapter 29 ➢ Worthy's Smokin Dat Shit

Although Worthy didn't attend Benét's Annual End of Summer Fest, she had spoken to Diandra and made up some story about why she couldn't make it. Hell, she has told so many lies, that she can't remember what reason she gave Diandra about why she couldn't attend. But Diandra filled Worthy in on what Benét told her about Shaeyla's issues with Mitchell Steele wanting them to be fuck buddies instead of a straight up couple. That's what Shaeyla's high sadity ass gets, always thinking shit can't happen to her, but guess what . . . it happened to her dumb ass, Worthy thought. Laughing out loud at her girl's dilemma may seem mean spirited but she didn't have time to worry about Shaeyla or anybody else's problems for that matter. All she could think about was getting her next hit.

Unlocking the door to her crib, she was giddy at the thought of that big ass rock she slipped from JJ's stash right before he left. Hell, he had only been giving her crumbs since he moved in. Saying she needed to keep her head on straight but all she wanted was a blast.

Moving to her bedroom, she slipped open the hidden drawer on the side, where she kept her stash. Smiling like a Cheshire cat at her loot, she was also excited because she didn't have to add ashes to the pipe, cause there were some already there from earlier. Pulling out the nickel size rock, she carefully broke off a piece, placed it on top of the pipe, and wrapped the rest to be placed back into her secret compartment for her next high. Lighting the fire to it, she looked at it in wonder as it reduces down, and the sound of the cracking and sizzling had her feigning for more. She was so jonesed out that she didn't see or hear JJ enter the apartment or the room. The pipe was knocked from her hand and the rock knocked to the floor and crushed under his size 12 Timberlands before she could even say or do anything. Normally, she was so high that she couldn't say a word, but that whole scene took her high, right the fuck away. "What the fuck is wrong with you!" she screamed at JJ, as she scrambled around on the ground looking to recover the smallest crumb, any crumb. Moving in his direction, she tried to lift his booted foot to see if there was any rock left. "Move your foot, boy!" she yelled at him, then stood up and kicked him.

"Bitch, what the fuck is wrong with you?" he asked, then punched her slam in her chest.

Knocking her head against the wall, she rubbed her head as she gasped for air. "Why did you hit me?" she asked between sobs.

JJ ignored her as she moved into the bathroom. The mirror showed her the bruise from his knuckles on her chest. Wetting a washcloth with cold water, she placed it upon body. That shit hurt! Fuck! Fuck! Fuck! Her mouth was watering for a hit. She could barely think straight, and was frantically trying to figure out how long it would be before JJ left so that she could finish off the rest of her stash, when everything went black.

Awaking hours later to an empty room, she could barely move. The urge to piss was incredible. Jumping from the bed, she dropped back down as her legs rejected the swift movement. She needed to get to her dresser, to get her hit. But first, she needed to go to the bathroom. Rolling over she placed both feet on the ground and as she attempted to stand, her ankle gave way and she crumbled to a heap on the floor. After many attempts she finally made it to the bathroom. Exhausted from her struggle, she sits down, and the first signs of urination caused her so much pain that she could hardly finish without crying.

The pain did not stop her from her mission, "*Girl hurry up so you can get that hit, she kept saying to herself.*" Getting up again

Worthy limped to her dresser where her stash was hidden and pulled out the rest of her rock. Walking back to the bed she fumbled under the mattress for her back up pipe, then frantically scrambled around for some ashes. Breaking up the now half size rock she placed took her second hit for the night.

In an attempt to prolong her high, Worthy broke the rock down into tiny pieces, trying to make her hits last. With each hit, she began hearing noises. Her anxiety level increased to the point where she thought that someone was looking through the window at her getting high. Running over to the shades, she saw no one, but her cracked up mind heard still thought that she was being watched. Her inner thoughts were projected at five hundred decibels. Scratching her chin, she went to take the final hit. When that was done, she walked across the room to put her pipe back in its drawer. The mirror showed her a pathetic sight. Looking at her reflection, she saw sallow skin, dead dry brittle hair, and glazed over glassy eyes. Her once white teeth were now a dank shade of ecru, and the smell of smoke permeated her place but her pores. Bursting into tears at her actions she tells herself that she needs to get help. Unfortunately, that is the same conversation that she has with herself each time she finishes getting high.

The ringing of the phone startled her out of her reverie. Worthy made a mad dash to answer it hoping that it was JJ on his way home. "Hello," she said trying to get her mouth to act right. The taste of that last hit still has her mouth twisted, hindering her speech.

"Hey girl, what happened to you today?" asked Shaeyla.

Fuck she did not want to deal with Shaeyla right now. She could barely think let alone talk, and of all people Shaeyla, would pick up on that because of her experience with Randy.

"Nothing much," Worthy replied.

"Well . . . what happened today? You know you missed Benét' annual cookout. We missed you and Jared we have been hearing some shit that we don't like about you, so I decided to call and see what's up said Shaeyla. What kinda shit?" Worthy asked as if she didn't already have a clue.

"Naw, we not talking about this until all of us get together." No way was Shaeyla going to say anything over the phone. Worthy would just avoid them and they would never get to the bottom of the rumors. Changing tactics, Shaeyla said, "Anyway I called cause I want you to go somewhere with me on Saturday. Are you busy?"

Shaking her head, Worthy said, "No I don't have any plans for next week. Why? What's up?"

"There is a festival I know you will enjoy, so be ready at three Saturday and we, I mean—I will pick you up," Shaeyla said.

"Okay, talk to you later," and Worthy hung up the phone.

Chapter 30 ➢ After Summer Fest

The drive from Benét's house had Diandra anxious to get away from Mason. His blatant disrespect of her at Benét's party was the final straw. Breaking into her thoughts, Mason asked, "What the fuck is your problem now?"

"Nigger, don't act like you don't know what my problem is. You sat there this evening and ogled everything that was there in a bikini! Hell Mason, you acted as if I wasn't even there," Diandra told him.

"You know what Diandra, I am getting tired of your drama," he said. "First, of all, your ass is still stink about my birthday party business, and second of all I was just looking. Damn!"

"Fuck you and your party Mason. That is not the point; the point is that you couldn't seem to do enough for them bitches. *'Can I get you ladies a drink? Oh here let me help you with that.'* Was all I heard you saying tonight! Hell you don't help me or assist me nearly as much as you did them," Diandra said, remembering how he was falling over himself to be helpful. "Knowing you, you probably want to add them to your list of fuck buddies."

"I added you to the list didn't I?" he said nastily. "In fact, your ass couldn't wait to get on my list," Mason threw back. "Now your ass acting like I belong to you alone . . . shit, you better check yourself."

His whole attitude shut Diandra up. As far as she was concerned, they couldn't get to her house fast enough. Feeling the tightness in her throat, she was determined not to let him see her cry. She mentally decided that this was the last time that he would be with her, because no one, and I mean no one was allowed to treat her like just a everyday ole fuck. That is not how Diandra Johnson was going down, she thought to herself.

Bringing her out of her musings, Mason said "What, now you have nothing to say." as he touched her arm.

Snapping at him, Diandra yelled, "Don't fucking touch me." Noticing that they had arrived at her place, she decided to be nice and said, I'm sorry, "I do have something to say." She licked her lips and leaned over to whisper in his ear and said, "You don't have to worry about this 'fuck buddy' anymore, as of now I am removing myself from your list." With that said, she didn't even give him the satisfaction of slamming his door, because she got out and left the door wide open.

Not believing that she had done that, Mason yelled "Hey, bitch, shut my fucking door." Diandra didn't break a stride when she heard, "Fuck you! You trick!" He drove off.

When she finally entered her apartment, Diandra threw down her bag and purse and flung herself onto her chenille covered couch and burst into tears. The pounding on her door woke her from her misery. With a face ravaged with tears, she opened the door to find Seven standing there. "What the hell is wrong with you?" he asked. Not allowing her to respond, he said, "What happened? Did that motherfucker do something to you?" he asked with concern.

Moving to permit him into her space, he noticed the tears welling up in her eyes. Seven gently pulled her to him, lifted her into his arms and moved to sit on the couch. The feel of her in his arms felt wonderful, but the tears of pain, made him wanting to fuck Mason up. Whispering soothing words, he slowly calmed her and eventually she stops crying. "Are you ready to tell me what's wrong?" he asked caressing her back.

Shaking her head negatively, she asked, "What are you doing here? I thought you would still be with your *date*." This last word said with sarcasm.

Squeezing the bridge of his nose and releasing a sigh, he said "Diandra, we need to talk. But now is not the time." He wanted her completely over Mason before he bared his soul to her.

With her head resting on his chest, Diandra admits to herself that she liked being in his arms; sitting on his lap while his hands caressed her back and shoulders. Why not tell him what happened, she thought to herself. *Yeah right, so he can tell you I told you so.* Conflicted she knew that Seven only had her best interest at heart. Having reached the decision to talk to him, Diandra slid off of his lap and faced him. "What's wrong?" Seven asked, placing his hand on her neck and rubbing his thumb across her jaw. "Talk to me Dia," he said using his nickname for her.

"Mason and I had it out on the way over here and I told him that I wasn't going to be seeing him anymore."

Nodding his head in understanding, he attempted to pull Diandra back into his arms. Stilling his actions, Diandra said, "That's not the complete truth. The truth is I accused him of wanting to add some of the women that were lounging around the pool to his fuck buddy list, and he said that I was anxious enough to be added. One thing led to another and I told him he didn't have to worry about me being on his list anymore, because I was removing myself."

Bursting back into tears, she fell upon his chest.

The grin on Seven's face was one of elation, but it quickly disappeared. As his mind reminded him that he had forgotten one minor detail *just because she broke it off with Mason, doesn't mean she wants him.* Pushing his feelings to the back burner, he decided to use this opportunity as his window to get closer to Diandra. She is vulnerable at this point, and he is going to make sure that she really sees him this time. Making him self a promise to take it slow, he massaged her back relaxing her into sleep.

Chapter 31 ➢ Benét's First Day

Fall

Reviewing her schedule again, she looked at her surroundings and realized that she was lost. Normally, Benét's not one to be lost, but today is her first day of school and she has a little more than half an hour before her first class starts. Yes, she is early, but she was so anxious this morning to get up and get ready for school, that she didn't even stop to have breakfast with her family. Instead she chose to get to campus early enough to eat in the *school cafeteria.* Her excitement was only increased by the surroundings of the beautiful oak trees scattered throughout. The vibrant colors of red, yellow, and green leaves scattered along the sidewalk from the brisk fall wind. Pulling her windbreaker closer together, she can't help but do the bank-head dance, because today is the first day of the rest of her life. Switching from the summer term to the fall term upon Kendra's suggestion was a good move, because Benét was feeling like a kid again. Moving to place a hand over her stomach, she tried to calm the butterflies that were floating making her more nervous with each step that she took. Having stood around daydreaming for the last ten minutes, she decides to get it in gear and find her building or else she would be late.

Trying to remember the directions given to her in the admissions office on how to get to the Humanities building, her concentration was broken by someone calling out her name.

"Mrs. Grier! Benét!" she heard from across the campus courtyard. Putting a hand up to shield her eyes from the morning sun, she sees a tall dark suited man heading her way. As he ran towards her with his coat tails flapping in the wind, recognition set in. Christian Kane, the young man she saw at Kendall's lecture and later at their annual summer fest. Damn! He is one fine young man, Benét thought to herself.

Smiling, Benét greeted him with a welcoming hug. "Good morning, Christian. How are you?"

"Good morning, Mrs. Grier. I'm fine and you."

"The name is Benét and I am fantastic. Today is my first day of class and I am excited." Are you a student here as well? asked Benét. Just then she recalled that the day they met Kendall on campus, he told her that he worked there and again he reminded her when they were reintroduced at the summer fest.

Thinking back to that night, she remembered how Kendall and her didn't say one word to one another and ever since then the rift between them has grown. She hasn't tried to have sex with him since he accused her of wanting to screw his co-workers. Snapping herself back to the present, she missed what Christian asked her.

Noticing the perplexed look on his face she said, "I'm sorry. I drifted for a moment."

"I asked if you were familiar with the campus. If yes, I will walk with you, and if no, I will escort you," Christian said determined to spend the any time with her that he could.

"No I am not familiar with the campus, and I would love for you to show me where I need to be." Laughing she told him she was standing there when he called her name because she was lost.

"I see the math, science and library buildings, but where is the Humanities?" Benét asked.

"Oh! Humanities. That is what is known as our hidden building, because it is obscured from view by the math and science buildings," Christian said, "Follow me."

"Wait. Let me get another cup of cappuccino," Benét said.

Turning them around to go back to the cafeteria, Christian couldn't keep the grin from his face. He'd thought about this woman since the party at her home remembering how the sight of her in that sexy one-piece bathing suit and sexy wrap that had him hard for most of the day. He was so embarrassed when Kendall caught him staring but her beauty mesmerized him. Her casual yet elegant style wrecked havoc with his senses and made having to appear nonchalant an act of purgatory. That's why he chose to sit down, because her presence seemed to take his breath away.

Daydreaming, Benét could not help but think about the feel of Christians hand in the small of her back, guiding her through the cafeteria doors. The thought made the small hairs on the back of her neck stand on end. "Talk about chemistry!" she mused. The shit she could do to this boy, Mmmm, Mmmm, Mmmm, she mumbled as she shook her head. I have got to get some…*soon* or else I am going to go nuts. Chastising herself for her adulterous thoughts, she distanced herself from her thoughts and his hand on her back.

After getting her cappuccino, Benét reached into her purse to pay for her drink when he placed his hand over hers, "This is on me, pretty lady. It's my way of welcoming you on your first day at Harris State College," he said, lifting his cup for a toast.

Clicking her cup against his, she let out a breathless, "Thank you." As she found her voice she clarified by stating, for the coffee, directions and for the toast. The intent of his eyes could not be disguised, he wanted Benét, and he could see a flicker of interest mirrored in her own but it was quickly extinguished as she looked away.

By mutual agreement, they walked in the direction of the Humanities building, all the while, enjoying natures silence and the sounds of the campus coming to life around them.

Reaching room 203 for Humanities 101, Benét turned and said "Well, here I am." Holding out her hand for him to shake, she said, "Thanks, again."

Ignoring her proffered hand, he pulled her in for a hug while murming, "Thank you! You have truly made my day, and my students will be eternally grateful," he said as he slowly released her.

Although he had on a suit, the athletic build of his body was still marked by his broad shoulders. Damn his body was solid, Benét thought, returning his hug. Benét could feel the muscles in his shoulders bunch as she placed her hands on them, and stepping closer into his embrace she could feel the strength in his thighs. Damn Damn Damn . . . the last thing she needs is to be thinking about another man this way, not to mention a man that is young enough to be her son. *But he's not* a voice reminded her, and the scent he wore was seductive, subtle, masculine and sex personified. Shaking herself, Benét pulled away, smiled and entered the lecture room closing the door behind her.

Promising herself not to think about him she seated herself, opened her Coach briefcase and retrieved her first assignment while mentally preparing herself for her very first class.

Going around the room the instructor asked everyone to introduce humor herself, and to relay their expectations of his class. Benét knew upon reading her course syllabus that she and her professor were not going to get along. She could see that this professor was going to be a complete asshole.

Chapter 32 ➤ Events to Remember, Inc.

The sound of the ringing phone in the outer office has Shaeyla miffed. *Where the hell is Bilal, my so called trusty assistant?* He must be out back on a smoke break. Picking up the headset and pressing line one, "Good Morning, Events to Remember, this is Ms. Andrews, how can I help you," she said in her politest voice. God knows that she was not a morning person, that's why it was mandatory that her assistant Bilal be at his desk and on the phones until at least noon. By that time, Shaeyla would have gotten a couple of cups of her decaf hazelnut cappuccino and maybe even a sandwich down to help her disposition. Once that is out of the way, she becomes once again the efficient and successful businesswoman and not *that bitch named Shaeyla.*

"Good morning Ms. Andrews," said the voice on the telephone. Perplexed, Shaeyla tried to remember where she has heard that voice before. But she couldn't place it, at least not yet.

"Good Morning. How can I help?" she repeated.

"This is Solomon Jackson," the voice stated.

The smile that washed over her face was replaced with confusion as she wondered at the reason for the call.

"Hello Mr. Jackson. How can I help you?"

Clearing his throat, he said, "I am calling to set up an appointment with you to discuss the Black Charities fundraising gala. Is now a good time?"

"Couldn't be better," said Shaeyla. Inwardly Shaeyla had been dreaming up ideas for the gala since their talk at the summer fest. Pulling the palm pilot from her purse, she asked "When would you like to meet?" Solomon Jackson knew he shouldn't feel the attraction that he did for her, especially as she was one of his boy's women. But the sound of her voice caressed something deep within in him compelling a need to see her. Unbeknownst to Shaeyla, Solomon had already questioned Mitchell about his relationship with her and whether or not he had told her about his fiancée. After being told that it was none of his business, Mitchell proceeded to state that "Ms. Andrews and I are just friends". The million dollar questions was, whether or not Ms. Andrews knew that Mitch viewed them as just friends.

Unknowingly breaking into his thoughts Shaeyla said, "Listen, if you have time today I can show you the board's I have that reflects the theme. I started working on them after the summer fest and I have to tell you that this event is going to be the hottest ticket in town, not to mention the large dollar amount that it will bring in for charity."

"Are you free this afternoon?" Shaeyla asked.

Glancing at his calendar, he asked, "What time did you have in mind?"

"One O'clock, if that is good with you. I know of this quiet little café off of Charles Street, that would be perfect for us to strategize," said Shaeyla.

"Okay, Ms. Andrews, I will meet you there at say one o'clock?"

"One o'clock sounds good. I'll see you then," she said and ended the call.

After Shaeyla replaced the receiver, she heard the front door open and close in the outer office. She walked towards her door to make sure that it was Bilal. "Good Morning!" Shaeyla stated.

Noticing the frown on her face, Bilal wondered what was wrong. "Good Morning," he said hesitantly.

"Bilal, how many times have I told you that the phones need to be covered in the morning? You know that I'm not good in the mornings."

"I'm sorry; I was on a smoke break, he said. "What happened?"

"Solomon Jackson is what happened," she said. Shaeyla brought her assistant up to speed on the gala, "So I am going to take him to Carembe Books and Coffee House on Charles Street for lunch to go over the boards we have."

Bilal knew how important this account was to Shaeyla, so the two of them spent the majority of the morning pulling together the very last details to make sure that Mr. Jackson, could not help but be impressed.

When Bilal left her office she opened her planner and began jotting down dates in her timeline as reminders when to order the flowers, book the band, have flyers printed up, tickets made, go over menus and a host of other details that she would delegate to Bilal.

Shaeyla arrived at Carembe a little early to browse through the current favorite reads recommended by the staff. The owner, an entrepreneurial spirit like herself, opened this bookstore a year ago. Shaeyla and the girls enjoyed coming to listen to the owner and her family, discuss their latest book of the month. Besides, this gave her a moment to unwind before Solomon arrived.

The atmosphere at Carembe was that of an eclectic ambiance. When you walked into the store the smell of incense and the *Sounds of Blackness* filled the air. Solomon didn't know what to think when she first suggested this place. His assistant raved about it, the poetry slams that they have on Thursday's and the number of famous black author's that have come in to sign and read their books. Stepping further into the room, he looked around and spotted Shaeyla standing near the "Carembe Book of the Month" aisle. Damn, she is one beautiful sister, he thought to himself as he walked up and placed his hand on her shoulder.

The touch of a strong male hand on Shaeyla's shoulder had her turning to find Solomon. Damn, he caught her unaware and she arrived early so that she wouldn't be put in that predicament. But, putting her in a bookstore is like letting a child loose in a candy store.

"Ms. Andrews," he said as he softly called her name causing goose pimples to rise to his occasion.

"Mr. Jackson. How are you? I am so glad that you could make it." She then slid the latest E. Lynn Harris novel onto the counter and asked the owner to hold it for her. "Please follow me," she said as she turned to lead him towards the back of the store to their meeting room. This is another reason why Shaeyla loved this place. You could come in, sign up for a room, free of charge, and conduct business, study groups, and other meetings.

Opening the door to room number one, she placed her briefcase and laptop on the table. Shrugging out of her coat as Solomon steps around her, he said, "Allow me," as he assisted her with her jacket. Then he held out her chair, and Shaeyla inwardly smiled because she loved gentlemanly men. Thanking him, she opened up her briefcase to pull out his file and turned on the laptop to start the presentation.

As she settled in her seat, she saw him remove his jacket before taking his seat across from her and pulling out a writing pad from his briefcase.

With a nod from his head, she started her presentation all the while, her enthusiasm showing through her eyes as she explained each of her ideas. The board portrayed a stunning ballroom, with a huge crystal chandelier as the focal point, a rich red carpet, and fifty tables draped in black and white tablecloths. Each chair was covered in a rich black-skirted apron with a white tie in the back. The floral centerpieces consisted of calla lilies in a vase designed to rest on its side allowing the flowers to cascade to the table without hindering the attendee's views. When Shaeyla presented the menu, she indicated that she felt the menu should offer hot and cold foods, with Italian, Chinese, American, and seafood stations placed around the room. The Hors D`Oeuvres would be, which depicted the charity logo of uplifting hands towards the sky. Putting down the last board, she pulled out a mock invitation for him to peruse.

As Shaeyla presented her ideas, Solomon heard the excitement in her voice and could see the sparkle in her eyes.

"I think the event should take place on the 12th as it gives us ample time to plan and get the invitations printed and mailed."

Placing a hand on her arm, Solomon said, "I think your ideas are fantastic."

He sat there gazing at her as she smiled, thinking that her smile had the ability to light up the entire room. Damn he thought to himself, Mitchell is a fool!

"Thank you Solomon. I promise you will not be disappointed. If I say so myself, I am the best event planner in Baltimore and your event is going to be front page on every society page from USA Today to the *Baltimore Sun.*"

Shaeyla removed the contract from her briefcase and passed it over to him, "I will forward the particulars to your assistant in the morning. And going forward I will keep her abreast of all of the proceedings."

After saying goodbye and shaking hands, Shaeyla went to purchase her book. While at the register, the cashiers Carian and Deidre, said, "I know that you are not letting that fine man leave by himself?" Shaeyla just smiled and thought to herself yes, the women were right, Solomon was fine, but she was not trying to get involved right now. Having had two assholes in her life, she simply was not interested in acquiring another . . . at least not right now.

Chapter 33 ➢ Worthy is MIA

Shaeyla returned to her office after a prosperous luncheon with Solomon Jackson. Bilal informed her that Benét on was her private line. Before she could get on him for leaving her on hold he said, "She just called here, and I saw you pulling up so she said she'd hold."

"Oh, okay," she said entering her and picking up the phone as she shrugged out of her jacket. "Hey girl! What's up?"

"Good Afternoon." Benét said.

"What's been going on stranger?" she asked. Since Benét started school they hardly had a chance to talk.

"Girl nothing much. Can you talk?" Benét' asked.

"Yes, but only for a minute. I am swamped, just got back from a business lunch and I have another appointment in about twenty minutes," Shaeyla said looking at the slim Movado on her wrist. "So how are things going? How's school?"

"Girl. This is the best move that I have made so far. You know what I mean?" Benét asked. "I love my family, but this is something that I am doing just for me! And I can't tell you how good it feels."

"I feel you girl, we are all so proud of you. It takes guts to go back to school and I am just glad you finally did it. Now, what's up with the honies on campus?"

"Phew! Girl!" Benét exclaimed over the phone, "You know I love my husband, despite our problems, right? But girl, the men walking around here, makes you wanna scream."

Benét said laughing at that statement."

"Now don't get me wrong, they have some brotha's down here that, lets just say, if I was single, I'd be something to reckon with."

"I don't even know why you go on like that, all you're doing is looking," Shaeyla told her knowing that Benét wasn't going anywhere.

The silence on the other end of the phone had her saying, "Benét, are you still there?"

Clearing her throat, "Yes, I'm still here . . . but I have to tell you something and you can't tell the other girl's."

The secretive yet serious tone from Benét did not give Shaeyla a good feeling about what was to come. "Oh damn! What happened?"

"Remember that young man that was at my party, the one that asked Kendall to lecture at the university?"

"Yes, I remember. What about him?"

"Well I ran into him on campus the first day—."

"And . . ."

"I couldn't believe my eyes when I saw him on campus. I completely forgot that Kendall told me he was an associate professor here."

"Girl, talk about putting temptation in your face. But, what's the big secret about that?"

"The secret is that I find myself attracted to him and from the way that he looks at me, I know that the feeling is mutual. Benét said.

"Okay. You need to hold that down." Just then Bilal knocked and poked his head in to remind her that her next client was due in fifteen minutes. As much as Shaeyla wanted to continue the conversation with Benét, she had work to do. "I hate to cut this short, but I have to finish reviewing this file before my client gets here. But do me a favor, you know I hate cheating, so don't do anything stupid . . . I don't care how fine he is or how attracted you are to him, it aint worth loosing everything that you have built over the years"

"I can't promise that, but I will take what you've said under advisement."

"I don't even know why you mentioned it to me then if you weren't willing to take my advice," Shaeyla said vexed knowing that it was time for her to go. "Hold on Benét my other line is ringing."

She pressed down the button to the second line, "Good Afternoon, Shaeyla Andrews".

"Hey girl," Diandra said into the phone.

"Hey girl what's up?" Shaeyla said adding "Hold on let me conference you in, I have Benét on the other line."

Pressing the conference button, "Hey Benét, I have Diandra on the other line."

"Hey girl," Benét said, "What's up?"

"I was calling to ask ya'll a question...have either of you spoken with or even seen Worthy lately?" Diandra asked.

"No, why? What's wrong?" Benét asked.

"Damn, come to think of it, it has been a minute since I've seen Worthy." Shaeyla added.

"You're right, it has been a while." Benét agreed.

"I know," said Diandra, "I talked to her the night of your summer fest to see why she didn't come and she gave me some lame ass excuse, but I didn't pay attention cause I was mad at Mason. But I haven't seen or heard from her since and I am starting to get worried."

"Did you ask Kendra has she heard from her? Or even seen her?" asked Benét racking her brain as to where she could be.

"No, she has been so happy wrapped up with Niall, I didn't want to spoil anything for her. You know how worried she is about her," Diandra said.

Shaeyla and Benét understood what Diandra meant by that statement because this is the first time that Kendra has been truly happy with herself and a relationship.

"Ya'll hold on a minute. I'm going to call Kendra so that we can all talk." Depressing her third line, Shaeyla dialed Kendra's office, as soon as she hear the first ring she hit the conference button, “Hey can ya’ll hear me?” she asked Diandra and Benét.

“Yeah,” They responded.

“Good Afternoon, Kendra Thompson.”

“Good afternoon girl, it's Shaeyla.”

“Hey girl,” Benét said.

“What's up girl?” Chimed Diandra.

“Damn!” Kendra said laughing, “What's up with all ya’ll on the phone?” Diandra filled Kendra in on the phone call, “No, I haven't heard from her and now I am worried,” Kendra fretted.

“Well I called her house and when some dude answered I hung up, because I figured it was JJ,” Diandra said.

“Well I am going to drop past her house when I leave my office today.” Kendra said, “I'll check out the situation and give ya’ll a call later. Okay.”

“All right,” they replied and hung up the phone.

Chapter 34 ➢ Diandra

Hanging up the phone from her conversation with her girls, Diandra tried to call Worthy again. She couldn't help but think that something was terribly wrong, it's just not like Worthy to go this long without contacting anyone. Although it has only been three weeks since Benét's fest, that was a long time for her to not have been heard from. Diandra said as she heard the answering machine pick up again. Leaving a message to call her or any one of the girls, she turned to flip the sign onto her door that read 'open'. Yes, she closes for lunch and what.

Damn! She just realized that she was still wearing her Timberland's and she never does hair in them, she quickly ran into the back of the shop and changed into her work shoes. She purchased a pair of nursing slides to wear since she is on her feet all day, plus she didn't mind messing them up. The ringing of the bell over the door alerted her to a customer. Sliding her feet into her shoes, she rounded the corner just in time to see a deliver man with a bouquet of flowers, which automatically tells her that he has the wrong address. No one ever gets a delivery in her shop. Before he could open his mouth, she told him that he had the wrong address.

"Well the card says DJ's House of Styles," the deliveryman responded.

The wrinkle in her forehead showed that she was trying hard to think who would send flowers, "Who is the delivery for?"

"Diandra," he said.

As her heart started to race, she immediately thought that they were an apology from Mason.

Inhaling the scent of beautiful fall colored roses, in a crystal vase and rust colored bow she discovered that they were too big to place on her station, so she moved to place them on her desk. Sitting them down, she moved around to sit in her chair as she pulled out the card to read it.

Diandra,

If these caught you by surprise, then wait for the other surprises that I have in store. I will pick up at 7 o'clock sharp.

Seven

Leaning down to smell the bouquet again, Diandra couldn't help but wonder what Seven was up to. He has been so kind and thoughtful since that night she had the fight with Mason. Hell if she were to be honest with herself, it felt good lying there in his arms. She had felt loved, and protected…like she really mattered to him. Seven has always been a good friend, and she needed to realize that before she looses him for good. *Hell she has to face the fact, that he will probably get married some day and his woman will have issues that her man has a female friend as close as Seven and I.* 'Damn! Now why does the thought of him getting married give me a sinking feeling in my stomach?'

Before she could dwell on the subject, her first client came through the door. Walking out from her office to greet them, she had the biggest smile on her face for the rest of the day.

"Good Afternoon Diandra," Mrs. Clemmons greeted.

"Good Afternoon Mrs. C, how are you today?" Diandra said cheerily.

"Well, you seem unusually cheerful this afternoon," said Mrs. C.

"My best friend sent me flowers," Diandra said, grinning like the Cheshire cat. She knows that no matter what happens, receiving those flowers will rule out all bad today.

"Well from the look on your face, I can see that it has made you happy."

"Seven is his name, and we have been friends for the longest time. He helped me through a rough patch a few weeks ago and ever since then; he has been kind and thoughtful., "Diandra said. Moving into her office, she picked the vase up and brought it out to show Mrs. C.

"Ooh, well he sure is thoughtful. Hmm, makes an old woman like me wonder if he has more than friendship on his mind. Cause honey, friends don't send roses . . . they send potted plants or maybe a card-but not roses."

"Naw, Seven and I are just friends," Diandra informed her returning the flowers to her desk.

* * * * *

Geesh! Diandra sighed as she thought her day would never end. All day long, she wondered what Seven could be doing for a surprise. If only Mason had acted as kind and sweet as Seven did. Laughing out loud at this thought, *who am I kidding, Mason would never act this way. None of the dude's she'd messed with in the past would act that way. Give women roses...oh hell naw!* All women should have a friend like Seven; he is really helping her to get over Mason.

Opening the door to her apartment, she puts the vase down on her coffee table. Hell yeah she bought her roses home with her. Shit had she left them in the shop someone was bound to take at least one from the vase, she thought. No way, this is the first time she had received flowers from a man and she was bringing them home. Looking at the mirrored clock on her living room wall, she realized that she had less than twenty minutes to get ready for Seven's surprise. Taking off her clothes she walked down the hallway, she wrapped up her hair and stepped into the shower. After dousing her body in her favorite body wash, she was generously applying her favorite cocoa butter body oil to her legs when her doorbell rang. Damn, Seven is always on time, she thought. Tightening up her silk robe, she ran down the hall and opened the door for Seven. Only it's wasn't Seven at the door but a uniformed waiter with a table romantically set with candles and covered dishes. "Ms. Johnson," the young waiter asked.

"Yes, I'm Ms. Johnson. How can I help you?"

"I have a delivery for you," he said then handed her a card.

Taking the card from him, she stepped back to let him wheel the table in. "Is this area okay?" he asked. As she looked up, she noticed that he placed the table in front of her sliding glass doors that lead out to her terrace.

"Yes, that's fine," she told him, moving to get her purse to give him a tip.

"The gratuity has been taken care of."

Looking at the card in her hands, she opened it and read,

Surprise!

Seven

So this is his surprise, she thought as she picked up the phone to call him. She thought he was going to pick her up, but that must mean he is coming over. The sound of his answering machine had her hanging up to Diandra his cell phone number. That too went to the answering machine. Damn! This is so thoughtful, she mumbled as she started to uncover what was hidden under the silver domes. The first dome revealed cheese and fruit, and then she uncovered a stuffed rockfish, with steamed veggies in a garlic cream sauce. There were hot dinner rolls, and a creamy New York style cheesecake for dessert. The sound of the doorbell told her that it has to be Seven, but again she was wrong; it was Kendra.

Opening the door to let her in, Diandra gives her friend a hug. "Hey girl, it's so good to see you."

Seeing the table set and the state of dress or rather undress that Diandra was in Kendra asked, "Oh am I interrupting anything?"

"Girl, Seven sent this over to me as a surprise. He has been cheering me up since I broke it off with Mason."

"Girl! No he didn't." Kendra shrieked, "Look at this, this man went all out to surprise you—cheer you up to help you get over another man?"

"Yes, he is such a good friend."

"Friend my ass Diandra. You better wake up and smell the coffee. That man want's you. He is romancing you, you big dummy,"

Kendra declared. "You better get that man before someone else does."

Dismissing Kendra's statement, Diandra said, "Girl he is not romancing me. He is just being a good friend."

"Yeah right!" Kendra scoffed. "We all saw how pissy your ass got when he bought home girl to the cookout, so don't go there with me! Did you at least call him and thank him for the meal?"

"Yes, but all I got was his answering machine," Diandra informed her, and seeing Kendra's lips about to ask another question, she said, "A*nd* I called his cell and I got the voice mail on that too."

"Well all I'm saying is that I have had plenty of male friends and none of them would ever think about doing something like this without a hidden agenda." Kendra said trying to get Diandra to think. Everyone could see how Seven felt about her but *her.*

"Anyway, I came over to tell you about Worthy."

"What's going on now?" asked Diandra.

"I don't fucking know!" Kendra replied, "She wasn't there when I called, so I dropped past on my way home and no one answered the door. But I could've sworn I heard movement inside, almost like she didn't want to let me in." Hell, Worthy has always been somewhat of a stray bullet, doing her own thing only worried about Worthy, but she never went without talking to at least one of them on a daily basis.

Seeing the turmoil on Diandra's face, Kendra was sorry that she even brought Worthy up and ruined Diandra's night. "Girl I'm sorry for dropping this shit on you like this and ruining your night," she said. Standing up she turned and saw the vase of beautiful flowers on the coffee table. "Damn! Who sent you those and how did I miss them when I first came in?"

"Seven sent me those. I told you he has been very thoughtful since I broke up with Mason. He takes me to the movies, or just calls to see how I'm doing," Diandra said.

Looking at the roses and back at her friend, "Uh Yeah right—a friend? Girl every woman should have a friend like that." Kendra said disbelievingly. Diandra still doesn't get it, or does she Kendra wondered while searching Diandra's eyes.

"Why are you staring at me like that?" Diandra asked.

Playing dumb, Kendra said, "Staring at you like what?"

"Like you are looking for something."

"I think I have already found it . . . the question is have you?" Kendra asked her, gave her a hug and walked to the door. "I have to meet Niall for dinner downtown; call that man back again and ask him to join you for dinner." Before Diandra could respond, Kendra closed the door.

Picking up the phone again to call Seven, she popped in a CD, damn, his voice mail again, oh well this time Diandra leaves a message. Bopping to Stevie Wonders "*Don't you worry 'bout a thing . . . Don't you worry 'bout a thing mama,*" she decided to dig into her meal.

* * * * *

Sitting in his living room, Seven listened for the third time to Diandra's message. *Seven are you there?* After a pause she continued on *Hey, your full of surprises today. The roses are beautiful and the dinner is wow! I wanted you to come and join me for dinner so that I could thank you in person. You're the best friend a girl could have and I'm glad I have you. You know that you're the first man to send me flowers or anything like this. Thanks again.*

Hitting the save button on his machine, Seven listened to the message one more time. He could hear the happiness in her voice. Thinking to himself, Seven said she doesn't know it, but I am going to make her forget all about Mason and any other dude in her past that ever existed. All he had to do was bide his time, court and woo her. How could she not fall in love with him? For him it was easy because he could feel the effects of that blazing hot kiss they shared at Benét's party. Sitting with her on his lap in her crib after that fiasco with Mason, was a start. She felt so good and right in his arms that he refused to think about failure. He has nothing but time on his side, so he decided to wait her out.

Chapter 35 ➤ Benét

"Professor Donnegal, can I talk to you for a minute?" Benét asked. She hated to have this conversation, because she knew he would suggest a tutor. Math has never been her strong point she mused.

"Mrs. Greir," Professor Donnegal said cutting into her thoughts.

"I'm sorry, Professor, what where you saying?" she asked.

"I was saying that it would be in your best interest to invest in tutoring sessions. If you check the board in the student center, I'm sure you should be able to find someone to assist you at a reasonable cost," he informed her.

Damn, how is she going to find the time to fit this into her already tight schedule? Kenny and the kids are not going to like this; it's only going to take up more of my time. "So your saying without a tutor, I won't pass your class?" she asked.

Shaking his head in the affirmative, "Yes, I'm afraid so. You've failed the mid-term, you had a low C prior to this test, and without tutoring your going to fail. I know that sounds bad, but I know you can do the work. Don't let it intimidate you, master it like I'm sure you've done the rest of your courses and move on," he said to her as they walked out of the class.

"I know, but math has never really been one of my favorite subjects. The farthest I went was Algebra in high school and that was over twenty years ago. And you're right, I am carrying a 3.46 grade point average and I don't want this to bring me down. I will check the board for a tutor and I promise to pass your exam with flying colors," Benét said to her professor.

As the two parted, she resolved to go into the student center and read the board. "Benét! Hold ON!" yelled Christian from the steps of the math building.

Running to catch up with her, she scratched the back of her neck thinking *this boy is fione!* As he nears her, he reaches out and gives her a hug. "How are you doing?" he asked.

Returning his embrace, "I'm fine. How are you?"

Christian has to control himself, as he feels his loins constrict from the embrace. "Well I know you're fine" he told her and smiled as she blushed, "That is the second time that I have complimented you and you've blushed. Not many woman can do that." Christian smiled.

Putting her head down, she replied, "Thanks, but you don't have to compliment me every time that you see me." Damn, just one time, she would like to know what he smelled like, what he tasted like, what it would feel like to be under him.'

Damn, Christian thought to himself, *I wonder what she smells like, taste like when she makes love. I wonder how she would look under me just before I take her?* Stopping this train of thought, he said, "Hey, I saw you talking to Professor Donnegal earlier, is everything okay?"

"No, I got a "D" on my mid-term and he suggested that I get a tutor if I want to pass his class. So I'm on my way to the student center to do just that," she said.

Damn that Christian thought if anyone is going to tutor her it is going to be him. Hell anytime spent with this woman is worth it. Thinking along those lines he said, "What are you looking for a tutor for? I can tutor you and it won't cost you a thing."

The look of surprise and apprehension on Benét's face had him asking, "What's wrong?"

What's wrong he asks, I'll tell you what's wrong, Benét thought. The two of us together on a one on one basis is like adding fuel to the fire. There she'd said it, at least to herself she admits to the attraction especially since the situation between her and Kenny hasn't changed. He still has issues and she is still masturbating. You mean to tell me that you can't be alone with this man and keep it platonic Benét asked herself. Mentally coming to the decision that she is an adult and that she can do this she says, "Thanks. I really need the help, but you have to let me pay you something."

Okay, Christian thinks. "Pass your final exam with flying colors, and you can treat me to an elaborate dinner," he said.

"Deal. Now when can you start because my midterm is in three weeks?"

"Let me ask you this? How much tutoring do you think you need?"

Pulling out her mid-term exam to show him her grade, she laughed at the expression on his face.

Suppressing a smile, he said, "Judging from this mid-term, I would say at the least three times a week no less than an hour."

Taking the paper back from him, Benét said, "I can do Tuesday and Thursday evenings after six and Saturday afternoons if you are available."

"Those hours are fine for me. We can meet here on the campus in my office. Now that we have that out of the way, do you want to get some lunch?" he asked.

Benét said that she would love to have lunch with him but she was already late for her English class. "Can I take a rain check?"

"Sure. I'll see you tomorrow," Christian said with a smile as he watched her walk towards the English building, thinking that he couldn't get her out of his mind.

Walking into the English building, Benét felt as giddy as a kid, because she couldn't wait until tomorrow.

* * * * *

At the dinner table, Kenny and the children were quiet as Benét told them about her day. "So if I want to pass this class, I need to get a tutor. Fortunately, I already have one lined up so that won't be a problem."

Throwing down his napkin, Kendall said, "Shit your ass ain't home now. I hardly see you since you started back to school."

Seeing that their parent's are about to go at it again, Zaria and Kenny, excused themselves and went downstairs to finish their meals.

Arching one eyebrow, Benét said, "Oh really. You haven't acted like you wanted to see me, so what's your point? I mean really Kendall, you supported me going back to school so I know this isn't an issue for you. Why don't you tell me what's really on your mind?"

"All I'm saying is that—" stopping in frustration Kendall doesn't even know why he's mad, "Fuck it Benét, do whatever you want."

"I had planned on doing that anyway," she told him. "Talk to your doctor Kenny," pleaded Benét, "Ask him to prescribe that new medication that is supposed to help men with ED?"

"I ain't asking for no fucking pill to get my dick hard," Kendall said between clenched teeth, "I'm forty fucking years old, what the fuck I look like taking some shit to get hard?"

"Like a mother fucker who needs it." Hissed Benét, "Shit, you act like the problem is just yours and not ours! Don't you think it affects me?" Benét stopped talking and started cleaning off the dining table.

Moving the plates into the kitchen, she scraped the food into the garbage disposal, "It's been over three months since we were intimate. Don't you miss me?" she asked. Putting the plate down to hug him, he pushed her away.

"Yes I miss you," he told her, "But this is something I have to deal with Benét, I'm sorry I can't help you and I can't talk to you about this."

Turning back to the sink so he didn't see the tears running down her face, Benét made a decision to call the doctor in the morning and discuss this problem without him.

* * * * *

"I'm sorry Mrs. Greir, but I am not at liberty to discuss your husband's medical condition with you," Dr Charles informed Benét. "However, I can give you some literature to read on the disease. I'll leave a packet at the reception desk for you."

"Thank you Doctor," Benét said disappointedly. Hanging up the phone, she grabbed her school bag and walked out of the door. On her way to the car, her cell phone rings. Glancing at the caller id, she see's that it is Shaeyla. She clicked the talk button, "Good Morning," Benét said.

"Good morning! I know you're on your way to school so I won't keep you. I am calling everyone to remind you about the bike fest this weekend," Shaeyla said.

"I thought you didn't like motorcycles," Benét asked.

"I don't," Shaeyla said, "But I love me some men, and I love dick even more. She giggled and asked Girl do you know how many might show up! All dressed in leather and shit!"

Laughing out loud, Benét said girl, you are a trip! But no, I haven't forgotten and I am going to be there with bells on."

"Hmm with bells on? Is that right?" questioned Shaeyla. "Your right, ain't no harm in looking, but I'm going to watch your ass to make sure you don't touch, cause I don't like that 'with bells on' comment."

"Shaeyla, if I don't get me some soon, my eyes are going to cross!" Benét jokingly told her friend.

Uh oh, she sounds serious Shaeyla thought to herself. "All jokes aside Benét, you sound serious."

"I am serious," Benét told her. As much as her girls loved Kendall and supported her marriage, she knew that this conversation would stay between the two of them. Well between her, Kendra, Diandra and Worthy, cause if she didn't tell them, Shaeyla damn sure would, thought Benét. "Listen I tried to talk to Kendall again last night and he wouldn't talk to me. So this morning I called his doctor."

"No you didn't call the man's doctor," Shaeyla admonished.

"Yes I damn sure did! Shaeyla. I am a young woman and I love my husband, but he is being stubborn on this subject. Hell not just stubborn but mean and selfish, this problem is ours not his, although that is how he is thinking. So I'm thinking fuck it, if he doesn't care about our marriage then I can't be bothered either. I have been patient for three months; which may not seem long to a lot of people, but the one thing that you, Diandra, and I have is common is our healthy sex drive. I've been kind and considerate, I've tried every trick in the book to help him and he won't let me in."

"I know, Benét, but . . . but you are married. Can't you try harder to work this out? Just don't give up. Don't throw it away for a meaningless romp, it isn't worth it. Besides, we're not men, you know how they are about their manhood, can you imagine how he must be feeling right now?"

Shaeyla could plead all she wanted to, Benét thought, but it's too late. Kendall has pushed her away one too many times. If he isn't trying to work this out with her, then she will work it out without him. But to shut Shaeyla up she said, "Shaeyla, you're right and I am going to try my best."

Before Shaeyla let Benét hang up, she asked her to purchase two tickets for the Black Charities event. It was taking place in a few weeks and she wanted to get all of her girls on the guest list. Knowing that Shaeyla could be a pain when it came to one of her events, Benét agreed and hung up the phone.

Chapter 36 ➤ Christian the Tutor

Christian stood in the entryway looking at Benét sitting in the student center at a computer terminal, unaware of how concentrated she looked and that she was being watched. Glancing down at his gold Rolex he made his way over to her. "Hard at work or hardly working?" he jokingly questioned her.

Jumping at the sound of his voice, "Oh, you startled me." She said, "Is it six o'clock already?" she asks as she looked at her watch. Seeing that it was six fifteen, she apologized and gathered her books. "Sorry about that, but I was researching a paper for class," she informed him.

"No problem. It wasn't my intention to startle you," he said by way of an apology. Picking up her jacket from the back of the chair, he helped her into it and headed for the door.

Placing his hand in the small of her back, he guided her into his office. After opening the door, Christian offered to take her coat.

Looking around Christian's office, Benét was delighted at his sense of style and the afro centric vibe that she felt as she entered his office. "I love the way your office is decorated." Benét told him with a huge smile on her face. "It reminds me of my family room at home. I have it decorated with masks and black art. Although, I added the leopard print rugs to finish the room off."

Christian looked around his office proudly saying, "Well my home is decorated in the same way." Christian moved to a statue of an African tribal man holding an arrow in the corner, "I got this statue from a Mobotu tribal chief in Zimbabwe. I try to pick up a new piece of art on all of my travels."

Crossing the room to stand beside him, Benét excitedly comments, "Really! Are all of these items from places that you've visited?" she asked as she reached out to touch the statue and slightly brushed up against him. She felt her nipples tighten at the unexpected rush of pleasure. Blushing she turned away and focused on another part of the room.

"Yes, they are. I love traveling and I have a few more countries in Africa to visit then I will have seen the entire African continent," he told her.

"Tell me about some of the places that you've seen in Africa" she begged as she took a seat on the loveseat situated in front of his bookcase across from his desk. *You're here to study girl, not listen to his stories of traveling or anything else.* She chastises herself.

"I went on a safari last year and to actually see animals in their natural habitat was awesome," Christian said.

Benét had always wanted to visit Africa, but she just never got around to it. Sitting beside him, Benét found herself fascinated by his voice and his stories. Laying her head onto the back of the loveseat, Benét closed her eyes and tried to imagine what it would've been like to visit half of the places he did, even the safari would've been great. Snuggling deeper into the seat, she yawned and tucked her arm under her head.

Seeing her yawn, Christian asked, "Are you tired or am I boring you to death?"

"No not at all," she denied. The look he gave her was like yeah right. "Well maybe just a little," she admitted.

Glancing at his watch he saw that it is almost eight o'clock, "I have talked so much, that we haven't cracked your math book yet and that is why we're here." Beginning to rise from his seat, Benét places a hand on his arm, "I know why we are here. But I wanted to hear about your trips, so don't feel bad, okay," She said easily.

Putting his hand over hers on his arm, he said, "I don't feel bad at all. In fact, I've enjoyed talking to you so much that math completely left my mind." Squeezing her hand to emphasize how much he enjoyed it, he looked into her eyes and knew that she was attracted to him as much as he was to her. He never pursued married women, it went against his beliefs, but he had never met a woman like Benét before. From the first time he met her at the light he has wanted her. He moved his hand to cup her face and the light kiss that she placed in his palm sent a chill up his spine.

Benét felt the goose bumps on her own flesh and could see the goose bumps on his as she placed a light feathery kiss in the palm of his hand. It looked like he was struggling with something. "What's wrong Christian?" she asked cupping his face in her hand. The feel of his skin was so smooth and he seemed so receptive of her touch. She knew that this was wrong, but the attraction she felt for him was so strong.

Christian knew that what he was about to do was not right, but he couldn't help himself. Pulling Benét closer to him so that part of her was in his lap, he put his hands in her hair and pulled her face towards his. When she didn't resist him but moved even closer, the urge to kiss her was so overwhelming that he could barely control his breathing.

Benét felt his breath on her face and in her ear as he places his first kiss onto her right ear lobe. The beating of her heart mounted when his tongue he traced her ear followed by sweet kisses to her neck, forehead and face. When he finally moved his attention to her mouth, he traced her lips with his thumb and then his tongue.

As Benét licked her lips, her tongue encountered his thumb and her excitement grew. *I need this* she justified to herself, *Kendall is not willing to change our situation, but just this once she needed to feel loved and wanted again.* The anticipation of Christian's lips had her insides doing flips. Feeling her hands getting clammy from the excitement, she wiped them down her pants, placed them on his shoulders, and moved in closer to him. "I've been trying to ignore the attraction mounting between us, but no longer am I willing to wait. I want you just as much as you want me," she told him.

Her confession only deepened his desire for her as his fingers tighten in her scalp and his loins tighten in anticipation.

"Kiss me. *Please*," she begged.

He looked her over seductively. Heaven help him but he wasn't going to make her wait any longer. His body hardened from the feelings that she aroused in him. Christian moistened his lips and gave her what she wanted. Tracing her top lip with his tongue, he enjoyed teasing her as he felt her mouth open to receive him. "I have wanted to taste you since the first time I saw you," he told her. Not able to hold back any longer he wrapped his fingers in her hair and gently kissed her lips. The spark between the two of them was so intensely tangible, that he could swear he saw a small lightening bolt illuminate throughout the room. Opening his mouth, his tongue plunged into and explored the depths of her mouth. Her soft moans escaped her mouth and resonated in the air. His tongue battled in a duel with hers thrusting and sucking arousing her with each kiss.

"Ooh," Benét moaned as her hands travel from his shoulders to his chest. Releasing his tie, she moved to the top button on his shirt and began to unbutton them one by one. The feel of his smooth chest and hard muscles under her hands, had her pulling the shirt from his pants so that she could see his upper torso.

At the same time, he began pulling her sweater over her head, while refusing to release her mouth. Quickly he pulled it over her head and continued kissing her. Moving her slowly, he gently pushed her into a reclining position so that he could lay on top of her. She could feel his manhood pressing into her stomach. The path of hot moist kisses had her writhing beneath him Benét couldn't believe how wet his kisses were making her. Damn, she thought to herself, *I have to get his pants open so that I can see if this is real or not.* Her private thoughts must have penetrated his mind as he raised himself and said, "Let me undress you first." Placing her hands above her head, he leaned down, placing first her right then her left nipple into his mouth, as he suckled them gently. Her nipples hardened as he licked and suckled a little harder. "Ohh yes, Christian," Benét said out loud clutching his head to her breast. She loved what he was doing to her. She lifted up as he pulled down her jeans and placed his hand over her hot wet area.

Christian threw her pants across the room and couldn't believe what he was about to do. Licking his lips he placed his hand over her and could feel the heat through her panties. "Ahh Benét, I want you," he sighed, as he never let her finish undressing him and kicked out of his pants and silk boxers. Turning back to Benét, and kneeling onto the floor he lifted her so that his mouth could taste the sweetness of her hot center.

The first contact of his mouth on her made her jump. The reaction was pure electric; he gently folded back her lips and ran his tongue around the outside of her vagina, and caressed her clit gently before thrusting his tongue deep inside. Grabbing him by the head, Benét couldn't control her reaction; she hadn't had this in so long that her excitement had built up to the point where she was about to explode.

Feeling her legs flex and the pressure of her hands on his head, Christian broke free to pull her closer and buried himself deep inside of her. With the first thrust he felt her walls constrict around him. With the second thrust she clawed his back and leaned up to come face to face with him. Kissing him, he lifted her completely and sat on the love seat so that she was now on top of him. Thrusting upwards, her eyes rolled back into the back of her head as he felt the release of her juices.

Benét loved riding Christian as she squeezed herself around his thick shaft. Damn she could feel him in her stomach, and she wanted more. With each thrust, her walls constricted around him. "Aaah . . . Oooh . . . Christian," she said bouncing up and down, taking him deeper and deeper inside of her. "I'm about to cum."

"Cum for me Benét. I want to feel you." He placed his hands on her shoulders and gave one last thrust as his own release spilled into her.

Benét collapsed into Christian's arms and he maneuvered them on the settee with her lying on top of him. Wrapping his arms around her, Benét snuggles closer. "Benét that was incredible. I have to see you again. When can I see you again?" he urged.

Kissing him back, Benét thought, *but what about Kendall. Damn Kendall, I told him this would happen. Damn! You can't do this to your kids or your marriage. I didn't plan for this to happen, but I am so happy that it did. Christian has made me feel whole again.* After struggling with herself mentally, Benét said. "I want to see you too."

"When?"

"You know my situation Christian, so I don't have to explain discretion to you." She hated to be abrupt but her situation warrants directness. No area can be left open for interpretation.

"No, I understand your situation . . . I don't like it but I understand and I would never do that to you. But let me ask you a question. Does Kendall know where you are right now?"

"He knows that I am with my tutor, yes. But I haven't told him who my tutor is. And that's the other thing; I will not discuss Kendall, my children or my marriage with you."

"I don't want to discuss any of that either. It's just that your husband's firm and mine still do business together, and we are going to meet from time to time," he told her feeling uncomfortable already.

"Well then, we are going to have to act normal if we are going to continue to see each other," Benét said. Seeing that he was about to say something else, she placed a finger over his lips, "Shhhh, you're talking too much," as she replaced her finger with her mouth.

Christian was going to tell her that he forgot to use a condom, but as her mouth touched his all thoughts of everything left his mind.

* * * * *

Walking into her house a little after eleven, Benét double checked herself in the foyer mirror to make sure every hair was in place and showed no signs of her night with Christian. As she dropped her books onto the floor, Kendall came out of his study, "You've been studying all of this time?" he questioned.

Looking at him with a raised eyebrow, she snapped, "Yes, I have been studying all this time. Why do you ask?"

Benét saw that his feelings were hurt as his head dropped to his chest. "I was just asking that's all."

Feeling bad for snapping at him, she apologized and headed upstairs to take a shower. Preparing for her shower, she noticed a mark on her neck. It immediately brought images of Christian on her, in her and all around her body. *I have to make sure he doesn't put any marks on me in future.* Putting on her shower cap, she stepped into the shower singing the words of "Jungle Boogie."

* * * * *

Kendall felt powerless as he watched Benét move up the steps. He wanted to stop her and ask her to come back and talk. *Hell why is he mad, she has done everything in her power to help him with his problem and he continues to push her away. Their situation was his fault not hers. He can't blame her for any animosity she might feel toward him. If he were Benét, he would've gotten an outsider to help him. Probably some young college boy who is more interested in getting in her pants than helping her study.* These thoughts have Kenny seething with jealousy. *Who wouldn't want Benét, she is beautiful.* The sound of breaking glass startled Kendall out of his musings. Looking down he saw that he had smashed the vase on the table in his silent rage. *You have to get yourself together man* Kendall silently berated himself. The only problem is how? He was ashamed to admit his problem to his wife let alone outsiders. The hardest thing he had to do was tell his wife about it, the second hardest was talking to that damn doctor who suggested that he join a support group to hear how other people have dealt with it. Benét even suggested he take a pill. Picking up the broken pieces of glass, Kendall laughed at the irony because his life was shattering into pieces like the shards of glass in his hand.

Chapter 37 ➢ Intervention

The knocking on the door slowly started to penetrate Worthy's drugged mind. Glancing at her clock, she saw that it was three o'clock in the morning. Opening the door without looking through the peephole, she was surprised to see Diandra, Kendra, Shaeyla and Benét on her doorstep.

Looking at her watch, "What the fuck Worthy." Diandra exclaimed, "It's three o'clock in the afternoon and your ass is still in bed! What the fuck is going on with you?"

Damn Worthy thought to herself, she could've sworn it was morning time, but maybe that's because she was just getting up. Looking at her calendar she saw five days in the month of October have been marked off. Damn, where did her week go she wondered?

Pushing Worthy to the side, the four women walk into her apartment. Placing a hand to her temple Worthy knew that she and the place looked a mess. Her thoughts were confirmed as she passed the cracked mirror in her living room.

"What are ya'll doing here?" she asked them as she fumbled around trying to pick up the empty beer cans littered throughout the room.

Shaeyla looked at Worthy, and instantly knew that the rumors Diandra had heard were correct. Her friend was gone; strung out on a drug that had taken the lives of so many of their loved ones.

Her hair was sitting all over her head spiked at the corners and matted in the back with small balls of what Shaeyla hoped was lint and not lice. The gnats flying around the trash bags and the sink in her kitchen made her angry and sad at the same time. *How does a person let themselves get this way, Damn Worthy!* Turning on her heels, she walked twirled her eyes around the dingy room. She placed her hands on her hips, and with her foot lifted the top of a box that revealed two slices of molded pizza. Clothes were strewn on the back of the two mix-matched chairs placed around a wobbly round table.

Walking over to her girls, she saw Diandra's face screwed up with rage, Kendra fished around in her purse and came up with a tissue to wipe the tears spilling down her face and Benét stood wrenching her hands worriedly as they eyed the woman that was now a shadow of their friend. Shaeyla took control of the situation. "Worthy I have been calling you for the last week. You don't answer your phone, you don't return calls. What's wrong with you, what's going on?" Shaeyla asked plaintively.

"Yeah," Kendra piped in, "What's going on? Where's Jared and who is that man?" she asked looking past her to a half-naked man in the entrance to the living room.

Shaeyla and her friends turned at the same time as Worthy to see the object of Kendra's question. There in the doorway, in Calvin Klein briefs and nothing else stood who Shaeyla knew only as JJ.

The look he bestowed upon Shaeyla and her friends was probably meant to scare, but after seeing their girl, it would take heaven and earth to move them from Worthy. Shaeyla watched him walk cockily towards Worthy then he asked her loud enough for them to hear, "Who the fuck are these ho's?"

Shaeyla saw how Worthy reared back and nervously moved away from JJ as she explained that they were there to take her to lunch. Seeing how Worthy jerked at each movement JJ made Shaeyla realize that it was not just nervousness that made Worthy play with the frayed hem of her nightshirt, but it was fear. Her eyes widened when she turned and noticed that her friends realized her fear. Shaeyla heard the muffled cry rip from Kendra and saw how she tried to calm herself down by pacing from side to side. Shaeyla watched Kendra shake her head and witnessed the hate in Kendra's eyes each time they landed on JJ in silent accusation of Worthy's appearance. Shaeyla nodded her head toward Kendra then motioned to Diandra and Benét telling them without words that they had to remove Kendra from the room. Diandra and Benét each placed a comforting arm around Kendra's shoulder as her anguished tears wracked her body. As they slowly turned Kendra towards the door and from the apartment Shaeyla sprung into action. She knew that she had to get Worthy away from JJ. They had to try to make her see what she was doing to herself and what she was allowing him to do to her. Shaeyla didn't know how, but they had to somehow convince her to seek counseling.

Ignoring JJ completely Shaeyla left him to his own devices in the living room then grabbed Worthy, and ushered her towards the bathroom to shower.

While Worthy showered Shaeyla began to rummage through the piles of junk scattered throughout the small bedroom. The scent of smoke made the room smell dank and musty. Moving to open a window to let in some fresh air, she spotted a small blue bag with white residue and knew that it was a rock bag. Tears immediately welled up in her eyes but before she could succumb to her distress, she heard the shower turn off and heard the door open and Worthy step into the room. Shaeyla pulled herself together and turned to watch Worthy pull a pair of jeans and a shirt from the dilapidated dresser along with a bra and underwear. Worthy turned her back to Shaeyla and she got her first glimpse at Worthy's emaciated body.

"Worthy, what's going on with you? Where's Jared?" Shaeyla watched as her friend stilled and yet she did not turn around nor answer her question. Shaeyla let it go, but as soon as they reached the car, the questions would come from not just her but all of them. As soon as she clasped her pants together, Shaeyla grabbed her by the hand and marched her through the apartment, past JJ and down the steps to her car.

As they reached the car Kendra jumped out from her position in the back seat and with her finger pointed at Worthy she yelled, "What the hell is wrong with you?"

"Kendra calm down!" Shaeyla watched Worthy's head dropped to her chest in shame.

"No I won't calm down. Hell, look at her! She was sleeping at three in the afternoon, for Gods sake. Her home is a mess. I . . . I . . . I can't do this," Kendra said shaking her head as the tears started again.

"Yes you can Kendra," Benét said moving to put a comforting arm around her. "All we can do is help, but if Worthy doesn't want help, we can't make her get help."

Shaeyla held onto Worthy's arm as they followed Kendra and Benét to the car. Shaeyla could feel the anger emanating from Diandra as her crossed arms over her breast.

Shaeyla took her seat, strapped herself in and started the car, but no sooner had they pulled off Diandra started the ball rolling.

"Worthy, what the fuck is up with you. I mean you and JJ?" Diandra scoffed.

"Girl, I've been seeing JJ for a minute," Worthy told her. Then looking at the way Kendra and Benét were all looking at her, even Shaeyla looked like she didn't believe that as she cut her eyes in the rear view mirror.

"How can you say that shit all nonchalant?" asked Shaeyla.

"Look, I ain't stupid. Okay. I know JJ, I know what he sells and I spotted the rock bag in your house. So are you smoking that shit or what?" Diandra asked her.

Putting on the best performance of her life and her poker face, "No I am not smoking crack ya'll. Dang, ya'll supposed to be my girls. How could you think that of me?" Worthy asked.

"Well your ass has lost a lot of weight. Your skin looks horrible, all oily and dinghy and your hair is as hard as a brick," Kendra told her. "What else do you expect us to think?"

"You never return our phone calls," Shaeyla chimed in.

"And you've missed the Summer Fest," Benét told her. "That's just not like you at all Worthy, so what's up."

"Nothing's, up. I've just been spending my time with JJ that's all. I really like him and he loves me so get off my back okay," Worthy replied because she was tired of them questioning her like she was a child.

"Okay, suit yourself. But we know differently and I think you're on that shit," Diandra said distastefully, "But if you want to deny it so be it. Just don't call me when he whips your ass." Shaeyla watched as she edged closer to the door and knew she had to stop somewhere soon because Diandra had a look on her face that said if she didn't get away from Worthy's ignorant behind soon she was liable to slap the taste out of her mouth. Shaeyla noticed that they were a few blocks from Diandra's and swiftly changed lanes.

"Sorry ya'll, but we have to go somewhere and talk privately and Diandra since your place is closest we may as well go there," she told her friends amongst the cries and gasps from the sudden movement.

Kendra picked up where Diandra left off and asked, "Has he hit you?"

There was no need to answer Kendra's question because Worthy gave her answer by putting her head to her chest in embarrassment. Shaeyla could tell from Worthy's body language that her friend was in a situation that she didn't know how to get out of and was probably doubly afraid because Shaeyla could see JJ telling Worthy not to involve them in her business or his business rather. Shaeyla could even see him telling Worthy that he would hurt one of them if she did. Shaeyla wondered why Worthy was trying to kid them because they all knew that the trash she spouted was bullshit.

Sighing, Kendra leaned back on her seat in disgust and anger. "This was supposed to be a good day for us. But you had to fuck it up didn't you Worthy?"

As they walked from the parking garage to the elevator, the deafening silence was released as soon as Diandra opened her door. Diandra let loose as she turned around with her hand out. "Sit your simple ass down," she said to Worthy pushing her onto the couch.

Shaeyla watched Worthy's face as her eyes pooled with tears. Stopping Diandra before the whole day turned into a fiasco, she said, "Diandra! That's enough. We are here to help her not scare or hurt her."

"Why! She ain't afraid to smoke that shit is she? So my yelling at her won't mean anything."

Shaeyla watched as Kendra chewed worriedly on her bottom lip and she knew that the silence coming from Benét was a ruse, as she sat to think about what she was going to say. Shaeyla walked up to Worthy and placed a hand to her arm, "It hurts us so much to see you like this. Look at you? Your hair is matted Worthy, your house is filthy and it smells. Come on, now we all know that you may not have kept the neatest place but damn, it never smelled." Shaeyla tried to make her see what they saw earlier at her place but the blank eyed look she gave her told her that she was not getting through.

The sound of Diandra's dining chair scraped across the hardwood floor caused Shaeyla to turn in time to see Benét walking towards them and stop in front of Worthy. As she crouched down with her hands on Worthy's knees to glare into her eyes, she turned a dark eye on Shaeyla who did not need to hear the words they conveyed as she knew Benét wanted to speak her peace without interruption.

"Listen we can talk to you until we're blue in the face, but if you don't admit you have a problem then we cannot help you."

Worthy threw Benét's hands from her legs and jumped up from her seat. "I am not listening to anymore of this bullshit! I am a grown ass woman and I don't have to sit here and take this from ya'll."

At Worthy's outburst Diandra gave Shaeyla the *I told you so* look, threw her hands in the air and said, "You know what's really sad, about this whole fucking situation is the fact that you don't even see how much we love you."

Shaeyla didn't know what to do. The whole thing was getting out of control but none of them had ever conducted an intervention so they didn't know what to do or how to say it. Shaeyla saw Worthy's mouth open about to say something then close. She must have thought better of it because she remained silent and that is when she started to walk towards the door.

"Where do you think your going?" Shaeyla asked.

"I'm going home. I have told ya'll a thousand times today that I am not getting high, damn! What do I have to do or say to convince ya'll of that?" Worthy wailed plaintively to her friends.

Benét strode over to her and steered her to the dining table. "You ain't leaving until we say so. So sit down, I'm going to order us a pizza, and we are going to play some cards. But one way or another, you are going to have to tell us the truth."

For the next few hours the women played cards and continued to question Worthy who continually denied getting high. Shaeyla watched as Kendra placed a hand to the back of her neck and dropped her head back as if it hurt, then she got up and signaled for her, Benét, and Diandra to come to follow her to the back of the apartment. Shaeyla could tell that Benét and Diandra was thinking the same as her but since Worthy was their friend they knocked their reason away and followed Kendra. Once in the room Kendra informed her friends that she was tired of the whole thing and that she was calling Niall to come and get her because she'd had enough. She said Worthy wasn't going to tell the truth because she still hadn't hit rock bottom. As the women agreed with her they returned to find the dining room empty and Worthy's purse gone.

Shaeyla knew that they shouldn't have trusted her to be there when they came back. That was all the evidence they needed to know that their girl had crossed over to the nether world of drugs and degradation and that the only thing they could do was pray for her to come to her senses and seek help. When she did they would be there to help her.

* * * * *

Kendra filled Niall in on how the intervention with Worthy went. He was supportive of any endeavor she wished to take with helping Worthy out. She should've known he would be there for her because he was that type of man. His natural kindness shone through everywhere he went, Kendra noticed he always made a friend.

Noticing her surroundings, finally, she asked, "Where are we going?"

"I think it's time that you met my mother."

Looking away from him, she couldn't believe he'd sprung this on her like this. How can she meet his mother dressed the way she was? "I am not dressed to meet your parents." She said hysterically. "Why didn't you warn me first? I smell like smoke and beer and—and outdoors."

Catching her hand as she waved it in the air, "Baby, you look gorgeous. My mother and father are very down to earth. They are going to love you as much as I do," he stated.

That statement stopped Kendra, as this was the first time he had said those words to her. Looking at him, she asked him wonderingly, "You love me?"

"Yes, I do. That's why I want you to meet my parents." He said, "It's time that the three of ya'll get to know one another."

Kendra was so glad that he said the words first, because she has realized she loved him a few weeks ago. She was afraid to say the words for fear of rejection, but she was not afraid anymore. Hugging him she said, "Thank you Niall. I love you too."

* * * * *

Seven could not keep his hands off of Diandra. Tonight she did not seem to mind the numerous times he had touched her. He found himself always moving in closer to talk in her ear or he found any excuse to flick an imaginary fleck of dust or something from her hair. He loved her and tonight was his lucky night. He could feel it.

Glancing at Seven as he pulled up in front of her building, Diandra said, "Want to come up for some coffee or something?"

Seven pounced on the suggestion like Tigger, "Yes. Go on up and get it ready and I'll meet you there."

Getting out of the car Diandra could not believe how nervous she was; *It's just Seven.* No it's not just Seven, it's a new Seven that Diandra was seeing for the first time. She was beginning to think her girls were right about him wanting more than friendship. Everyday she received a delivery. Early this morning it was two white roses, one for today and the other for tomorrow since it was Sunday and the card simply had the number seven on it penned in his distinctive scrawl.

Opening her door, she grabbed the remote to her stereo and the sounds of Stevie Wonder filled the room. She had just put the water on, when Seven knocked at the door. Lighting an incense opening and dimming the lights Diandra opens the door.

As soon as he entered, she didn't think or give him a chance to move, she grabbed him by his lapels and kissed him. As soon as their tongues met, they both sighed contentedly and with lips joined he moved them to her sofa and deepened the kiss.

Breaking away Diandra stated firmly, "I want to thank you for the cards, flowers, and gifts. I can happily say that I am over Mason."

The relief that swept through Seven's body had him doing two things, he hardened and lowered his lips back to hers, prompting him to ask, "Can I make love to you tonight?"

Diandra thought he would never ask. "I thought you would never ask," she told him. "I've been anticipating this moment since I started receiving your thoughtful gifts. I figured after the first week they would stop, but you kept it going through the whole month of September and now here it is October and they are still coming."

Cupping her face and looking deep into her eyes, "I wanted you to know that you are worth more than anything in this world to me and that you are too good for men like Mason."

The whistling of the teapot had him jumping up and running to the kitchen to turn the pot off. When he came back into the living room, he saw a trail of clothing leading into Diandra's bedroom. Following her lead, he dropped his clothes as well and picked up her thong. Entering her bedroom saw her laying on her stomach across her bed. Seven held up the thong and said

"Did you loose something?" Her gaze was a soft caress.

"No." Diandra said as she rose up to eye level with him. "I think I've found it, *finally*."

Leaning her back onto the bed, Seven plunged her mouth with his tongue. Caressing her breast, he moved to put one juicy chocolate nipple into his mouth.

The shock of his mouth on her breast has Diandra urging him to go lower. Her body ached for his touch.

Seven tangled his hands into the coarse curls of her middle and parted her lips. Dipping his finger inside of her made his dick grow harder as he felt how hot and ready she was. Replacing his finger with his mouth, he gently lapped at her middle until she begged him to stop.

She wove her fingers aound his locks. "Please stop." Diandra begs breathlessly, "I can't take anymore."

Reaching down on the floor for the pack of condoms he pulled from his pants before dropping them in the living room, he ripped the top off of the pack and placed it on. Placing a pillow under her hips and sank into the moist depths of her he felt as if he had come home. Diandra returns his excitement as he feels her sugar walls grip him bringing him deeper into her being.

"Ahh yes Seven. You feel so good," Diandra told him. Wanting to prolong the feeling, Seven moved in and out of her slowing to build up the moment.

"Please! Stop teasing me," She implored.

Unable to hold back, Seven raises up for the final thrust and explodes on a wave of feeling that he has never felt before, instinctively he knew it would feel like this with Diandra.

Wrapping her arms around him with the feelings running through her had tears welling in her eyes. *Damn, this nigga done made my ass cry* she thought.

Seven rolled over with her in his arms and asked, "Say that you don't regret what just happened?"

Looking into his eyes, she saw doubt and uncertainty. "I will never regret what just happened. How could I? I've just come home."

Feeling her even breathing, Seven pulled her closer as he realized that she was sleeping. "I've come home too," he said kissing her on her forehead and falling into a contented sleep.

Chapter 38 ➢ Shaeyla

With the Black Charities gala fast approaching Shaeyla took her assistant to lunch as a reward for his dedication and hard work. She especially liked the idea he pitched during their meal on doing events for rap artists and other musicians, because it showed her that he was committed to success. He called them album release parties that would consist of various individuals in the music business. Shaeyla told him to work up the numbers and get back to her as she dropped him off. Her meeting with Solomon to review the final details for the charity ball was to take place in another few hours giving her just enough time to run to pick up her gown for the event.

Swinging her beamer into the parking area of *Sundie's Collection's,* an exclusive boutique in Towson, Shaeyla parked and locked the car as she headed inside. Crossing her fingers, she hoped that there were no more alterations that needed to be made on her dress.

Opening the door, her feet sunk into plush mauve carpet as the discreet bell marked her entrance.

"Ms. Andrews How are you?" Sundie greeted her with a thick slavic accent. Chanel No. 5 surrounded Shaeyla as the owner grabbed her hands and bussed her cheeks with air kisses, before turning to lead her into the dressing area. "Take off your clothes. Your dress is ready for you to try on."

Shaeyla placed her handbag on the velvet-covered mint green chair in the corner of the dressing room and started to remove her clothing. Behind her Sundie had placed a long black garment bag on the far wall. Unzipping the bag the sequined garment blinded her and Shaeyla's excitement built as she revealed the exquisite garb. Removing the gown from the hanger, Shaeyla stepped into the sheath style halter dress and zipped it up. As she gazed at her reflection in the mirror she smoothed the specially designed black georgette skirt over her shapely hips. The splits on each side went to her mid-thigh and were only revealed as she walked or moved, standing still the material of the skirt relaxed back into place hiding the splits. She twirled to view her backside, smiling at the material floated up and outward. The frog clasp of the halter bodice aided in giving her breast a lift, as well as, highlighting her dark chocolate back. Stepping out of the dressing room onto the podium to get the full effect in all of the mirrors surrounding the raised area, she made a three hundred and sixty-degree turn. The gasp of delight from the owner prompted Shaeyla to exclaim her gratitude over the beauty of the dress.

"This is simply beautiful Sundie, please tell me the shoes that I wanted came in because they would set the dress off."

Shaeyla watched as the owner stepped forward and revealed the platinum-heeled slides that were perfect for the dress. Shaeyla almost fell trying to slide her feet into the designer mules she gave one last twirl before walking back to the dressing room to prepare for her meeting. As she walked from the boutique her arms held the black garment bag and the red trimmed shoe bag bearing the trademark from the high brow store.

After paying for the dress, she called and informed Solomon's secretary to advise him that she was on her way. His assistant informed her that he was unavailable and advised that he would call her to reschedule. He also left instructions that he had complete confidence in her abilities and directed her to move forward with her plans.

Chapter 39 ➢ Creeping

Benét could not wait to see Christian again. From that first day that they spent together, it catapulted her into a world of ecstasy. She hated lying to her family, but Christian had become an addiction to her. He made her feel young, needed and wanted, which was something Kendall hadn't done in the past few months. Thinking about her husband, she couldn't see their relationship getting better. Ever since that night when she came home from her first 'tutoring' session, they have been distant strangers to one another. Truth be told, all they do was argue. Their king size bed that once was a haven for them to escape, now finds one of them going to bed earlier than the other to avoid any conversation whatsoever. If they had to talk, it concerned the kids and nothing else. Pulling into the driveway of Christians home and parking, she pushed the depressing thoughts from her mind and walked to the door.

Reaching into his mailbox she retrieved the key that he left for her as he told her he would be a few minutes late getting to his house. Opening the door, she turned on the light and placed his key on the stand near his door beside a card with her name on it. Picking up the heavy embossed card, she opened it to reveal a note stating '*light the candles in the living room.*' Placing the card back on the table, she moved into the living room and found candles all over. The remote control to his stereo had a note taped to it that read *push play.* Pressing play, the sounds of Maxwell permeated the air. Another card on the sofa beside a beautiful black negligee that made chills run up her spine with anticipation read *Put this on and get the goodies from the fridge.* Undressing quickly and donning the outfit, she moved to the kitchen to find a platter of fresh chocolate dipped strawberries, cheese and grapes. A bottle of Moet and two crystal flutes sat beside the fridge on the drinks trolley. Wheeling the savory delights into the living room she realized that she had forgotten to light the candle over his faux fireplace mantle. Setting the candle alight she spotted another card that read,*'turn out the lights and lie down on the sofa'* doing as the card instructed she turned out the lights and lay down on the sofa.

Outside of his townhouse, Christian was waiting in his car until he saw the light's go out in his living room. Making his way to his door, he opened it to find the house a romantic delight that he was sure Benét would love. Ever since she came into his life, his mission was to make her happy. Even her current situation and status hasn't deterred him from wanting to do things for her and to her in his pursuit to make her happy. Thinking about how much he enjoyed going to Victoria's Secret to purchase the sexy teddy nightie made him smile because the sales lady commented on how lucky the lady was that he was buying it for. He couldn't help the thought of her wearing it for him had him semi-erect all day. Undressing in the foyer, he put on the silk robe that he had place earlier behind the door leading to the living room. Upon entering the sight before him of Benét lounging and singing softly brought a smile to his face.

Benét didn't know what it was that made her open her eyes but when she did, she found Christian in the doorway in a navy blue silk robe smiling at her. Rising up on her elbow she asked, "What are you smiling for?" then held out her arms to him.

Crossing the room to get two glasses of champagne, he sat them down on the coffee table before pulling her into his embrace. Kissing her deeply and passionately he said, "I was looking at how beautiful you looked sitting here—waiting for me."

"Thank you. You don't look bad yourself," she said sliding out of her peignoir to show him the full effect of the teddy.

Resisting the urge to rip the teddy off of her, he has to stick to his plan. He was going to make her body his feast of fortune tonight. Stepping back, he pulled the drinks cart closer to them and told her to lie down. Under the cart, he had massage oils warming on a tray. Removing the oil he poured a large amount into his hands and slowly started to massage her body.

From her feet to her head front and back he aroused Benét to a fever pitch with moans of pleasure escaping her mouth. Her attempts to kiss him were gently thwarted as he grabbed her hands and kissed each finger saying, "Anticipation is the best part of foreplay." Then holding her arms in one hand he reached over to the cart, plucked a ripe juicy strawberry, and proceeded to feed it to her. Teasingly he placed the ripe fruit just out of reach as she tried to lift her head and opened her mouth to receive it.

Looking down at her mouth, Christian wondered what it would feel like wrapped around his hard shaft. All of the things that they have done, Benét refused to perform oral sex on him because she's married and he respected that, but that didn't mean he couldn't fantasize about it.

After feeding her fruit, cheese and champagne, Christian moved between Benét's legs and gently splayed his large hand over her wet mound. In the pocket of his robe, were small squares of Godiva chocolates that he opened and placed inside of her. The chocolates started to melt immediately as it came into contact within her moist folds. Christian with pleasure slowly started to devour the chocolate waterfall as it flowed out of her center determined not to miss a drop. He was caught up in the essence of the liquid mix of chocolate almost sent his body into premature ejaculation. *Damn* he said to himself, *I want, no need to be inside of her.*

As he started to rise Benét intoxicated with pleasure could no longer wrestle with her self imposed boundaries of never pleasuring another in the fashion as to what Kendall jokingly refers to as his 'private ball park girl'. He always plumped when she cooked him.

"Oh God Christian you feel so good. I want, no I need to explore" Overcome with desire her sighs of pleasure made her catch her breath before she continued, "I know what I said before but I need to taste you." She said looking from his eyes to his shaft, "All of you."

"You're already doing it," he told her not wanting her to embark on another journey that will surely deepen his already unmanageable desire for her, yet wanting to satisfy his longing to have her hot moist mouth wrapped around his shaft.

Benét knew that she told him that she didn't think it fair of her to perform oral sex on him because of her marriage, but looking down at him she threw her convictions out of the window. Pushing him away from her, she stood and pulled his robe from his back and gently pushed him onto the couch.

Reaching under the cart she grabbed some oil and gave him a sensuous massage that had Christian flexing his muscles as her hands gently held and caressed his manhood. Just when he thought he couldn't take anymore, he felt her slide between his legs and take him full into her mouth. It was all he could do to contain himself as he raised up to look at her as she pleased him.

Looking into Christian's eyes as she had him in her mouth had her juices flowing down her creamy caramel thighs. Why she waited so long to do that to him, she would never know but now that she did, she was hooked. Christian's eyes rolled back and he placed his head back against the sofa, she took him from her mouth and straddled him.

Grasping her hips, he thrust upwards in his quest for release. Meeting him thrust for thrust, his penis throbbed within her slippery tunnel driving her over the edge. She wrapped both of her legs around him as their tongues danced a dual of delight and with one final thrust; Christian deepened the kiss on a wave of erotic bliss.

Contentedly lying in his arms until their breathing returned to normal, reality came crashing into Benét's happiness because as much as she doesn't want to she knows she has to leave.

Christian could feel Benét starting to separate herself from him. Stopping her from moving, he held her tighter and asked,

"What's wrong? I can feel you distancing yourself already," he sadly stated.

Reaching up to hold his head between her hands she smiled and said, "Everything and nothing. I am going to have to leave soon but I don't want to."

"I know, I don't want you to leave but we both know you can't stay," he said dejectedly.

Not wanting to think of her husband and the guilt, she felt she justified to herself that she warned him this could happen. *She warned him.*

Feeling Christian's hands slide under her to pick her up, "What are you doing?" she asked as she placed her arms around his neck.

Nuzzling her neck, he said, "Well you have to shower, so I figured why not shower together."

* * * * *

Sitting in his chair watching the game on television, Kendall stopped himself from looking at the clock again. *What kind of tutoring takes this long?* He wonders to himself. Ever since that last argument, they had become more and more distant. They didn't talk to each other about anything anymore other than the children and that wasn't often as they were teenagers. So, he took on more responsibilities at work. He didn't think it would make any difference anyway because between her classes and studying Benét didn't have time for them anymore, so why not work more he reasoned to himself.

When he heard the car pull into the driveway, he sat back down trying to pretend interest in the game.

As Benét walked into the house, she heard the sound of the television on in the game room. It's probably Kenny watching the game she thought. Walking into the room, she was surprised to see Kendall watching the game.

"Oh. I though Kenny was in here," she said as she turned to walk out of the room.

"How did the studying go?" He wanted to say something to her to try and change their situation but he didn't know how or where to start.

"Fine," she said as she waited for him to say something else. When he didn't she started back out of the room. "I'm going to bed."

Damn, why didn't he say something anything he thought instead he said, "Good night. I'll be up later."

After getting undressed, she sat down to look at the list on her dresser. It was the list for her upcoming New Years Eve celebration. *Hell, with the way things are between us I might as well cancel this party* she thought. Placing the pad in her drawer, she moved to her side of the bed and slid under the covers. About to turn off the light, Kendall entered the room. Deciding that now is as good a time as any she says, "I'm thinking we should cancel the New Years party."

Stopping where he stood he asked, "Why ?"

"Come on now Kendall, things aren't the same around here between us. Why should we still have the party?" Benét asked.

"Because we always do and canceling it will just lead to people asking questions." Namely your girlfriends he said silently.

Shrugging her shoulders, "Okay. I'll get Shaeyla on it Monday. Oh by the way, don't forget we have that Black Charity event tomorrow. Is your tuxedo clean?"

He had forgotten all about that damn ball. "Yes it's clean," he responded and with that said he walked into the bathroom to shower.

Kendall entered the room after his shower and crossed over towards Benét in the bed only to find her asleep. He settled down beside her watching the rhythmic rise and fall of her body as his mind longed for things to be the way they once were.

Chapter 40 ➢ Black and White Ball

Shaeyla moved the poster from its current home in the lobby of the posh Baltimore hotel, and posted it near the entryway that led directly into the banquet room for the Black Charities gala. The opulent red carpeting was the backdrop for the fifty tables draped in black and white tablecloths. The chairs were cloaked in an opulent black-skirted apron accented with a white tie in the back. The calla lily floral arrangement centerpieces were inside an art deco vase designed to rest on its side, allowing the flowers to cascade to the table without hindering the attendee's views the room or their table mates. The crystal chandelier reflected a sunburst of sparkling lights that bounced off the glass panes of the Windsor room from the Renaissance Hotel. This effect was also mirrored in the crystal champagne flutes held by patrons of tonight's event.

Well I've out done myself again, Shaeyla congratulated herself. The hand on her shoulder made her turn to see Kendra and Niall all dressed up in their finest. Kendra wore a georgette pantsuit whose pants gave the illusion of a long skirt with a matching black blouse that tied at the waist. Hugging her friend to her, "I'm so glad that you both could come."

Shaeyla eyed the look of happiness on Kendra's face and as she gave her another hug whispering, "Hold on to him because I can see how much this man loves you."

“I plan on holding with both hands. I realize how lucky I am.”

Stepping back, she could see that she had lost some weight. It looked good on her. “Okay now you both need to mingle. Benét is at table seven.”

* * * * *

Walking up to the table Kendra was surprised to see Diandra and Seven smiling into each other's eyes. But the look Kendall wore was one of bored indifference. Hmm she wondered what his problem was.

Looking over Seven's shoulder, Diandra jumped up as Kendra and Niall reach their table. Hugging her girlfriend, she exclaims over how good she looks and the amount of weight she's lost.

“I decided right after the party to exercise and get this weight off,” Kendra said.

“Well I loved you just the way you were,” Niall added.

Kendra raised her head to the ceiling to thank the man above for sending her this wonderful man. She reached up to kiss him on the cheek, “I know baby, but I didn't.”

“Awww isn't that sweet.” Benét replied as she hugged her friend. “You both look fantastic.”

“All of us look good,” Diandra declared as she stood up and took a bow.

* * * * *

Sitting at the table with Solomon to check the last of the guest in before the dinner was served Shaeyla looked up and froze. At the door was Mitchell Steele and he was not alone. On his arm was a beautiful Latino woman draped in a fuchsia gown that left very little to the imagination.

Seeing the stricken look on Shaeyla's face, Solomon followed her eyes to the couple at the door to see his partner and his fiancée. At that moment he wanted to shield Shaeyla from Mitch's callus behavior, so he placed her hand in his and gave it a reassuring squeeze. He saw her mouth open then close as she reached for the dark amber liquid and raised it to her mouth. He saw her hand tremble and reached over to pluck the glass from her hand. Solomon felt his partner and friend stop at the table, but he was intent on looking at Shaeyla silently telling her he was there for her.

Solomon and Shaeyla turned their attention to Mitchell as he cleared his throat. "Good evening," he said as he pulled his fiancée closer and smugly presented his tickets.

Solomon's mouth tightened at the look Mitch gave Shaeyla and he felt her indignation as her nails dug into his hand, he could feel the anger emanating from her, because Mitch acted like he did not know her.

Her chillingly delivered "Good evening Mitch" was said so quickly that Solomon could see the regret she felt for having giving in to her anger. But Solomon knew the worst was not over because although he knew that this was Mitch's fiancée, Shaeyla did not. He had wanted to talk to her so many times about her relationship with Mitchell but he never got around to it. He had even made attempts to warn her prior to the event, but the frantic pace in which she worked provided no time.

The woman with the other half of Steele Consulting turned to him asking, "Mitch do you know this woman," revealing a slight accent?

Solomon watched as Shaeyla quickly closed her eyes and surreptitiously shook her head and placed her hand out in greeting, "Yes, I'm Shaeyla Andrews. Mr. Steele and Mr. Jackson and I are business associates." Once Shaeyla had her hand clasped with the woman's the glint of light drew her eyes to see a ring on the other woman's that was a replica of the rock of Gibraltar. Noticing how Shaeyla was looking at the ring the woman informed her that Mitch had proposed to her on the prior evening.

Solomon was proud as Shaeyla lifted her head and smiled to Mitch and his companion. "Well congratulations," she said unclasping her hand with his she turned and calmly walked away.

After checking his friend in, Solomon admonished Mitch by calling him a fool and went in search of Shaeyla. He found her on the balcony of the hotel trying hard not to give in to what he suspected were tears. Placing a comforting arm around her shoulders, she acknowledged his presence by placing her hand over his. After twenty minutes of silence, the announcing of dinner reached them outside. "Come on," he said, "Let's go inside and eat. It's almost over and then I'll take you home." He didn't want her driving at all.

Without saying a word, she turned to follow him back into the ball.

* * * * *

"Oh my God!" exclaimed Benét. "Look who just sat at table ten," she said pointing to Mitch Steele.

"Ah shit! Where is Shaeyla?" Diandra asked.

Kendra had spotted her and Solomon going outside. Looking in the same direction she saw them coming back inside, "There she is right over there," she pointed.

As soon as they spotted her they all jumped up to see how she was handling the situation. "Girl what is going on?" Benét asked.

"Yeah, what is your man doing here with another woman?" Kendra asked.

Excusing himself Solomon went to take his seat on the stage and left Shaeyla to her girlfriends. From the looks of it, they didn't know that Steele wasn't her man anymore.

Moving her girlfriends out into the vestibule, she explained to them that he didn't want a permanent relationship and then shocked them with the news of that woman being his girlfriend.

"Oh hell no!" Benét yelled then clasped her hand over her mouth. "No the fuck he didn't tell you that and then proposed to that bitch," she seethed.

This was not the time, nor the place to show out. "Calm down Benét," Kendra said. "Although, I agree with her a hundred percent."

Seeing Mitch tonight was a shock but it also was an eye opener, because she finally realized that what she thought was love was only lust or the love for something new. Explaining this revelation to them, they looked skeptical but since they were her girls, they let it go.

"Well I say good riddance." Benét stated. "If I were you I'd hook up with Solomon. Ya'll seem to get on."

"I ain't jumping into anything anytime soon. Now lets get back, take our seats and move on."

The rest of the evening was a success. The charity proceeds were over a half million dollars which would go to a homeless shelter and for her hard work, Shaeyla made four new business contacts.

As she gathered up her items to leave, Solomon asked her to wait as he insisted on taking her home.

Chapter 41 ➢ Solomon

Relieving Shaeyla of her belongings Solomon helped her into the elevator and pressed the down button. When it looked like she was going to topple over he put his arm around her to hold her close. That was the wrong move, because he could feel her body beneath the beautiful gown that she wore. Taking in a deep breath, he filled his senses with the smell of her perfume, which was a heady essence of musk. When the elevator stopped he fished in his pockets for his car keys and disarmed the alarm. Opening the door to his C-Class Benz, he gently placed her in the passenger seat, reached over, and strapped her into the seat. That was another wrong move because his arm grazed her breast, which had her turning those bedroom brown eyes in his direction as if questioning his actions. Not knowing what to say, he apologized and shut her door and moved around to the driver side of the car. Before taking his seat, he placed her belongings on the back seat and took his spot at the wheel.

Locking his belt, he decided that he didn't want her to be alone tonight and urged her to rest her head on the ride home. The drive from the hotel to his home wasn't long as he pulled into his driveway and turned to her. He found her asleep and didn't have the heart to wake her.

Feeling car stop, Shaeyla woke up took in her surroundings. Disoriented and still groggy with sleep she asked, "Where are we?"

"We are at my house. I didn't feel that you should be alone tonight. After what happened," he said by way of explanation.

"You're probably right. But right now I am too tired to argue with you," she told him and took off her belt to get out of the car.

Taking off his own belt, he got out of the vehicle to follow her to the house. When he opened the door his dog made a beeline for her and she froze. "Remember he just want's to smell you. That's all he want's to do, after that he will leave you alone," Solomon assured.

Doing what he said, he took her coat and headed to the back of the house. Hoping that she didn't get the wrong impression he led her into his bedroom so that she could rest. Handing her a robe, he said, "You can sleep here. I'll sleep in the guest room."

Taking the robe from his hand, she thanked him and moved into the ensuite bathroom. After she finished dressing, she moved to sit on his king-size bed. The plush cashmere blanket in muted gray felt excellent under her hands.

Standing at the bedroom door he found her caressing the blanket with her hands. "It feels good doesn't it?" he says startling her. "Sorry I didn't mean to scare you."

"That's okay and your right it feels exquisite. Is it cashmere?"

Holding out a cup of hot chocolate to her he said, "Yes it is. I purchased it a while back during a stint overseas in the military."

Welcoming the hot cup of brew, she thanked him and moved over so that he could sit down beside her. Reaching into the closet for extra pillows, he handed her one and kept one for himself so they can relax their backs while drinking their cocoa. Amusing her with stories from his past, he noticed that she was drifting off. Taking the cup from her loose grasp, he eased the pillow from under her and turned to get off of the bed. Her arm shot out to him, "Don't go."

He didn't know whether she was awake or asleep, but he didn't want to leave. Moving his own pillow to the floor, he pulled her close wrapping his legs around her and dozed off.

* * * * *

The warm arm around her and the hand clutching her breast slowly penetrated her mind. Then the feel of something wet on her hand hanging over the bed has Shaeyla jumping to see Solomon's dog licking her hand. Elbowing Solomon, she pulled the covers up, and said, "Solomon your dog."

"Max get down!" Solomon yelled. "I'm sorry, he just want's to go out," he explained in the process of getting up.

What the fuck! That damn dog scared the shit out of me Shaeyla thought. Why wasn't his door closed and what was I thinking asking him to stay. "No problem. I'm going to get dressed and get down the road," Shaeyla said.

"Let me walk him and I will get dressed and take you to your car." He said.

Damn, how could I forget that I didn't have my car, Oh well so much for an easy escape. "Okay," Shaeyla said hoping to get him out of the room as soon as possible.

Gathering her clothes, she moved into the bathroom showered and dressed. Reentering the bedroom, he was sitting on the bed tying his running shoes in a blue velour sweat suit. "Are you ready?" he asked.

"When you are. I'm starving. Can we stop to get something to eat on the way?" Shaeyla asked.

"Sure," he said grabbing his keys and leading them out to the car.

Once in the car Shaeyla had no idea what to say to him other than thank you.

Brushing aside her thanks Solomon explained, "You were in no shape to be alone and I was glad to be here for you. I wanted to warn you about Mitch, but I did not know how. I'm so sorry that he hurt you."

"Thank you for being there for me. But it's still embarrassing that I acted like a child instead of a grown woman," she said.

"Let me ask you this?" he said, "Are you in love with him?"

Turning to him after a moment of thought, she answered, "No, I'm not. That's what I found out last night—I was never in love with him. So don't feel sorry, actually it was a relief. Although for a minute there I thought he was my ideal man, but I realize now that wasn't true. Mitchell entered my life for a reason, one that no longer exists," Shaeyla stated matter of fact.

This was welcome news to him because he wanted to see her on a personal level and he didn't want any emotional baggage or drama.

After the meal, he dropped her at her car and decided that he would wait a few weeks before calling her up. Maybe he would see what she had planned for Thanksgiving.

Not knowing his thoughts, Shaeyla says good-bye and drove off.

Chapter 42 ➤ Thanksgiving Dinner

Setting the final touches to the dinner table Benét and her daughter moved back to the kitchen to bring out the platters of food and placed them on the dining hutch. "Zaria, call everyone in to eat," Benét instructed.

Her table was set in coffee brown, rich gold, rusty red, and dark orange that represented to her the traditional colors of fall and Thanksgiving. She pulled out her copper cornucopias and filled them with oranges, apples, banana's and nuts, with deep purple grapes spilling out onto the colonial inspired runner atop the white linen tablecloth. The place mats were in the same pattern as the runner as were the cloth napkins that were held in place by a bronze leaf napkin holder. Stationed on either side of the large dining room were three-tiered wrought iron candle-holders that stood five feet in height. In them, Benét placed large russet candles whose flickering red flames danced, lacing the atmosphere with a hint of apples and cinnamon. As the small crowd of friends and family moved to take their seats, they stood and joined hands as Benét's father-in-law blessed the table.

Sneaking a peak at her watch, Benét wondered how soon she could slip away without looking suspicious. She had promised Christian that she would meet him today to spend some time with him, but she told him not to be upset if it did not happen because they could spend all day tomorrow together.

During dinner the mood of the guest was jovial. Only Shaeyla and Diandra picked up on the tension permeating between Benét and Kendall. Trying to ignore their questioning glances she finally gave in and mouthed to them that she would talk to them later. Seeing the knowing looks that passed between her friends, she knew that the interrogation was going to be long and arduous. To get their minds off of her Benét stated, "Too bad Kendra couldn't be here, but Niall is taking her to have dinner with his family."

"Yeah! She seemed so excited, this being their first holiday together," Diandra said then turned to Seven. "This is our first holiday together too."

Wrinkling his brow he asked, "How do you figure? We've spent the last few holidays together."

"Yes, we have but as friends, not as a couple," Diandra said kissing him on his nose smiling from ear-to-ear.

"Mom, make Aunt Diandra and Seven get a room," Benét's son, Kenny, said from his end of the table after witnessing the couple's kiss.

"Yeah," Benét piped in laughing, "Kenny's right."

"Whatever," Diandra told them giving them the hand.

"So has anyone spoken to Worthy lately?" Benét asked her friends.

"Nope. Home girl is missing in action. She doesn't answer the phone and I've stopped going over there since we picked her up for bike fest," Shaeyla said.

After the meal, the men moved into Benét's game room to watch the game while the women cleared the tables and washed the dishes.

"So, Shaeyla, you're a dark horse. How long have you been seeing Solomon?" Benét asked.

"You know what, I'm glad you asked that because I have something to tell both of you." Looking at Benét as if she was crazy, Shaeyla told them she knew that the thought of juicy gossip would have them believing she had something to tell them but she wanted to find out what was going on with Benét.

Throwing down her dishtowel, Diandra grabbed them by the arms and pulled them from the room to run up the steps to Benét's bedroom. "What's the 4-1-1?" she asked Shaeyla.

"Nothing about me." Directing her gaze to Benét, "I want to know what's going on with you and your husband," Shaeyla asked. "I could cut the tension between the two of you with a knife."

Benét knew this moment was going to come but she was trying to put if off for as long as she could. Asking her friends to sit down, she crossed the room to close and lock the door. Turning back to them, she took a deep breath and blurts, "I'm having an affair." There she said it.

Shaeyla and Diandra looked at each other then back to Benét. "An affair? Benét no. Tell me your lying," Shaeyla begged.

"I wish I was, but I can't," Benét murmured contritely.

Shaking her head from side to side in disbelief Shaeyla states, "It's Christian isn't it?"

As Benét shook her head yes she explained, "He was tutoring me in math and one thing led to another and I've been seeing him for the past couple of months." Knowing how her friends held her relationship with Kendall as the poster-child for marriage she begged them not to be upset. "I fought the attraction between the two of us for as long as I could. But I couldn't hold back any longer. He's an intelligent young man and he makes me happy."

The two women look at each other as they absorbed what Benét was saying. "I am not saying that I agree with you. But it's your life and I can't tell you how to live it." Diandra said as she hugged her friend and walked from the room.

Turning to Shaeyla, "So what do you think?" She valued her opinion most of all.

"I'm like Diandra," Shaeyla said, "I can't tell you what to do, I just ask that you understand what you're doing and how the consequences of your actions affect everyone around you."

Knowing what her girls were telling her was true, Benét realized that she had some major decisions to make in her life. She just didn't know where to start.

* * * * *

The dinner with Niall's family was fantastic, but Kendra noticed that Niall seemed anxious all day. Sitting on the arm of the chair beside him, she rubbed his head asking, "Is everything okay? You seem really jumpy today."

Damn! He thought he had cleverly disguised his nervousness. But the box in his jacket was burning a hole in his pocket. "Everything's fine," Niall assured her.

Receiving the signal that he and his father had arranged yesterday, he stood up and moved to the middle of the room, "Can I have everyone's attention please!" He said to his family. Everyone ignored him. Slamming his hand down on the coffee table, he finally got everyone's attention.

"Hey man, what's wrong with you?" his cousin asked.

"I have an announcement to make," Niall said wiping his forehead. Holding his hand out to Kendra, he pulled her to join him in front of his family. As she approached, he dropped to one knee, "Kendra. from the first night that I met you, I knew you were the woman for me. Your generous heart won me over and I want you in my life forever." Reaching into his jacket, he pulled out the black velvet box and handed it to her.

Standing in front of his entire family with tears streaming down her face, Kendra took the box from his hands afraid to open it yet unable to leave it closed. The sparkle of the emerald cut Diamond made her gasp. Taking the ring from the box Niall placed it on her finger, "Will you marry me?" Niall asked.

It seems that all of Kendra's dreams were finally coming true as her body was wracked with tears of joy. "Yes Niall Adams, I'll marry you," she said tearfully.

Getting off of his knee, he swept her in his arms for a soul-searing kiss amid the sound of cheers from his family.

* * * * *

So, it was Thanksgiving! Worthy thought. So the fuck what! She was tired of everyone calling her to see if she was coming for dinner. Hell no she wasn't going anywhere for dinner. First, her eye was still swollen from where JJ hit her on Monday and secondly, she didn't want the interrogation from her family or her friends. That's why she didn't go over Benét's. Worthy and her girls always spent the holidays together, but in the last few months she'd ignored their phone calls so much that they seem to have given up on her. That thought filled her with sadness because she always counted on them to be there and here she had pushed them out of her life. Rising from the couch at the sound of the keys in the door, she turned to see JJ entering and holding what looked like a dinner plate.

Smiling at Worthy he held out the plate, "I bought you a plate from my mom's house."

The look of surprise on her face was evident as he said, "It's to apologize for you having to stay here today because of that." He explained as he pointed to her eye. "But you know that I had to do it for your own good. You need to understand that you have to listen." JJ said sternly.

Taking the plate from him, she said, "Thank you." She took the foil off to reveal turkey, dressing, sweet potato casserole, mashed potatoes and gravy and what looked to be a homemade roll. *What no macaroni and cheese* she thought and was about to say something until she moved the turkey, which was hiding it. *Boy am I glad I didn't say anything cause he would've knocked me out for being ungrateful.*

Sitting on the couch to eat, her phone rang and she looked up at JJ to see if it was okay to answer it.

"Go ahead and get that. It's a holiday today," he said as if that explained everything.

Picking up the phone, she said "Hello."

"Happy Thanksgiving!" Kendra said into the receiver.

Smiling at the sound of her friend's voice Worthy leaned back on the couch, "Happy Thanksgiving to you too. How are you?" she asked.

"Girl today is the happiest day of my life!" Kendra exclaimed.

"Why? What's going on?" asked Worthy excitedly.

"I'm getting married!" Kendra screamed.

Screaming on her end JJ looked at her like she was crazy, "What! Oh my God! Congratulations! When did this happen?"

Worthy asked barely able to contain her own excitement. She placed her hand over the receiver to tell JJ Kendra's news.

"That's all," JJ scoffed. Bitches are crazy as shit screaming and cackling over somebody getting married.

"Girl, I'm on my way over to Benét's to give them the news," Kendra told her. "Are you just getting back from your mother's house?"

"No I stayed here today, because I'm not feeling good," Worthy lied.

"Oh," Kendra said in disbelief. Kendra found it odd that Worthy didn't go to her mother's for Thanksgiving. "So Jared is with you then?"

Worthy was waiting for that question; now Kendra was really going to let her have it when she answered, "No. I felt it best that he stay with Momma and them to have dinner."

Shaking her head to herself Kendra couldn't believe that her girl has let that shit control her to the point that she'd rather get high than see her family on a holiday. "Worthy, what is wrong with you?" Kendra asked. She couldn't help it. She lost it. "It's Thanksgiving and your ass wasn't feeling good!" Kendra yelled in disbelief ending the conversation with, "You need to get your shit together. You're thirty six years old and a fucking crack head." There, Kendra had finally told her friend what she knew all along.

Worthy couldn't believe that this was Kendra on the phone talking to her like this. Being lambasted like this was so unfair! They have no idea what it's like! They are always judging people, and it's not fair. Unable to take anymore she lashed out at Kendra, "Fuck you! You don't know what the fuck I go through everyday. All of ya'll think you know so fucking much and don't know shit. I know it's a holiday and I ain't no fucking crack head!" Worthy yelled into the receiver before slamming the phone down in Kendra's ear.

Looking at her cell phone Kendra couldn't believe that Worthy cussed her before hanging up. "She just hung up on me," Kendra said to Niall.

"Why did she do that?" questioned Niall.

"She didn't like what I had to say," Kendra responded. Then shaking her head she said, "My girl needs help, but as long as she is in denial there is nothing I can do about it."

"Maybe you and the girls can have an intervention to try and make her see how this is affecting her life, her son's life and the relationship she has with ya'll."

What Niall said was right, but that didn't make Kendra feel any better about the situation. She knew that unless or until Worthy hit rock bottom there was nothing any of them could do.

Sighing she leaned her head back onto the headrest for the rest of the trip to Benét's house silently thinking about her girl and how she let her life get so messed up.

* * * * *

At Benét's Shaeyla sat quietly talking to Solomon all the while thinking about how easy he was to talk to and get along with. After that disastrous night at the gala when she ran into Mitch and his fiancée, he called to ask her to go bowling. Nonplussed at first she figured why not, and since then he has taken her roller blading, ice skating, to the movies, and they have shared the occasional light meal. Shaeyla liked him though because he was so easy to talk to and very down to earth. You wouldn't know that he was a millionaire because he was so personable. He didn't have any of Randy's issues or Mitch's demands. Outside of her father he and brother he was a positive man who knew what he wanted and how to go about getting it.

"Thanks for coming with me today," she told him.

Solomon covered her hands with his, "Thank you. You have great friends that love you very much and that's good to see."

Putting her head down to her chest she blushed at the compliment from him and it made her wonder what it would feel like to lie in his arms as his woman and not his friend. Despite her best intentions she was increasingly aware of him and she was going to have to be deal with it soon. Just before she can respond to his statement the sound of the doorbell ringing distracted her as she turned to see the new arrivals.

"Hello! Happy Thanksgiving!" Benét said holding out her arms to embrace Kendra and Niall. "I'm so glad ya'll dropped by."

Moving into the house amongst good wishes and cheers, Kendra asks everyone for their attention. Getting the group of raucous holidaymakers to settle down took only a second because rarely did Kendra command the center of attention.

Holding out her hands to Niall she turned to her friends and said "Niall asked me to marry him and I said yes."

Diandra, Shaeyla and Benét converged on her all at once. "Congratulations!" Benét said.

"Let me see the ring," Diandra said.

"I'm so happy for you," Shaeyla said.

"Thank you all. We just left Niall's mothers house and I couldn't tell you guys over the phone. I had to do it in person," Kendra told them.

Kendall opened another bottle of champagne to toast the couple he asked if she had told Worthy.

"Yes, I called to tell her and she was very happy," Kendra replied.

With the rest of the guests returning to their conversations, Kendra motioned to her friends to follow her. She moved into Kendall's study to tell them of the conversation she had with Worthy.

"I can't believe she cussed you out," Diandra said. "Now we know that shit got her ass."

"How many times do I have to say it?" Shaeyla said with exasperation. "I went through the same shit with Randy, and unless she is ready to admit her problem there ain't shit we can do about it."

"We know Shaeyla, but it's not that sorry ass Randy this is our girl Worthy. Don't nobody give a fuck about Randy," Diandra said to her.

"Diandra's right Shaeyla," Kendra said, "I mean come on ya'll, that's our girl. We have to do something! Intervene in some way." Kendra implored helplessly as she plopped down on the couch.

"Look let's not think about this right now. Today is your day," Benét said as she sat down beside her and placed a comforting arm around her shoulders. "We all love Worthy, and we are going to try to help her. So let's go back out and let you be the center of attention. Okay."

Looking around at three of the most important women in her life, Kendra nodded in agreement and the ladies returned to the party.

Chapter 43 ➢ Shaeyla and Solomon

Winter

The sound of Donnie Hathaway singing "This Christmas" piped into the stereo system and sent throughout her office had Shaeyla singing along as she went over her books. Her favorite time of year was Christmas, because people were nicer and more respectful to one another and they also loved spending money to throw those holiday parties she thought as she danced around her office.

Shaeyla could not believe it, but she was actually one percent above her profit margin and the year wasn't done yet. Glancing at her booked calendar, the onslaught of the holiday prompted her to hire extra help just to remain on schedule, which brought her to the party this weekend, "Bilal, can you come into my office please?"

As the outer door to her office opened Bilal entered. "You wanted to see me Shaeyla?" he asked wondering what she needed. He tried not to get upset with her, but she became anal for her weddings and holiday parties. At other events, she was cool, but at Christmas, Bilal knew to tread lightly with Shaeyla.

"Yes, let's go over my calendar for the parties this weekend. Christmas is still three weeks away, but I don't' want anything to go wrong," she told him. "We have the Hamilton's party this weekend, and I don't want any problems. She was my first client when I started out and I always, always go that extra mile for Mrs. Hamilton."

"I know and you know that you don't have anything to worry about. Mrs. H and I get along great," Bilal responded in his unflappable not to worry voice.

"Great. Thanks Bilal, I knew I can count on you. And thanks for not getting upset at me for going over the details a thousand times, but you know how I get and yet you're still here," Shaeyla told him with a smile in her voice. That made the decision even easier to give him a good bonus for the holidays, he deserved it.

"So what's going on that you can't work Mrs. Hamilton's party this weekend?" Bilal asked.

Standing up to move to her file cabinet, she turned back to him with a huge grin on her face, and said, "I have a date."

"Really!" Bilal hadn't seen her happy since she was dating that Steele character a few months ago. "Anyone we know?" he asked thinking it was Solomon Jackson, because he saw that they had become friends as he called the office often and his charity ball was back in October.

What was the harm in telling Bilal who it was, Shaeyla thought. Bilal had to notice the number of calls that I get from Solomon daily, so what the heck, "It's Solomon Jackson."

"Well, I've talked to him a few times and he seems like a decent dude. I wish you luck and have fun okay. Don't be worrying about the party," Bilal told her as he exited her office.

*****

Solomon pulled his Mercedes to a halt in front of Shaeyla's home and glanced at his dashboard radio to realize that he had arrived twenty minutes early. Retrieving the bouquet of yellow and white roses from the passenger side along with the bottle of Merlot from her favorite winery he stepped from the car and walked to the door. Placing his hand on the doorbell, he rang it twice and waited for Shaeyla to open it.

Shaeyla heard the doorbell ring and panicked *Oh no! He's early and I'm still in my robe.* Pulling her robe tighter around her and belting it almost to the point of cutting off her circulation she runs down the steps to her front door. As she looked through the peephole, she sees Solomon standing on the other side of the door handsome as ever. The frantic beat of her heart had her questioning what was wrong with her, she took him to Benét's for Thanksgiving, so why was she so nervous today? *That's because today is a date, and that was just a friend thing so we didn't have to spend the holidays alone.* Calming down she turned the knob and opened the door.

Solomon had his hand raised to ring the bell again when the door opened to Shaeyla in a beautiful black silk kimono style robe with a bright yellow and red rose emblazoned on the side. *His beautiful Shaeyla* he said silently, how is he going to get through the night without touching her he didn't know but it was going to be an exercise in self-control that he won't want to go through again. He has done nothing but think about this day since Thanksgiving. He was ready to move this friendship to a relationship but he didn't want to push her too fast and he damn sure didn't want to be a rebound man.

Holding out the bouquet and wine to her, he pulled her into his embrace for a friendly welcoming hug. "Hello, beautiful," he said to her placing a sweet kiss to her cheek.

Taking the proffered gifts, Shaeyla was speechless as Solomon pulled her into his arms for a hug and kiss. As he released her, she turned to move into the living room. Tucking the wine under her arm and holding the roses with one hand, she smoothed an errant piece of hair back behind her ear and dipped her head to smell the roses. "Thank you! These are lovely," she told him. Nervously she laughed, "As you can see I'm still not ready and I apologize. Let me put these in water and I'll get ready."

Taking the items from her hands he instructs her to get dressed advising that he would take care of putting the bottle in the fridge and placing the roses in water. As she hesitated, he prodded her out of the room as her nearness was having an overwhelming affect on him to throw her onto her red velvet couch and take her right then and there.

When Solomon moved closer to prod her out of the room, his talk dark form elegantly encased in slate gray pen striped suit swayed gently as he stopped in front of her. The heat emanating from his body was like a magnet pulling her to his nearness sending a ripple of sensation down her spine. Quickly exiting the room, she ran up the stairs to the sanctuary of her bedroom. Closing the door and leaning back against it, she felt sure that Solomon noticed the effect his closeness had on her. *How am I going to get through this date?* Shaeyla agonized. Shaking herself into action, she removed the robe and layed it across the bed. Underneath she wore a red lace push up bra, matching thong and a red jersey knit dress that draped her body like poured chocolate. The movement of the dress around her legs gave Shaeyla a feeling of sexiness as the side split would give Sol a peek of her thigh with each movement. With its draped neckline it didn't call for a necklace so Shaeyla wore ruby studs in her ears a gift that Mitchell Steele had given her in one of his better moments. Pulling the red duster that matched the dress from the closet she gave herself one final check in the mirror and headed back to the living room and Solomon.

In the living room, Solomon heard her door close and moved to stand in the entryway to see Shaeyla rounding the corner and descend the stairs. He could tell she wasn't expecting his presence in the doorway as she stopped then started down the steps again. Her hair hung about her shoulders a shining curtain of black silk as it moved with each step she took and the dress she wore was designed to tempt the imagination as well as stimulate the senses. It hugged her figure in all the right places and he could feel his loins stir at the thought of her naked beneath him waiting for him to plunge into her folds.

Seeing the look on Solomon's face as Shaeyla approached him had her licking her lips as she thought about what it would be like to kiss him. *Where are these thoughts coming from* she berated herself, *maybe it's time I got laid or something because he is a friend, just a friend.* Coming to a stop in front of him, "Thanks for waiting." She said as she noticed he placed the roses in a vase and placed them on the foyer table. Moving down to smell their scent before they left, "These look great here. Thanks again," she said. Somehow, this thoughtful gesture pleased her *and* he found and used her favorite vase too.

Taking his coat from the closet, he donned it and asked, "Are you ready?"

As ready as I'll ever be Shaeyla said silently.

Moving to set the alarm, they make their way to his car. He opened the door and assisted her into his sleek ride before moving to take his place at the wheel.

The ride home later that evening Shaeyla couldn't help but relive the enchanted evening that she and Solomon shared. The evening started with a fantastic meal at a famous soul food restaurant in Philadelphia followed by dancing at a jazz bar featuring Najee. Although they had been out several times Solomon revealed more of himself. Shaeyla found that he loved to read as much as she did, although where her reads are contemporary romances his were mystery, horror and quite a few technical books. He didn't mind a chick flick every now and then, but he said he didn't want to be inundated with them. Like his reading, he preferred suspense thrillers and horror movies to which she told him that she didn't mind a suspenseful picture but horror was out of the question. Yawning and stretching she snuggled into his heated leather seats and dozed the rest of the way home.

Looking over at Shaeyla, Solomon's eyes trace her relaxed face as he pushes the control button to recline the seat making her more comfortable. He thought that the evening was a huge success and he couldn't wait for them to do it again. Shaeyla opened a floodgate of feelings that he had never experienced before with any woman. Shaeyla stimulated his mind and he had never been able to separate the intellectual from the physical, unlike Mitch who only saw the physical and disregarded the mental. Pushing a lock of hair from her face, he turned the volume up on his satellite stereo system and relaxed in his seat for the rest of the ride home.

Chapter 44 ➤ The First Time

Shaeyla didn't feel the car come to a stop in her driveway until Solomon touched her face with a gentle caress.

"Wake up sleepy head." Solomon said as he rounded the car to open her door. Solomon held out his hand to help her step onto the pavement as she handed him her house keys for him to open the door. Quickly moving to the alarm to deactivate it she shrugs out of her coat and taking it from her, he hangs up both in the closet. Following her into the living room, she turned to him and asked, "Do you want a nightcap? Coffee?"

"Coffee would be great."

Shaeyla was in the kitchen standing on a stool to reach her fresh bag of Jamaican coffee beans when Solomon appeared in the doorway.

"Anything I can do to help."

She took down two mugs and they went back into the living room to wait for the coffee to finish.

As nervous as a cat on a hot tin roof she could not sit still. "Would you like to listen to some music," she asked him about to jump up from the couch to turn on the stereo.

He placed a restraining hand on her arm. "No! This is what I want," he said before placing his lips upon her. The first touch of his moist lips rendered her motionless. This was their first kiss and it was blowing her mind.

On a soft moan of pleasure, Solomon gathered her closer to him and deepens the kiss. As her mouth opened to accept his sensual assault, she eased against him on a sigh of pleasure.

Feeling her body move into a reclining position heightened his awareness of her as his body moved on top and pressed her into the settee. Solomon rambled unintelligibly against her mouth as his arms tightened jerkily. "My beautiful, sexy Shaeyla, I have wanted, needed this for so long," he rasped.

As the kiss went on and on it fired her blood that matched a fire of his own. The beeping from the kitchen made her wrench her lips from his mouth. "The coffee—"

Solomon cut off her protests with, "To hell with the coffee. I need you." As he took her mouth again but this time in a slow gentle force that had her clinging to him in shameless, abandon.

The heat pooling at her center had her shaking beneath him as she felt his erection pressed against her stomach. Thinking how much she wanted this man and to feel him within her, Shaeyla must've voiced these thoughts out-loud because he whispered in her ear, "I want you too Shaeyla."

Sitting up he pulled her onto his lap and answering the question in his eyes, she linked her hands behind his head and kissed his lips in answer. As he got up from the couch with her in his arms, he carried her up the steps and to her room as if she weighed no more than a feather. Placing her on her feet in front of the mirror, he turned her around to unzip her dress and unhook her bra allowing them to puddle around her feet. Reaching around he kneaded her breast in his hands, while gazing at the sight of the two of them in the mirror, as he dropped to his knees to peel away her hose he places sensuous kisses along the his path before guiding her to the bed.

"Not yet. Allow me," she told him reaching up to remove his tie then slowly unbuttoning his shirt to reveal a hard chest and flat stomach. Placing her hands upon his chest, she felt the beat of his heart against her palm rhyming with that of her own rapid heartbeat. Moving to the belt at his waist, she released the clasp and undid his pants, letting them fall to the floor. As he stepped out of them, he picked her up again and dropped down onto the bed.

"I've been wanting to see you like this since we met," he said as his hands beneath her behind to remove her panties. Gently he caresses her hairless mound and tested her readiness for him. Ridding himself of his silk boxers, he stood up to remove a condom from his pants and returned to her side. The bed dipped as he sat down, "Are you sure this is what you want?" He didn't want her to regret a minute because he knew in his heart that she was *the one.*

Not knowing until this moment that she wanted him more than anything she reached up and pulled him down to her mouth, "Yes I want you, Solomon. Please love me," begged Shaeyla in between kisses that she traced along his body on her way to his manhood.

Solomon gripped her shoulders to slow down her ravaging his body and prevented her from tasting his manhood. "Not yet," he said then pushed her back to take up where he left off. "Now where was I?" He spoke with a wicked grin on his face as his thick fingers moved inside of her. "Ahh yes…now I remember." He rasped as he moved them in and out of her slowly as her suckled upon her breast. Shocking waves of pleasure rippled through her system, she grasped his head in one hand, and with her other pressed him deeper into her so that he wouldn't stop.

Easily removing himself from her grasp, he slid down between her legs to spread them and taste her glory. At the feel of his tongue, her body jerked in an upward motion. The second time he traced her outer lips before placing his tongue inside her slippery walls she gave a deep guttural sound of pleasure that seemed to come from the depths of her soul. He continued to tease her until she climaxed then putting on protection he arched above her and buried himself completely inside of her.

Looking up into Solomon's eyes as he sheathed himself within her melting folds, she saw him tremble from his own desire. Never has she wanted a man more than she did now as she met him thrust for thrust until they climaxed together. As their bodies convulsed upon waves of ecstasy she felt as if she'd come home. *Never before has it been like this, not with Randy and not with Mitchell. With them it was sex, not love which is what I've experienced for the first time in my life* I silently exhaled.

Brushing the damp hair from her face, "You're incredible." Solomon sighed into her mouth, "Absolutely incredible!" Then placing his head upon her chest, he promptly fell asleep.

Solomon woke her two more times that night and each time their loving was different. The second time was slow and gentle with them finding out each other's sensitive spots and the final time was a frantic race to reach their pinnacle as if they were in a marathon.

That morning she awoke to the smell of bacon and fresh coffee. Slowly she started to rise from the covers just as Solomon strode into the room with a tray full of food and a smile. "Good Morning beautiful," he said placing the tray on the dresser and stooping down to ravage my mouth *morning breath and all.*

Pulling the sheet up to her neck in a sudden fit of embarrassment, "Good morning to you too. Somebody's been busy." she said eyeing the tray of food. *Damn even in the morning he's sexy and so very thoughtful. No one has ever cooked for her before.*

Seeing how Shaeyla was clutching the covers Solomon knew he had to talk to her to make his intentions clear so that she won't retreat into that wall he broke through. Every time he thought of her two ex-boyfriends and how they callously played with her emotions, he wanted to *fuck them up.* Leaving the tray on the dresser for now, he sat on the side of the bed and unwrapped her steely grip from the sheet to take them in his own. "Shaeyla last night was amazing and one of the best of my life. I don't want you to regret anything that we did, because I don't."

She didn't regret what had happened how could she? This man taught her how to make love by showing her how he wanted to please her. He put her desire first not his. About to answer him his next statement blows me away.

Deciding not to beat around the bush Solomon told her how he felt. "Shaeyla, I have waited a lifetime to meet a woman like you and now that I've found you I have no intentions of letting you out of my life." To make sure she understood what he said he held her face in his hands saying, "I'm falling in love with you," he said looking deep into her eyes before he kissed her.

In love with me. What did she say to him? How was she supposed to react to him now that he's dropped this bombshell on her? She was beginning to care for Solomon but *love*? She was in love with Randy and he took that and threw it away until her love turned to hate. Then, she thought she was in love with Mitchell and found that she loved what he could do for her. The material items he bought. He fit her idea of the man she thought she wanted. About to tell him what she was thinking he placed a quieting hand over her lips, "Think about what I said." Then he moved to get the tray from the dresser and placing it across her legs he instructed her to eat while he went to shower.

Sitting on the bed remembering the past loves of her life she could not help but think of Solomon. He was thoughtful, insightful, exciting, and kind since the black charity ball. He saw her distress and promptly took care of her by coming to her side. Since then they had went out on friendly outings and he had escorted her to various functions and to listen to her vent about her problems. Placing the tray beside her, Shaeyla got out of the bed and moved to the bathroom. Standing in the doorway, she looked at Solomon's excellent form through the haze of steam and walked to the shower door. Solomon turned around and opened the door upon her soft tap.

Shaeyla had to say what she came to say before she lost her nerve. "Do you mind if I join you?" she asked. The pleasure this statement gave him showed in his face as he smiled and without saying a word, he stepped back to allow her to enter.

"I promise not to rush you Shaeyla," he said as he folded her into his wet arms. "I am going to follow your lead and go at your pace."

"Where ever this *thing* between us goes I am willing to hang on for the ride." She told him. Then I dropped her head onto his chest and she didn't care that her hair was getting wet. All she wanted was for him to hold her tight and never let go.

Chapter 45 ➤ Benét and Christian

Benét had been rushed off of her feet, what with finishing her exams before the Christmas break and seeing Christian, had been a whirlwind of activity. She'd juggled, shoved, and moved several things to get the time to spend with Christian to exchange gifts before the holidays. She planned this carefully as she knew and he knew as well that it would be hard to see him without raising suspicion. Just thinking about Christian raised the hairs on the back of her neck. He invoked a mountain of pleasure in her that left her spent every time they made love.

She could not get enough of him and that worried her because that was not how it was supposed to be. Her plan was to have a passing affair, get her feet wet and hopefully the problem that her and Kendall were having would be cleared up. But now she was conflicted. Kendall moved into the guest bedroom right before Thanksgiving claiming that the mattress was better for his back but that was an excuse. His real reason was because of his impotence, which Benét still thought at this point was self-imposed. And Kenny and Zaria had questions but they were either too scared or too polite to ask what was going on between them. Hell, she didn't know what was going on, other than the fact that her marriage was crumbling at her feet and she was powerless to stop it. She loved her husband and still believed that they could make their marriage work but she was no longer willing to put herself out there. He has to come to her if he wanted their situation to change. Other than that, Benét planed to live her life, *period.*

Snapping from her musings it dawns on her that she has driven to Christian's house on autopilot. Parking the car, she got out and retrieved the packages she had hid in the trunk of her car. For the past month she has shopped for Christian's presents and she cannot wait to see his face when he opens them. Benét stepped to the front door and before knocking took a deep breath to calm the butterflies in her stomach, then knocked.

Christian is putting the last box for Benét under his tree when his doorbell rand. It can only be Benét because he wasn't expecting anyone else. As his excitement builds upon seeing her, again he ran from the living room to the few feet it took to get to the door and flung it wide open to the love of his life. He couldn't remember what his life was like before she came into it and although this train of thought was dangerous, he could finally admit to himself that he loved her. Pulling her into his arms, he placed a hot pulsating kiss amongst her lips not caring that they were still in his doorway in full view of his neighbors.

As Christian swept Benét into his arms, she forgot about the bags she had as they slid from her loose fingers so that she could caress the nape of his neck as he kissed her. Consumed instantaneously with passion and desire about to spin out of control she felt the December breeze on her hands and realized they are still in Christian's entryway. Breaking the embrace, she picked up the bags and pushed past him into the house. *She couldn't believe how careless she just acted, what if someone saw them* Benét silently swore. As she placed the bags down once again, she whirled around and ask him what he was thinking.

When Benét swiftly turned, the hair she had been letting grow at his request flew into her face and taking his hand, he swept it back from her eyes and helplessly gave into the desire he had building in him. Crushing her to him, he forced her lips apart then gentled as he controlled his desire. "I know that we promised to eat and everything first but I can't wait Benét. I need you now," Christian said to her as he led her up the steps to his bedroom.

Wanting and needing him as much as he needed her Benét didn't deny him *anything*. Slowly undressing each other, he gently lays her down on the bed to take each breast into his hands. Caressing the burgeoning peaks, he allowed his thumbs to linger over her throbbing nipples. Benét found that this never before sensitive area was tender and that the slightest touch had her inner walls clenching with desire. Placing his hand to cover her mound, he slowly dips each finger inside of her and felt his insides melt. Benét almost lost it. Clinging to him shamelessly Benét allowed her fingers to scrape his scalp as her desire for him mounted.

Christian was just as hopeless as Benét as he knew that if he let her go he would die. Quickly protecting them, he moves over and into her, his manhood seeming to swell and surge within her hot folds. Riding the storm together, they seem to loose conscious thought as their desire for one another spirals out of control climaxing as one entity, mouth-to-mouth, soul-to-soul.

Chapter 46 ➢ Seven and Diandra

The first day of winter was a bright beautiful forty-eight degrees in a clear blue sky. Peering through the cases at the exclusive jewelry store in Annapolis, Seven cannot make up his mind as to which one he was going to purchase for Diandra. In his mind he has always seen her in a platinum ring with a marquise cut diamond surrounded by no less that six baguettes, one stone for each year he as known and loved her. He plans on proposing to her New Years Eve and although he knows many women say it is taboo to propose on holidays, he has a feeling that the day won't matter to Diandra. He knows that Diandra looks at the holiday as another day for them to grow closer together.

This is the last item on his list for Diandra. He has gotten her all of the things he has wanted her to have for Christmas. He even went back to the shoe store and got her the outrageously priced boots that she wanted although he kicked up a fuss when he was with her. That was to divert her to something else because he had planed to get the boots, purse, gloves and hat to match. They are going to go perfectly with the long cashmere coat he got her trimmed in sheared rabbit. Seven is just lucky that he was blessed with a gift that enables him to pick and choose his jobs. His occupation as a freelance journalist, allows flexibility in his schedule and the articles fetch him no less than fifteen hundred a piece. That along with sound investments he is able to give Diandra that life he wants her to become accustomed to. There is no doubt in his mind that she is going to accept his proposal and when she does, he'll pick up the phone and call his realtor to make an appointment to show her the house he has picked out for them.

Finally deciding on the ring that he wants he pulls out his debit card and pays for the ring in full. No payments for him, when he decided on something he always purchased it. The only payment he wanted was a mortgage that he hopes to fill with smaller versions of him and Diandra. Pocketing his purchase, he turns to walk out of the store, happily whistling to his car.

* * * * *

Diandra was finishing her last client when the door buzzer went off. After a certain hour, she locked the door and the only way to get in was to be buzzed in. Seeing that it is Seven coming to pick her up, she depressed the button to release the door and watched him walk into the shop. Noting the curious look in her client's eye Diandra explained that he is her best friend *and* her man.

As he approached, she slid her arms around his neck smiling Diandra kissed him saying, "Hey baby. You're early." Wanting to deepen the kiss that she placed upon his mouth, Diandra steps back before he can act on it. The wicked gleam in his eyes tells her she is going to pay for teasing him later.

Focusing on her client, she puts the last pin curl in place and whips the cape from around her to send her to the cashier. Diandra removes the register till and receipts from the cash register after her client pays and heads for her office. Giving the till to Seven, he counts the drawer and places the deposit in the night deposit bag for her. This allowed her to help her assistant with the clean up. Setting the alarm, they lock the store and Seven places Diandra in his truck and followed her assistant to her car parked down the street.

Getting into the passenger side of his vehicle Diandra pulls him to her saying, "Thanks for walking Stacey to her car."

Taking her mouth in a breathless kiss Seven responds, “No problem.” He continues his sensuous onslaught until Diandra pulls away from him to remind him that they were going to be late for the movie.

Reluctantly releasing her, Seven puts on his seatbelt and drives to the newest movie complex in the county.

* * * * *

Diandra cannot wait to get back to her house after the movie. She has a surprise for Seven that she knows he is going to love. As they move through the lobby of the theater to leave, a woman yelling Seven’s name stops them. Turning to see whom it is, Diandra recognizes his colleague Leslie Fordham. An instant wave of jealousy overcomes her and that is the moment she realizes that she is in love with Seven. When it happened Diandra can't say all she knows is that now he is hers and there is no way she is going to give him up without a fight.

Oblivious to Diandra's jealous thoughts Seven embraces Leslie and turns to reintroduce her to Diandra. “Leslie you remember Diandra.” He said.

Smiling at Diandra Leslie is unaware of Diandra wanting to fuck her up right now. *Look at how she is holding onto his hand.* Diandra thought. The green-eyed monster had her wrapped up in its grip so tightly that Diandra didn't hear anything that Leslie was saying to her. Nudging her shoulders to get her attention Seven said, “Diandra? Leslie was talking to you.”

Focusing on the woman, Diandra apologized and gave her undivided attention.

“I'm glad to see that Seven and you are together. You know that day he asked me to escort him to that barbecue was to make you jealous. And it looked like it worked too. Congratulations.” Leslie said to Diandra.

As Leslie hugged Seven, she whispered into his ear before returning to her group, “I want an invitation.”

Seeing the smile on Seven's face as he hugged his friend had Diandra wondering what she had to say to him that she couldn't hear. As Leslie walked away, she turned to Seven "What did she say that made you smile?" Diandra asked him.

Putting a loving arm around her shoulders he told her his words and not Leslie's, "She said that she is happy for me because I look truly happy." He told her smiling into her face. Seeing the smile this statement brought to her face has him saying, "I can't wait to get you home." With that, they broke from each other's arms to run to the car.

Arriving at her house, she heads toward her bedroom instructing Seven to wait in the living room until she calls him.

"Why can't I go with you?" he asked.

"Because I have a surprise for you," she told him.

Flopping down onto the couch to wait for Diandra, Seven' hears the sounds of the bath running. *Oh, Damn! Now she is taking a bath!* Seven thought because he knows how long Diandra can stay in the tub. Picking up the remote from the couch, he settles into his seat on the couch and turned on the television to check out what's playing.

In the bedroom, Diandra is running around grabbing the candles she purchased out of her bag and placed them around the bedroom and bathroom. Checking to make sure that the tub has enough bubbles in it she takes off her clothes and grabs her robe from the hook of the door. Placing two of her best towels on the heated towel rack her mother got her for Christmas last year Diandra scans the room again before calling Seven.

At the sound of his name Seven looks at his watch, *that was quick* he thought happily jumping up from the couch, he heads down the hall. As Seven opens up the bedroom door, the light from the candles cast a soft illumination about the room. Their fragrance instantly stimulates his senses and then he stopped in his tracks. Diandra was standing in the doorway to the bathroom in a sheer robe with nothing underneath. He hardened instantly at the sight of her and started to quickly undress. Moving forward to her he stands and looks her up and down while he counted his blessing at how lucky he was to have her in his life.

Holding out her hand to Seven, Diandra leads him into the bathroom, takes off her robe and steps into the warm sudsy tub. Instructing him to do the same, he sat down and she moved to kneel in front of him. The tub was small so his legs hung over the edges.

"I remember what you said about wanting me to give you a bath," Diandra said picking up the sponge and moved it slowly across his stomach.

Seven's stomach muscles compress as he felt the moist sponge make contact. "Yes, I can see that," He told her with a smile.

Gently and slowly, Diandra lathered Seven's body from head to toe not allowing him to return the favor. "Tonight is your night. I wanted to make your fantasy come true," she said stepping from the tub to pull one of the heated towels from the rack. Holding the towel open she told him, "Step out so that I can dry you off then set us off."

Seven didn't think he could be set off anymore than he already is but he succumbed to the feeling of love that Diandra was giving him tonight. She wrapped the towel around him and led him into the bedroom where he laid down while she rubbed and caressed the moisture from his body.

Throwing the towel to the floor, Diandra reach for her lotions and stroked him to a fever pitch. Turning so that her back is too him she straddles his legs and slowly lowers herself onto his ridged pike. When she felt him fully ensconced, she started the slow ride of movement to take them to the cusp of beyond. Their sighs and moans built into a cacophony of ecstasy. *Seven isn't deep enough* Diandra thought gripping his hands to her hips and grinding onto him as he trembled on the verge of release. Diandra can feel the first wave wash over him. His legs stiffened lifting her higher bursting forth the culmination that made them one.

Chapter 47 ➢ Worthy's Girl Thing

Standing on the corner of Fulton and North Avenue, Worthy is trying to find JJ. Looking down at the piece of paper in her hand to the address that he gave her, she heads up the block until she finds the house number. Coming to a stop at the bottom of the steps, she has a feeling that something is wrong but she can't quite figure it out. She honestly didn't want to meet him because she promised her mother they would go shopping for Jared's Christmas stuff, but he promised her that if she met him he would take her shopping to get her all of Jared's stuff on Saturday.

Trudging up the steps to the door the sounds of a dog barking has her stopping in her tracks. She didn't mind pets, but she did have a problem with large breeds or mean dogs and this one sounded mean. Seeing the curtain move she steps to the door as it opens to a beautiful young girl dressed in little denim shorts and a stomach-bearing shirt. "You must be JJ's girl," she said to Worthy pushing the door open further to allow her to enter. Pulling her coat around her tighter, she sees JJ sitting in the corner with two other women, one on each leg. They looked at Worthy in disgust with one of the women voicing their opinion to JJ nastily. "I ain't touching that!" she said pointing to Worthy. The other two ladies in the house agreed with her.

What in the fuck is she talking about touching me for? Worthy thought wrinkling her forehead earnestly trying to figure out what is going on. Then it dawned on her what JJ wanted. S*he knew she shouldn't have come here. This is just like JJ to do this shit on the sly. He has been trying to get me to sleep with women because the shit turns him on. JJ told me that if I loved him I would do it. I told him point blank no, I am not into no muff diving or bumping bushes or whatever it's called nowadays. But, here lately he hasn't been hitting me off with my hit's or nothing and he hasn't bought anyone to the crib either. Damn, what am I going to do?* Worthy thought anxiously.

Pushing both of the women off of his lap, he moves towards Worthy holding his arms out for a hug. *Now I know it's a show* she said to herself. He never shows me any affection unless he wants something. As he holds her to him, he says for her ears only, "I know your ass is feigning and I know you need a hit bad. So—"

Before he could finish his sentence Worthy pushed him away "Why am I here JJ?" Worthy asked. She didn't care if those other tricks heard her right now she didn't give a fuck!

Dragging her into the next room, that looked to be a den of sorts he closed the door and turned on her. The blow to her face came before she knew it. "Bitch, you know better than to pull that loud talking shit with me," Scolded JJ, "And your ass ain't dumb either. You know exactly why you're here. So I suggest you deal with it and put on your game face." JJ put his hands in his pockets, pulled out a bag of pure cocaine, and waved it in Worthy's face. "You give me what I want, and I'll give you what you want."

Seeing how her eyes lit up at the sight of the bag, JJ knew he had her. Taking her back out into the room with the rest of his whores, he picks up his video camera and tells them to get busy.

It was obvious to Worthy that these women knew what JJ meant because they couldn't wait to get out of the little bit of clothing that they had on. "Undress that bitch ya'll," JJ instructed the other women when Worthy continued to stand in the center of the room clutching her coat. Panicking she knew she had to get out of there.

Turning she tries to run to the door, almost there she is tripped by one of the women. Worthy fought off the three women as best she could, clawing, scratching, and kicking she did anything to get them off of her. "Grab her hands Cherry!" JJ yelled and the other two undressed her as she thrashed around on the floor. Worthy tried to bite the hand of the girl holding her down, while trying to kick at the other two. "Sit on her legs Candy!" This effectively pinned her down with no movement. Closing her eyes, she feels on the verge of tears.

"Worthy, open your eyes." JJ instructed her and when she did, he was standing over her with the camcorder zoomed in on her face. JJ dangled the bag of cocaine in front of her like a carrot to a horse. "If you want this, you'll do it," he said then returned to the couch.

Sighting the bag of cocaine has Worthy's mouth watering as she could taste the hit on her tongue. She could smell the burning rock in her nose and she knew she had to have that bag. Deciding not to struggle with the ladies anymore she lets her body relax. Feeling her movements subside, the women asked, "Are you going to stop fighting?"

Dejected and morose Worthy responded, "Yes."

"It's okay girl. JJ just wants you to enjoy yourself. He said you like to get down and we promise not to hurt you," Candy said, stroking the hair from her brow with what was supposed to be a reassuring smile to Worthy. But it only made Worthy resigned to the fact that no matter what she is their prisoner.

The girl named Cherry stood over Worthy holding a long red double-headed dildo. Placing it near Worthy's lips she instructed Worthy and Candy to suck it. "Show her what I mean Candy," Cherry said when Worthy hesitated to put the dildo in her mouth. She didn't know where that thing at been or who it had been in, *I am not sucking shit* Worthy thought clamping her lips together.

Afraid of what will happen if Worthy didn't do as she was instructed Candy said, "You better do what Cherry says or else JJ will step in."

Remembering the last beating she had received from JJ, Worthy followed Candy's lead, and did as she was told. The two of them made the dildo slick so that when Cherry pushed Worthy back and placed the dildo at her opening, it slipped in easily as Cherry worked it until it was deep inside of her. Then Candy placed herself on the other end of the dildo, facing Worthy and that's when Worthy realized that she couldn't turn back now. Worthy is shocked to feel her love juices start to flow. Clenching her eyes shut, she tries in vain to stem the rise of excitement coursing through her body but she can't. The toy moves into her even more, as Candy slides up and down on the long red shaft, which starts a chain reaction movement within Worthy. She feels her hips start to move to meet at the knot in the middle. Once there her lower lips graze Candy's lower lips and a ripple of sensation has her wanting more. Hearing a moan from the couch, she turned to see JJ holding the camcorder in his left hand stroking his dick with the right one.

JJ eyes Worthy through the camera, drops it down to look at her, and said, "See Worthy this isn't so bad after all."

Giving herself up and over to the sensations running through her veins Worthy and Candy's mounds bump and grind until the knot disappears as the women's bodies climatically convulse. Gripped in the throws of her orgasm Worthy agrees with JJ *this isn't bad after all.*

The women did whatever they wanted to her and for the rest of the night Worthy climaxed repeatedly as the women used her body as their sexual playground.

Chapter 48 ➤ Kendall's Office Party

The last thing that Benét wanted to do was go to Kendall's office holiday party. She loved to party especially now during Christmas, but she just didn't want to go.

Walking to his wife's room he is pissed at the state of her undress, "What the fuck Benét. You're not ready and you know that I have to be there on time. I am an executive in the company you know."

"Why am I going anyway?" Benét asked him. "Just to put on the show of the two of us being happy? You go and I'll meet you there," She threw over her shoulder.

"No! Be ready in fifteen minutes Benét," he demanded then stomped from the room mumbling under his breath.

We cannot go on like this Benét thought. This constant arguing and bickering is taking its toll. Their children didn't even want to go this party tonight for fear of how her and Kenny would act. The kids decided to stay with friends for the night, which was fine with Benét. Deciding not to argue and to go have a good time, Benét accepted the fact that she had to go and she was determined to have a good time. At least Shaeyla and Kendra would be there because Shaeyla did the event and Kendra will be with Niall. Thinking of Shaeyla, Benét can't help but smile. Shaeyla was determined to put Mitchell Steele and the insensitive treatment of her behind her and as she explained to

Benét what better way to thumb her nose at him and show him how little she cared than to do this party. Plus, the last time they talked Shaeyla had told her that she was seeing Solomon, so as far as Benét was concerned to hell with Mitchell Steele.

Pulling her white velvet cape from the closet Benét lifts her matching purse from the bed and descends the steps.

Kenny is standing near the door and as Benét moves down the steps, he turns to open the door and head to the car. He didn't want her to see the longing he had in his eyes for the way things used to be. He didn't want to see in her eyes the disappointment she had for him at this mockery of a marriage they have. Opening the driver's door, Kendall waits for Benét to get in and pulls off before her seat belt is fastened.

Just another way things have changed between them Benét thought. He used to open doors for her, but they have nothing now. She needs to decide what she was going to do and soon. New Years is in a few weeks and she was not going to start the New Year with her marriage the way it is. *Oh yes. A change is gonna come.* Benét promised herself.

Settling into her seat for the ride to the party, Benét laughs as the two of them sit like silent strangers.

Hearing her laugh, “What's so funny?” he asked.

“I wasn't laughing so much as reflecting.”

“Reflecting on what?”

“Reflecting on how we are with one another. The fact that we are in this confined space with nothing to say to each other yet the tension could be cut with a knife,” Benét said turning to see the reaction on his face to her statement.

“Benét I do not want to talk about this now.”

“That's the problem. *You* never want to talk about anything. So be it. So that you understand where I'm coming from, you need to be talking to me before the new-year because I refuse to start the year off with our marriage the way it is.”

He knew she meant business from the cold look on her face. The thought of his life without Benét puts a fear in him that he cannot explain. “What do you mean Benét? I—I mean what are you trying to say to me?” he asked.

Why is he acting, as though he doesn't have a clue, he has to see how they are; polite strangers, roommates sharing a space and nothing else. This is not a marriage thought Benét. "I'm saying we need to go to counseling and get this marriage on track, or maybe we need to be alone for a minute to figure out something else." She didn't want to be the one to say the "D" word. She doesn't want a divorce. Benét loves Kendall and the kids so much that she knows she wouldn't be able to function right without them. Don't take that to mean that she couldn't learn that if she had to, but if her marriage can be saved, then she was going to save it. As much as she felt for Christian, her marriage and family meant more to her than anything.

Kendall didn't miss the way Benét put her head down and wiped the salty tear from her cheek. The last thing he wanted was to see her crying. Wrenching his hands around the steering wheel, he doesn't have the answers and it scares him to death.

Their arrival at the party was met with half of the partygoers already on there way to sky-high land. The drinks and food were flowing and the music had everyone on the dance floor.

Kendall had more than his usual amount of drinks tonight because he wanted to rid himself of all of his troubles and woes. This was the first time he ever drowned himself in a bottle and looking across the room at his wife surrounded by his co-workers *again* he knew unless he agreed to something he was going to loose her for good. Tilting his head all the way back, he emptied the bottle and asked the bartender for another.

Spotting her husband at the bar, Benét breaks from his co-workers to go and stand near him. "What's wrong?" Benét asked him.

Swaying from side to side, her husband responded, "You know what's wrong." His words slurring and saliva flying in the air.

Placing a hand over her mouth so he won't see her laughing at him Benét said, "Your drunk." Taking the bottle from his hand, she placed her hand under his arm guiding him to the door. "Come on. Time to go." Benét wanted to remove him from the party before he did or said something to embarrass them both.

By the time Benét got them home it was still early, wasn't even gone midnight. Oh well too late to do anything but shower and go to bed she thought. Fleetingly thoughts of calling Christian played in her mind but yawning she pushed them away and settled down to sleep.

When she felt her bed depress on the other side waking her from a sound sleep, Benét opened her eyes frozen in place by fear.

"Benét," Kendall said reaching out to see if she was awake.

Upon hearing his voice she moved to turn on the light to see him holding his hand wrapped in a towel. "What's wrong, now?" she asked.

"I was trying to make myself a sandwich and used the knife to slice open the top of the package, it slipped, and I cut my hand," he said showing her the deep gash in his palm.

"Why did you do that in your condition?" Benét fussed because it looked deep enough for her to have to take him to the emergency room. Looking at the clock, she was only asleep for two hours and now she has to spend the rest of the night in the emergency room thought Benét with mock disgust.

"Go put on something so I can take you to the emergency room," she told him. Hell, she didn't want to be nasty about it, but all he had to do was say something to her and she could've made him the sandwich.

Meeting her in the kitchen where she cleaned up his mess, he apologized, "I'm sorry Benét, but I didn't ask you cause we ain't on those type of terms now." He sounded like a wimp, Kendall thought to himself.

Brushing off his statement, they walk out to the car to head to Harris County General. Thankfully, she can tell the kids what happened tomorrow as they both were staying with friends tonight. On the ride over Benét selfishly hoped and prayed that they could get in and get out. She wanted to get back home to her nice warm bed.

Chapter 49 ➢ Worthy

Worthy has had enough of this life. She can't take anymore of the abuse from JJ or his friends and she is tired of people talking about her and laughing at her behind her back.

She hasn't seen or heard from Shaeyla, Benét, Kendra, and Diandra for a while. The last time they were together was when they were at Diandra's questioning her about getting high. That day she lied through her teeth trying to convince them that was okay and that she knew what she was doing. Finally, she just got mad at their nosiness and ran out of the apartment. She had to make them mad at her because the alternative was JJ. He told her to be home by ten and she knew he meant for her to be there by ten. *What am I going to do? Christmas is a couple of weeks away and I have nothing. No job, no son and no life.* Worthy despaired. Worst of all she thinks she lost her friends. She should pick the phone up and call them but was afraid of how or what they would say to her. Moving from the couch to pace the room these feelings had Worthy wanting a hit. *There it is again, a hit—a blast, whatever, whenever, or however, so long as I get one.*

Moving about the room she was earnestly thinking on where was the last spot JJ had hid his shit. Right now she didn't care about herself or the consequences all she wanted was her hit. Worthy hit the jackpot on the last spot she looked in. Inside of a thermal can in the veggie bin in the fridge was at least fifty vials filled with rock cocaine. She was so afraid to move after she found it that she stood and looked at it for what seemed like hours but in reality was only five minutes. Stuffing her bounty into her pockets, she ran to her bedroom to get her supplies of an ashtray full of ashes and her pipe. Worthy never emptied ashtrays in her home because she always needed the ashes for her pipe. Looking at the clock on the wall and seeing that it's not quite midnight, she has plenty of time before JJ gets home and when he does she'll deal with him then. *In her quest to get high, she forgets that JJ always comes back around one in the morning to re-up.*

The first hit strikes her throat and goes directly to her brain giving her an indescribable sensation. She was on the second to the last piece when JJ came into the house and caught her, making her freeze like a deer caught in the headlights.

Cocking his head to the side, he slowly moved forward and picked up the thermos. Looking down and seeing that it was empty, JJ threw it against the wall. He came home to re-up and found Worthy smoking his shit. Slapping the rock that was beside Worthy to the floor, he pulled his arm back and punched her in the eye. *He is tired of this crack head bitch taking his shit. He is going to teach her a lesson this time* JJ raged to himself.

The blow to Worthy's face knocked her against the wall near the living room. *She had to get out of here* she thought. Holding her head in pain, she attempted to get up, but the dire pain made her fall back against the wall. Out of her good eye, she could see JJ moving towards her with both hands balled into fist. *He looks like he could kill me* she thought dazedly. *I'd be better off dead anyway.* Trying to get to her knees to crawl away, JJ takes his foot and kicks her in the stomach, lifting her from the floor and into the living room.

An uncontrollable rage took over JJ's entire being. He didn't want to kill her but this time he knew he would teach her a lesson that she wouldn't soon forget. This thought had him kicking her repeatedly in the stomach.

The second paralyzing blow was inflicted upon Worthy's head, then her abdomen, then her back. How long it went on she had no idea, but she knew she couldn't hold on any longer. Succumbing to the pain Worthy, was engulfed by dark nothingness.

With his boot raised to kick her again, JJ stopped when he noticed that she had stopped moving. Leaning down to her, he put his face near her bloodied nose to see if she was still breathing. Finding her still alive but not moving, he knows he has to get out there. He didn't bother to call the police, he gathered his things and rolled out.

Peering through the peephole in her door, Worthy's neighbor heard the commotion and waited to see JJ leave before she went next door and found Worthy unconscious on the floor. She immediately called the police and reported what happened. After reporting the situation to the police, she picked up the phone to call Worthy's friend Diandra.

Chapter 50 ➢ Head on Collision

Driving down the street to the highway, JJ is weaving in and out of traffic attempting to getaway from what he did to Worthy. He was on his way to his other girls place out in the county. Worthy had no idea of her or the place. Mired in his own thoughts he ran a red light and didn't see the policeman sitting in the alley. The sounds of the sirens alerted him to the police. Checking his review mirror, he saw that they were following him. *Oh, fuck! That bitch faked me out and called the police!* He thought. Stepping on the gas, he decides to run. *He is not going back to jail.*

* * * * *

Benét was sitting at the light three blocks from the hospital. As the light turns green, she starts to move through the intersection and that is when she heard the sirens. Looking to her left, she sees a car being chased by the police. Quickly moving to the side, she isn't quick enough as the driver of the car jumps the median and heads straight for her vehicle. It is too late to react or do anything as the sounds of the crash penetrate her mind. Benét winced at the sound of metal against metal before she was knocked unconscious.

* * * * *

Kendra was just getting to sleep after a vigorous love making session with Niall when her phone rung. Picking it up on the first ring, she is surprised to hear Kendall's voice on the other end.

"Kendra, thank God I've got you. You have to come to Harris County General quick," he said frantically.

"What? Kendall wait slow down," she implored. "What's going on? Is everything alright?" Kenny was rambling and not making any sense.

"Benét," he kept saying.

"Oh my god! Is something wrong with Benét?" Kendra asked.

At the sound of panic in his fiancé's voice Niall woke up and took the phone from her trembling hands.

"Hey man, its Niall . . . calm down and tell me what's going on," Niall instructed as he pulled Kendra close to comfort her.

Kenny explained to Niall that him and Benét were on their way to the hospital when this man jumped the median and hit them head on.

"Are you and Benét alright?" Niall asked.

"I got away with cuts and bruises but—" He stopped as his emotions got the best of him. "Benét is unconscious." Kenny finished as he hung up the phone in tears.

"Kenny is fine," Niall told Kendra as she looked at him with questions in her eyes. "But Benét is unconscious."

As soon as Niall told her that Benét was unconscious, Kendra knew she had to go to her. Without thinking, she threw on her sweats and hurried to Harris County General's emergency room.

* * * * *

Across town, Diandra received a similar phone call about Worthy from her next-door neighbor.

When the phone rung Seven, picked it up wondering who could be calling Diandra this late at night.

"Hello may I speak to Diandra," the voice on the phone said.

"May I ask whose calling?" he said while nudging Diandra awake.

"Who is it?" she asked rubbing her eyes.

Holding his hand over the mouthpiece of the phone, "It's Worthy's neighbor."

Puzzled Diandra took the phone, "Hello."

"Is this Diandra?"

"Yes, your calling about Worthy?" Diandra inquired.

"Yes, I'm her neighbor and I just had to call an ambulance for her. JJ beat her up real bad," the person on the phone said fearfully.

Sitting straight up in the bed and throwing the covers to the side Diandra yelled, "What! What do you mean he beat her up real bad?"

Rising from the bed Diandra pulled her jeans from the floor and starts to dress. "What hospital is she in?" she asked with tears streaming down her face. *I knew that nigga was hurting her. I just knew it!* She cursed herself. *We should've pushed her harder.*

Seven took over as he could see that Diandra was completely out of it. "Do you want me to call Benét, Shaeyla, and Kendra to tell them about Worthy?" he asked.

"Yeah, but let's call them on the way. I need to get to Worthy! We are going to have to call her mother and tell Jared," Diandra said on a fresh wave of tears.

Arriving at the hospital Kendra and Diandra saw each other and started to cry and began rambling about what was going on until they realized that they were not talking about the same thing.

"What do you mean about Worthy?" Kendra asked. "What's wrong?"

"JJ beat her up real bad," Diandra explained, "Isn't that why you're here?"

"No, Kendall called me and said that him and Benét were in an accident and she is unconscious," Kendra explained.

This tragedy only made the women cry even more at the thought of both of their friends fighting for their lives.

"Where's Shaeyla?" they asked each other.

"I tried calling her on the way over but she wasn't home and her cell is off," Diandra said. "I'll try it again."

While Diandra calls Shaeyla, Kendra is going to the nurse's desk to ask about Worthy and Benét when Kendall rounds the corner. Kendra can see how upset he is, so she hugs him and asked how was she.

"The doctor is working on her now. He said for me to have a seat and he would come and talk to me when he is finished working on her," Kendall said.

Diandra came back saying, "I just got hold of Shaeyla. She was out with Solomon and left her phone in his car. They are on their way now. Shaeyla is hysterical. Has the doctor said anything about Worthy? Benét?"

Kendall snaps his head up "Worthy? What's wrong with Worthy?"

"This guy named JJ beat her up and she is in there unconscious as well," Diandra told him.

"Get the fuck off me bitch!" JJ yelled out struggling with the female police officer.

At the sound of the commotion, they all turn to see what's going on. "That's the motherfucker right there!" Diandra and Kendra said recognizing JJ.

"Who is that?" Seven, Niall, and Kendall asked?

"That's the motherfucker that beat up Worthy," Diandra said.

"That's her man JJ," Kendra replied.

"Well that's the bastard that hit us," Kendall said starting to walk over to him." Niall and Seven held him back "Let the police handle him man," They told him.

The thought of his wife fighting for her life has him wanting to tear JJ apart.

Shaeyla arrived as the friends settled back down. With tears streaming down her face and her coat tails flying about her, she asked hugging her friends, "What's wrong ya'll how did this happen?"

"We have to wait for the doctor's to talk to us. Worthy's family is on their way over now," Diandra said. She knows her friend is upset but Shaeyla's ass will break on you in a heartbeat. She is a strong woman until tragedy strikes then Shaeyla crumbles like a tower of dominos.

Settling in for the night, the family and friends await word from the doctors.

Chapter 51 ➤ After the Accident

Kendall entered Benét's hospital room and walked up to her battered form as he eyed the tubes running from her hand and arms his mind only heard the sound of the monitor measuring the steady beat of her heart. The doctor had advised that she had some internal bleeding from the impact of the accident, but they were able to stem the flow of that. Cupping his wife's small hand in his own, he placed soft kisses into her palm urging her to come back to him. *Please Benét, I need you. Please wake up!* Kenny urged. Still Benét did not move her breathing steady as the myriad of machines that she was hooked up to attested. The sound of the door opening admits the doctor who asks to speak to Kenny in private.

Kenny reluctantly relinquished Benét's hand to follow the doctor into the hallway.

The doctor informed Kendall. "Mr. Grier we did everything in our power to save the baby. I'm sorry."

Pole-axed Kendall didn't know how to react to this news "Baby? What baby?" He hadn't had sex with his wife in over three months.

"Your wife was nine weeks pregnant. You didn't know?"

"No I didn't know. Let me be the one to break the news to my wife?" *Pregnant, Benét was cheating on him and she had gotten pregnant by another man.* This phrase was like a mantra in his head that he couldn't get rid of. Kenny needed to get some air. Turning back to the room, he starts to open the door, jerks away, and heads for the elevator. At the ground floor, he walked to the nearest bench to sit and think about what the doctor just told him. *Pregnant!* Benét is his life! The guilt starts to set in and eat away at him, chipping his soul piece-by-piece, as he believes that this is his fault. He remembered her words from their argument at summer fest when he accused her of wanting to sleep with one of his co-workers. *"What if I told your ass, that if you don't get your problem fixed, I'm going to find a man that can do what you can't!"*

He winced as he remembered his scathing reply *"You know what Benét. At this point, I don't give a fuck who you fuck!"*

Stupid he did care and he was a fool to think that he didn't'. Had he just went to therapy! Had he listened to her and gotten counseling! *She turned to the arms of another man and it was his fault.* These feelings of guilt and disappointment were too much, he had to get away and although he knew that Shaeyla, Diandra, and Kendra were going to wonder what happened to him, he had to make sense of this in his own mind.

Thoughts of the pregnancy made him remember that with the kids spending the night with friends they had no idea about their mother. Pulling out his cell phone, he call the children's cell phones and instructs them to get dressed as he was on his way to pick them up. Having done that, he moved to the cab parked beside the emergency room exit and went to get his children. He no longer had time to worry about his feelings; he was going to have to be strong for his children. He would deal with Benét later.

Kendall told his son and daughter about the accident on the way back to the hospital. Zaria burst into uncontrollable tears, while Kenny Jr. just looked out the window holding his in. Kendall could see that he wanted to let them go but was struggling over the thought of people seeing him cry. At the hospital, the kids run into the comforting arms of their "aunts". This only starts them all crying again as Shaeyla told them about their Aunt Worthy.

Shaeyla turned to Kendall and said, "When you went to see Benét the doctor came and told us that Worthy had a lot of internal bleeding. She has three broken ribs, a concussion, two black eyes, and a broken wrist." Thinking of how JJ had damn near killed her friend, Shaeyla was thankful that the policeman informed her that even if Worthy refused to press charges the city of Baltimore would.

The nurse came and instructed them that they could see Worthy but only for five minutes and only two at a time. Kendra and Diandra went first, while Shaeyla and the kids went to see Benét.

* * * * *

Worthy was floating and felt that she was wrapped up in a cocoon of cotton wool. She felt good. She felt free, *finally*. She didn't want to leave the place where she was but she felt that she couldn't stay. Worthy settled back to sleep. She gave over to the feeling of peace once again.

Kendra and Diandra stayed fifteen minutes, refusing to leave when the nurse instructed them. Making their way back to the waiting room and into the arms of their men they waited for Shaeyla to come from seeing Benét. Kendra and Diandra went to visit Benét while Shaeyla visited Worthy.

When the ladies once again met in the waiting room the nurse told them they may as well go home and rest as the women wouldn't be transported to their rooms for another few hours. Deciding to go home and changed clothes and come back, the women designed a schedule so that their girls would always have one of them in the room with them. Shaeyla took Zaria and Junior to her house for the night. Even though they wanted to stay Kenny agreed with her and told them to go, get some rest and that Aunty Shaeyla would bring them to see their mother in the morning.

Solomon stood back and witnessed how the love these women felt for each other encompassed everyone around them. The envious eyes of the strangers in the waiting room looked upon them with happiness and hopes of their loved ones sacrificing self for the love of others. Solomon pulled some strings at the hospital so that Worthy and Benét could be placed in the room together.

Chapter 52 ➤ Christian

Christian has been trying to contact Benét for the past few days. He hasn't heard from her and he's left several messages on her cell phone. *Where are you Benét* he asked looking down at his phone. This isn't like her not to contact him at all. Something has to be wrong with her. Pacing back and forth in his living room he is trying to remember the name of her girlfriend's business…what is it he wonders thinking hard. Christian walked to his den cum office and pulled out his day planner. *Benét's girl owned a party or event business of some sort.* Flipping through the pages of his book, he spots it under the letter E *Events to Remember Entertainment and Event Management*. Picking up his phone, he punches in the number to Shaeyla Andrews's office.

"Good Morning! *Events to Remember*, Bilal speaking. How can I help you?"

"Yes, may I please speak to Shaeyla Andrews?" Christian asked hoping that she was in. He had to find out what is going on with Benét.

"May I ask who's calling?" Bilal asked thinking Shaeyla has gotten herself a new man.

"Christian Kane."

"Hold on please." Placing the caller on hold, Bilal buzzed Shaeyla to see if she was available. "Please hold while I transfer your call."

Shaeyla was sitting at her desk wondering how she was going to tell Christian about Benét. Why didn't she think that he wouldn't call? Benét spent a lot of time with him. Damn this was not going to be a good phone call because she would have to convince him not to visit her in the hospital. Hell! What if he ignored her advice? What if he shows up anyway and the kids or worse Kendall was there. Although now that she remembers, Kendall had only been to the hospital once and that was the night of the accident. She knew that they have been having problems and all but still, she thought having almost losing his wife, he would've been more open to try and change their situation. Picking up her phone with dread Shaeyla says, "This is Shaeyla Andrews. How can I help you?"

"Hello Ms. Andrews. My name is Christian Kane and I am a—a friend of Benét Grier," Christian said not knowing how much Benét's friend knew about their relationship. Hell, she may not even know about him at all. Right now, that doesn't matter to him, all that matters is that he finds and speaks to Benét. "I've been trying to get in touch with her for a couple of days and I haven't been able to reach her. I was wondering if everything is all right. I mean I'm really concerned because it's not like her not to return my calls." He explained.

Shaeyla sat at her desk shaking her head. This man has it real bad and she hated being put in the middle of this mess. Expelling a huge sigh, "I hate to be the one to tell you this…but Benét was involved in an accident two days ago."

Christian fell back onto his chair. His heart was racing, his palms started to get clammy as he tried to breath evenly. "What happened? Is she okay? I've got to go to her! Tell me what hospital is she in!" He begged.

"I'm sorry," Shaeyla said at the sound of distress in his voice. "She is fine now, but I can't tell you the hospital Christian. Please don't get me involved in this. She has a husband and children that love her very much and I cannot allow you to go there and—and wreck havoc on an already fragile situation."

Christian didn't care about anything but finding and getting to Benét. If he has to call every hospital to find her he would...but he was going to see for himself that she was fine. "I'm sorry Ms. Andrews. I really am and I don't know how much if anything that Benét has told you about me—no about us, but I love her and I have to go to her." He really hoped she understood how he felt, but at this point, nothing and no one mattered but Benét.

"Please, please leave it alone. Once she comes home and is on the road to recovery I'm sure she'll contact you but until then I'm asking you to stay away," Shaeyla beseeched.

"I'm sorry, but I can't do that," he said as he replaced the phone and retrieved the yellow pages from his bookshelf. He would start with the beginning of the alphabet and work his way down, but he is determined to find her. However long it takes he thought to himself as he picked up the receiver to dial the first number.

Two hours later, he found her. She was at Harris County General and he is on his way. He would deal with whatever when he got there.

* * * * *

Benét was sitting up in bed when the door to her and Worthy's room burst open. Standing in her entryway was Christian. Her heart skipped a beat. Not at the sight of seeing him, but at the thought of what if Kenny or worse the kids came here and he is here. How would she explain his presence to them? Especially to Kenny? She couldn't use school because they were on a break. "Christian. What are you doing here?" she asked him worriedly attempting to look past him into the corridor. Glancing over at Worthy she was glad to see that she is still asleep.

Moving to her side, he gingerly lifts her hand to his lips and kisses her. "Benét I am so glad to see you! I've been calling you and you didn't return my calls!" He cried, "I didn't know what to do or think! I panicked!" He said wanting to rain kisses all over her but didn't.

"Christian you have to leave. My husband . . . my kids! Please. I—I—I we have to talk Christian but not here. Please," Benét begged him knowing that at any moment one of her family or friends could walk through the door.

Seeing the look of horror on her face, he releases her hands and questioned, "We have to talk? What is it Benét?" He had to ask because the tone of her voice told him that she may want to break things off and he can't bear the thought of that. Christian started to shake his head in denial but caught himself, "Okay, I'll leave," he said reluctantly then kissed her on her forehead and walked from the room. Before he closed the door, he stopped in the doorway to look back at her, because his instinct told him this might be the last time he saw her.

Falling back on the bed Benét takes a deep breath in order to get some control over her raging heart. She has never been so scared in her life…that she saw it flash before her eyes. This is the dose of reality she needed to know that whatever she and Kendall were going through they have to try and make their marriage work. She loved her husband and she was not going to do anything to jeopardize what they have by continuing her relationship with Christian. She has no choice but to stop seeing him.

* * * * *

Kendall was packing a bag to go and pick up Benét when he knocked her cell phone off the dresser. Picking it up he noticed that she had missed ten calls. Wondering who could be calling her that many times when all of her family and friends knew she was in the hospital. Kendall's hand hovered over the button that would show him the name or number or both of the person or persons that had repeatedly called his wife. Kendall asked himself, *What if it is the baby's father?* His blood is boiling as he pushes the button and saw the initials "C. K." on the phone. *This has to be the bastard* he reasoned. What should he do? Should he call the number and have it out with this man face to face or should he take the phone to Benét and ask her about it. *Hell man, what can you do? You still haven't told your wife about the baby, a baby that she kept hidden from him. She doesn't even know that you know she is having an affair* Kendall thought.

After thinking about the situation, he called Diandra and asked if she could pick Benét up as something came up at the office. He could hear the upset in Diandra's voice over the phone at the thought of him choosing work over his wife. Oh well. He had some business to take care of and soon. He then pressed the button to call the number that was labeled with the initials C. K. whom Kendall knew had to be Benét's lover. He told him to meet him in an hour at the Lake. It's secluded at this time of year and things might get heated, so Kendall dressed accordingly and headed over to the Lake.

Christian didn't know what to make of the phone call he received from Kendall but he decided that he should go anyway. Kendall didn't even ask him for his name all he said was, "This is Benét's husband. We need to talk about you and my *wife*. Meet me at the lake in an hour." Then he hung up. Christian saw from his caller id that Kendall called from Benét's cell phone. Now he knew how he got his number. All those phone calls he'd made to her phone were still there and Kendall must've found it and put two and two together, *but how* Christian wondered.

Kendall was sitting at the lake when a car pulled up and Christian Kane got out. Seeing him make his way over to his car Kendall steps out, "Hey man. What are you doing here?" he asked not wanting him to be around when Benét's nigga showed up. Kendall hated to have is private business made public.

Deciding to be frank, Christian said on his guard, "You called me."

This statement enraged Kendall. "What! Man are you telling me that you're the motherfucker that has been screwing my wife!" Kendall bellowed. Clenching his fists in and out, he wanted to lash out at Christian. He had befriended this *boy* tried to mentor him and woo him over to Steele. Instead, he stole his wife and has the audacity to act as if nothing is wrong. "You bastard!" Kendall wanted to wipe the look of resignation from Christian's face.

"I'm sorry you had to find out like this. You found her cell phone didn't you. That's why you called me today," Christian stated.

"Motherfucker I found out about Benét and *someone* on the night of the accident because the doctor expressed his condolences to *me* for not being able to save the baby," Kendall said crossly.

Baby Christian thought. Benét was pregnant! "Baby? Man what baby? What are you talking about?" Christian asked.

"Benét was pregnant!" Kendall said gripping the bridge of his nose. "Don't tell me you didn't know." Kendall scoffed. Kendall knew he didn't know because Benét didn't know he said it to make Christian believe that Benét knew and didn't tell him, as a form of betrayal.

"No I didn't know," Christian said stunned he started to walk back to his car.

"Wait. This thing between you and my wife is over. Understand. You will not contact her or attempt to see her. That is my wife! My property! And I swear I'll kill you if I even think you tried to contact her in anyway," Kendall said looking Christian directly in his eye.

Christian didn't care. This hurt him more than anything that Benét was pregnant with his child and didn't even tell him. He had to get away for a few days, time to think about what he is going to do. The woman that he loved had delivered him the ultimate betrayal and he didn't know how to handle it right now.

Watching Christian drive away Kendall had a feeling that he wouldn't have any more problems from him. Getting back into his car, he drove around for a while before going home.

Chapter 53 ➢ Benét

Benét was released from the hospital just before Christmas. She was still felt a little discomfort from the accident, but she was glad to be out of the hospital. When she finally woke up, Shaeyla and the kids were in the room playing three handed spades. Zaria was the first to see her and sprung from her seat to place kisses all over her mothers face. Junior was next then Shaeyla.

Shaeyla then told her about the person in the room with her. Benét burst into tears when she was told that JJ had almost killed Worthy and that he was the person that hit her and Kendall. He was running from the police when he hit them Benét remembered. A flash of memory entered her mind of the twisted wreckage making her head ache.

Sitting up on her couch, she brings her thoughts back to the present as Zaria walked into the room with a lunch tray.

"Here you go Mom," Zaria said placing the tray across her mother's lap.

"Thanks sweetie," Benét said.

"I'm going to do my homework okay. Yell if you need me," she said kissing her mother and walking from the room.

The one thing on Benét's mind is the fact that Kendall only visited her once while she was in the hospital. She knew that they were distant but tragedies have a way of bringing people closer together. Something is on his mind. Benét realized that he is avoiding her, but why. The object of her thoughts walked through the door and stopped when he saw her sitting on the couch.

"Wait," Benét said to him as he moved to go to his study. "Kendall what's wrong?"

What's wrong he thought? *Well Benét, how about the facts that you got yourself pregnant and didn't even know it, i*nstead he said, "Nothing's wrong. Why do you ask?"

"I just feel that you have something to say to me. I also feel like your avoiding me for some reason, I mean you only came to see me once in the hospital and now you act as if I have the plague or something."

"I don't see why you find that surprising. We were hardly on speaking terms before the accident why should that change now."

Holding her head towards the ceiling to stop her tears Benét realizes what he says is true, but still she at least figured they could talk about their problems since she was injured. "I just figured that accidents make people look at things differently. I thought we could at least talk about our problems, but I see nothing has changed with you Kendall. Your still closed minded about your problem."

Kendall was about to tell her exactly what the problem was but Kenny Jr. came into the room and he refused to involve the children in this mess of a marriage. He also didn't want them to loose or feel any differently about their mother if they found out about the baby and the fact that it wasn't his. At least Kenny respected and loved, yes loved his wife to the point that he wanted to spare her feelings, which is more than could be said for her, she didn't spare his feelings at all. It's been a week and he still didn't know what he was going to do. Walking from the room in disgust, he went into his study and closed the door.

Benét watched the emotions play over Kendall's face before he turned to go into his study. Benét knew at that moment that she was going to ask Kendall to leave. She had to. She could no longer take the mental abuse from her husband and it wasn't fair to the kids.

* * * * *

Sitting in his study, Kendall concluded that he had to leave. As much as he loves his family, he cannot stay here. He isn't thinking straight and all he sees is his wife in the arms of another man. *Christian Kane*. Images of the two of them flow in and out of his mind, skewing his vision, distorting his thoughts. *He had to tell Christian about the baby, he had to drive a wedge between the two of them* he repeated silently. The one thing he did know was that he was going to have to tell her what the doctor told him. Looking at his calendar on his desk he decides to leave after the New Years party. He would spend the time between now and then finding a place to stay and how he would approach Benét about the consequences of her infidelity.

Chapter 54 ➢ Christmas Day

Pulling the pancakes from the oven, Diandra sets them on the table. She is taking down plates to set her table for the first Christmas breakfast that her and Seven will spend together when she turns and finds him standing in the doorway.

"Good morning sexy," Diandra said extending her arms for her morning kiss.

"No you're the sexy one Ms. Johnson," Seven said kissing her in return.

"I'm almost finished setting the table. Take a seat so we can eat our breakfast," Diandra instructed.

"When are we going to open gifts?" Seven asked.

"When I was growing up the tradition was to eat breakfast then open presents." Diandra said laughing at him, "Damn your worse than Shaeyla. This is her favorite time of year."

Over breakfast, Seven shared some of his holiday moments that he treasured when he remembered to call his parents and wish them a Merry Christmas. Giving him some privacy, Diandra cleaned up the dishes and waited for him to join her on the floor in front of the tree. One of the boxes on the floor caught her eye and it was the outfit she had purchased for Worthy. Diandra knew her friend would look really good in it. But, Diandra stopped herself from thinking about the "what ifs" and reflected on the goods time her and her friends had and will continue to have. This will be the first time that Christmas won't be at Benét's since the women have been friends, and the first time that they all haven't spent the holidays together. Kendra decided that since Benét is still recovering she would cook Christmas dinner and Shaeyla said she would do the New Years Eve party this year.

Seven entered the room quietly and caught the errant teardrop with his thumb. Diandra was in her own world up to that moment. Pasting a smile on her face she said, "How is your family?"

"They're fine and mom said to tell you happy holidays," he said. As if he could read her mind, "You were thinking about Benét and Worthy." he said.

"Yes. I was thinking how lucky we are to still have them here," Diandra said.

"True. Now enough crying, tis' time to open gifts," Seven said and picked up the large box with her name on it.

It took less than twenty minutes for Diandra's living room to swim in a sea of gaily-wrapped paper. Seven had given her so many gifts and she felt just like a kid in a candy shop.Pulling Seven from the room to lead him to the bedroom, Diandra said, "Come on Santa. Let me show you how much I loved my gifts."

* * * * *

This morning sickness was a motherfucker, Kendra thought in between another retching session in her toilet. Standing up she dampens her washcloth and wiped her mouth and face. Moving back to her bedroom, she was glad that Niall was still asleep. She was still in two minds about it though, because she had been heavy all of the life, then she got motivated enough to do something about her weight. She met a wonderful man who loved her regardless of her weight only to turnaround to gain it back again. That was inevitable because with pregnancy came weight. She still hasn't told him that she is pregnant even though he has asked her to marry him. From the conversations that they've had, she knows he will be a great dad. As she placed a hand on her stomach an image of a little girl that favored her and then a little boy whose brow furled as Niall's when he was concentrating flashed in her head and she knew that weight or no weight, she was going to have a baby. The crazy smile she felt at her thoughts was interrupted by the sound of the phone. Running over to the offensive piece she snatched it up before it could wake Niall. *I swear that if this is Shaeyla again about dinner I'm going to scream,* Kendra thought.

"Merry Christmas!" Shaeyla said cheerily into the phone.

Damn! "Merry Christmas to you too," Kendra responded on a laugh because Shaeyla is the biggest kid on Christmas. "Girl you act like a damn kid all excited about Christmas like you still believe in Santa Claus."

"Girl, this year Santa Claus treated me good," Shaeyla said. "Anyway, I'll talk about that later. I called to let you know the caterer will be there in an hour so listen out for them. Tell them where you want everything to go and they will take care of the rest."

"Okay," replied Kendra.

"Cool. I should be picking you up at noon so that we can spend time with Worthy before we head back to eat dinner," Shaeyla said.

"Okay, I'll be ready. Niall, Kenny, and Seven are going to watch the game until we come back," Kendra said.

"Great. See you later," Shaeyla said and hung up the phone.

* * * * *

Kendall got Benét a pair of gloves and a scarf for Christmas and that was it. Benét got him a coat, two outfits and some boots. *All I got was a fucking scarf and a pair of gloves* Benét seethed. She knew it was the thought that counts, but she is his wife, not his fucking secretary. Hell, Christian gave her more than that. On the day she met him at his house, his hunger for her had them putting off exchanging their gifts immediately, but later as they wallowed in his huge bed he handed her several boxes. The exclusive black red trimmed boxes held three beautiful dresses, a watch, a sexy nightie and two pair of shoes. Throwing the items back into their box, she flung them back down not caring how they landed as she turned her flinty black eyes to her husband with a forced thank you Benét retreated in silence. She really didn't want to ruin Christmas but this motherfucker has been making shit hard since the accident. If he has something to say to her, he should fucking say it.

Kendall smiled smugly to himself at the look of outrage on Benét's face at the gloves and scarf he had his secretary pick out for Benét. He told her it was to go with the other gifts he had gotten her, but after what the doctor told him he took those items back and got his accounts credited. Petty yes, but it made him feel good. Almost like, he was getting her back, because he knew how much his wife liked gifts. Hell, she expected a lot because he always gave her a lot. But that was about to change, *and soon* he thought. Returning his attention to the excitement of the kids opening their gifts, he forced himself to enjoy the day.

* * * * *

"Merry Christmas!" yelled Shaeyla and Kendra as Junior helped their mother into Shaeyla's car. Kendra moved to the back so that Benét could relax the seat a little on the ride to see Worthy.

Turning on her friends like the exorcist, Benét yelled, "Shut up about Christmas!"

Shaeyla immediately knew that Kendall had gotten her a fucked up gift if Benét had this type of attitude on Christmas day. "What! Ahh shit, girl what did you or should I say what didn't you get?" Shaeyla asked.

"I got a fucking scarf and a pair of gloves. Shit he normally gives his secretary," Benét scoffed.

"Well it's the thought that counts," Kendra laughed at her friend's ire.

"That is not like Kendall." Benét told her friends, "You both know about the problems we've been having, but ever since my accident he has been even more distant to me. Almost as if he hates me or something."

Seeing the look of bewilderment on her friend's face Shaeyla asked, "You don't think he knows about Christian do you."

Benét blanched at this thought and turned damn near white. *Could he* she thought back. Then negating this thought, Benét said wondering what transgression he feels she has done, “No. I have been too careful. I have too much to lose so I know that isn't the case.”

All three women were trying to figure out what Kendall knew or didn't know when they picked up Diandra. Explaining the situation to her on the short ride over, Diandra said, “I told you what I thought when you told us. For your sake and the kids I hope like hell that ain't it.”

Not wanting to set Benét off again, Shaeyla said they needed to concentrate on Worthy and resume this discussion later.

When the women arrived in Worthy's room, the police were just leaving. Gingerly hugging and kissing their friend, they asked what the police wanted.

Worthy haltingly explained that they are going to press charges against JJ cause her neighbor gave a statement that she saw and heard everything. She was still in a great deal of pain.

Looking into Worthy's swelled face Benét asked everyone to join hands in prayer to thank God for their blessings.

The women opened up the gifts that they had for Worthy and tried to cheer her up for spending Christmas in the hospital.

On a faint whisper, “Listen. I want ya’ll to know that I am checking myself into rehab when I leave here. The doctor told me how lucky I am to be alive and had JJ kicked me one more time it would've been too late.” Worthy cried.

The mention of rehab leaves the women joyous at the thought of their friend finally admitting her problem. Gathering their items, they head back to Kendra's for Christmas dinner.

Chapter 55 ➢ New Year's Eve

Benét was lounging on the couch in her game room looking at television when the phone rang. "Happy Holidays," she sang into the phone.

"May I speak to Mrs. Grier?" the man on the phone asked.

"Speaking?" Benét replied.

"Mrs. Grier, this is Doctor Nunez from Harris County General. I was calling to check up on you and to see how you're doing."

"I'm fine doctor thanks for calling," Benét said. "Have a safe new year." She finished beginning to disconnect the call.

"Well I'm glad to hear that. I called because at the hospital I promised your husband I would give him information on support groups for the two of you to attend. The hospital found that after the loss of a baby other people in your situation could help the parents to overcome their loss," Dr. Nunez explained.

"Baby!" Benét said sitting up straighter. "What baby?"

"Your husband didn't tell you?" Dr. Nunez asked.

A sweat broke out on Benét's brow. "What is this about a baby?" Benét asked fearfully.

"I'm sorry to be the one to tell you this, but the injuries you suffered in the accident resulted in the loss of your baby. I did everything I could but I couldn't save her."

Sweating on her upper lip by now Benét has to ask, "Are you telling me that I was pregnant?"

"Yes, nine weeks to be exact. Uhh—you didn't know?" inquired Dr. Nunez.

It all makes sense to her now. Kendall's behavior after the accident and up to this point all makes sense to her now. *Pregnant! With Christian's, baby* Benét thought miserably. "No I didn't know," Benét replied dropping the phone. Benét was dumbfounded at this news placing her hands on her now empty middle. *Pregnant! And* Kendall *knew. He knows she's been unfaithful to him, he knew about the baby.* She had to figure out a way to fix this to make him understand how she was feeling to turn to another man. That it wasn't planned.

Kendall was working in his study when he went to pick up the phone to check his voice mail at work. The incessant annoying sound of one of the phones not being hung up properly has him moving from the room to see which phone it is. He went into the room where Benét was sitting with tears streaming silently down her face and her hands trembling holding the phone cord in her hand. Taking the phone from her hand he asked, "What's wrong?"

Turning to her husband Benét said, "The doctor from the hospital called to tell me about support groups for parents that have lost children." Benét accused, "Why didn't you tell me Kendall? She pummeled his chest with her fist in her anger, "Why?"

Kendall watched his wife's hysterics and roared, "Tell *you.* I have to find out from a fucking stranger that my *wife* lost *our baby* and you ask me why I didn't tell *you.*" Kendall shot back pushing her away from him. "Do you know how hurt I was? How hurt I am? I find out that your fucking around and got pregnant by the motherfucker to boot. And you wonder why I didn't tell you!"

The look of disgust and contempt on Kendall 's face humbled Benét. "I'm sorry. I—I didn't plan to have an affair. I didn't plan to get pregnant," she hiccupped, "I was lonely and miserable. I missed you." Benét implored. She had to make him understand he had to forgive her. "Please forgive me. I love you and I don't want to loose you."

"Love me! How can you say that? How can you stand there in all honesty and tell me you love me? You love me enough to sleep around. You loved me enough to sleep around without the thought of protection?" berated Kendall "I mean what am I supposed to think Benét. How long has this been going on?" he asked.

Crying hysterically, Benét spread her arms helplessly. "Kendall—" she hiccupped and stopped as he cut her off.

"You know Benét it doesn't matter when." Kendall said in defeat, "I decided I'm leaving. I need to decide where or how I want to go from here."

"No Kenny, please," Benét wailed moving as quickly as she could to him. Reaching out she tries to grab his arm but he flinched away from her.

"No Benét. I need to do this. I already have a spot. I just need some space right now. Please allow me this."

Benét wanted desperately to stop him but knowing that she couldn't she crumbles to the floor in a heap of regret, guilt and misery.

* * * * *

Shaeyla was putting the finishing touches to her tables when Solomon came into the room. He was about to tell her that Benét was at the door, when Benét wailed, "Shaeyla!" Benét cried flinging herself into her friends' startled arms.

"Benét, calm down. What's wrong?" Shaeyla asked frightened.

"Ken—Kend—, he's—he's gone Shaeyla he left me!" Benét cried harder.

Oh my goodness, Shaeyla thought. Why of all fucking days did he have to do this shit today? Moving to guide Benét into the bedroom for privacy, "Now calm down and tell me what's wrong."

"Shaeyla you were right! He found out about Christian and me in the worst way possible!"

"Tell me what happened."

Benét explained the call from the doctor and the discovery that she had lost a baby, Christian's baby. Shaeyla was shocked, but she isn't going to judge her friend. "Oh sweetie, I'm sorry . . .

about everything," Shaeyla comforted. "I am going to cancel the party okay and you can stay with me for a few days."

"Thanks. But as much as I would love for you to cancel the party, it's too late. He moved out. Said that…that we need time alone. He needed to think," Benét said sorrowfully.

Damn, Shaeyla has never seen or heard Benét sound as lost and alone as she did now. The guilt of what she did to Kendall is not going to go away soon. Turning to her bathroom medicine cabinet Shaeyla grabbed two powerful sleeping tablets and instructed Benét to take them. That should keep her zonked out until tomorrow. Sitting by her side until she fell asleep, Shaeyla immediately called Diandra and Kendra and come over early and bring a bag…she had something to tell them.

* * * * *

Diandra and Kendra descended upon Shaeyla demanding to know why they had to come early and what is going on. Moving her friends into her home office she closed the door and turned to them, "Benét is upstairs. She came here crying fran-tically . . . ya'll Kendall left her," Shaeyla told them. She didn't know how not to come right out and say it. "When they had the accident, Benét was pregnant—" Benét was cut off by Diandra's outburst.

"Pregnant!" exclaimed Diandra in disbelief.

"Yes, pregnant. She didn't know and the doctor told Kenny that night at the hospital—" Shaeyla continued when she was cut off by Kendra.

"Now I understand why he left the hospital, then came back with the kids. That also explains why he never came to visit. I put it down to the problems they were having about the impotence," Kendra said.

"Yeah I thought the same thing." Shaeyla added, "But that wasn't it. He told her today that he was leaving. He already got a spot and everything."

"I know Benét is broken up. She loves Kendall and this is the last thing she wanted," Diandra said. "Did you give her something to put her to sleep?"

Shaeyla nodded her head in agreement, "Yeah. She lost the baby. A baby she knew nothing about and her husband knew all this time and didn't say anything. Can you imagine how he felt looking at her knowing of her affair and the result of it? I just wish I could cancel tonight. To answer your question Diandra, I gave her two strong sleeping pills…she won't stir until the wee hours of the morning. By then the party will be over," she said crossing her fingers, because sometimes people just did not know how when to go home.

* * * * *

The sound of the door opening and the noise from the music from the party jerked Shaeyla backed to the present as Kendra and Diandra came in the room. *Damn…she didn't realize that she had been sitting there for so long.*

"Girl, I saw you go into the kitchen, and thought you were getting more crab dip, but when you didn't come back, I went in search of you but I got sidetracked refilling the trays of food. Have you been up here the entire time," asked Kendra.

"Yeah, I was just sitting her thinking about all the stuff that has happened this year," Shaeyla told them. This thought had the three women turn to look at their friend resting on the bed.

Silently mired in their own thoughts they could see the damage of the tears on her face, as even in her sleep Benét could not rest.

The women each took turns in kissing Benét on the forehead before heading back downstairs. The party was in full swing when Kendra grabbed Niall a few minutes before the sound of the New Year. She needed to tell him that she was pregnant.

"What is it?" Niall asked his fiancé as she maneuvered them through the crowd and out on the deck.

Turning to Niall Kendra took one of his large warm hands in hers and placed it on her stomach, "Niall, I have something to tell you and I thought what better time than the dawning of a New Year."

Kendra could see that the significance of what she was trying to say was lost on Niall. Pressing his hand more firmly to her stomach she said, "I'm pregnant Niall. I'm going to have your baby," she smiled.

Niall was speechless as Kendra told him of his impending fatherhood. Gathering her close, he slowly moved his hand over her abdomen in wonder, "A baby! You're going to have my baby." He repeated as tears of joy fell from his eyes. "But…you just lost all of that weight…" his voice dropped off.

Shaking her head, "Yes, I did. Don't get me wrong, I struggled with it for a long time. Hell, I almost contemplated not telling you. Then I saw a handsome and I imagined a boy whose brow furled as yours does when your concentrating on something, and a girl with my a head full of black curls and my eyes. But the bottom line is, my feelings for you and how I felt for you, which you solidified on Thanksgiving Day. Happy New Year sweetheart. I love you," Kendra said in between soft kisses to his face. *What better way to ring in the New Year* she thought in elation as they rejoined the party.

* * * * *

Inside Shaeyla's office, Seven was on one knee holding out the diamond ring he handpicked for Diandra. In stunned silence, she reaches for the ring through eyes cloudy with tears then slid to the floor in front of him.

"Diandra I have loved you for the last six years and I want to continue loving you for sixty more. Will you Diandra Johnson marry me and be the mother of my children?" Seven asked in tears.

"Yes! Yes! Yes!" Diandra said planting a hot wet kiss on his lips before sliding the ring onto her finger. *What better way to ring in the New Year* she thought. "Come on let's go tell Kendra and Shaeyla," she told him pulling him from the floor and running back to the party.

Shaeyla was making her way to Solomon when she was stopped by the shrieks as Kendra rushed in with Niall to tell them of their impending parenthood, while Diandra and Seven announced their engagement. As tears welled up in her eyes at the good news from her friends, Shaeyla's smile dropped, as she thought of Benét upstairs filled with sorrow and Worthy in the hospital broken with pain. She walked up to Solomon to place her hand in his as the countdown started, *bring it on* 10…9…8…7…6…5…4…3…2…1, Happy New Year! As they turned to each other and kissed, Shaeyla's mind whirled, *Whew! A baby, two marriages, a separation and a new beginning . . . wow what a year! Soon it's going to be time for another Party!*

Printed in the United States
50038LVS00004B/115-162